THE PROJECT

ALSO BY ZEV CHAFETS

THE BOOKMAKERS

INHERIT THE MOB

DEVIL'S NIGHT

MEMBERS OF THE TRIBE

HEROES AND HUSTLERS, HARD HATS AND HOLY MEN

DOUBLE VISION

HANG TIME

THE PROJECT

ZEV CHAFETS

WARNER BOOKS

A Time Warner Company

The events and characters in this book are fictitious. Certain real locations and public figures are mentioned, but all other characters and the events described in the book are totally imaginary.

Warner Books, Inc., 1271 Avenue of the Americas,
New York, NY 10020

 A Time Warner Company

First Printing: April 1997
10 9 8 7 6 5 4 3 2 1

Library of Congress Cataloging-in-Publication Data
Chafets, Ze'ev.
      The project / Zev Chafets.
        p. cm.
      ISBN 0-446-51886-7
      I. Title.
    PS3553.H225P76   1997
    813'.54—dc20   96-31674
                                                                            CIP

To Sue Jacobson Kutz

THE PROJECT

CHAPTER ONE

THE FIRST THING MOTKE VILK NOTICED WAS THE SANDwich platter. It looked normal enough, set out on the long green felt conference table next to the liter bottles of Coca-Cola and Diet Sprite and the plates of crumbly biscuits, but something was missing. All morning he had been hankering for open-faced Bulgarian cheese on slightly stale white bread. Now he saw with disappointment that there was no Bulgarian, just yellow cheddar and tuna fish.

The omission disconcerted Motke. The three varieties of sandwich constituted the standard menu of official Israeli meetings, served up automatically and invariably, without regard for occasion or protocol. Midlevel bureaucrats discussing traffic problems got the same fare as members of the Cabinet or even the Committee. As the prime minister's chief of staff, Motke could have easily changed this egalitarian refreshment policy, but in truth he liked the government sandwiches, and he counted on them for perspective. No matter how great or trivial the subject, how grand or mundane the forum, the consistency of the food testified to the essential proportion of things.

Motke Vilk at seventy was a realist; he had long ago learned that life contained surprises, many of them unpleasant, and that the best way of facing them was by remaining cheerful and making do. He was in the process of pondering his sandwich choice—whether to go for the cheddar with the little green pickle or the dark, flaky tuna—when he heard Marcus Broun, the head of the Mossad, say that the Iranian extremists had an atomic bomb.

"We've got hard confirmation," said Broun, emphasizing each word in his slow, slightly German-inflected Hebrew. "This time there is no doubt."

The faces of the six men gathered around the table registered varying degrees of concern, but none was astonished. Ever since the Gulf War a decade earlier, they had known that the Islamic extremists were trying to acquire nuclear weapons. In the three years since the fundamentalists had overthrown the Egyptian government, this prospect had loomed larger and larger. The difference was that, put into words here, in the most secret chamber of the Israeli government, the threat had become a fact. Moreover, it was the sort of fact that required action. Efforts to stop extremists from getting the bomb had failed; now something would have to be done to prevent them from using it.

Everyone in the room was looking at Prime Minister Elihu Barzel, who remained, as always, utterly composed. Motke knew each of them well enough to guess their thoughts. The director of the Shin Bet Security Service, a cautious career official, was obviously relieved that this wasn't his problem. The army chief of staff was silent and solemn, but he, too, looked relieved. Almost thirty years younger than Barzel, he was already wrapping himself in the protective cloak of the old man's authority. It was the prime minister who would decide what to do; the army's task would be to implement those wishes.

Marcus Broun was, as usual, impassive as a turtle, but he couldn't quite hide the satisfied air of a man who has done his job well. The Mossad chief prided himself on being unemotional and detached, but Motke had long since observed how eager he was for the prime minister's approval.

Foreign Minister Yarkoni cleared his throat. A former professor of political science at Hebrew University, he was the only one in the room with an independent political base; the dovish party he led was a junior partner in the coalition government. "The only sane thing for us to do now is to open a dialogue with the extremists and look for common ground," he said. "If we had done this five years ago, we wouldn't be facing this situation now."

"Common ground," mused Adam Reshef, in an almost perfect imitation of Barzel's own habit of restating the absurdities of others in a flat, faintly amused tone. Reshef, the prime minister's adviser on special operations, was, at thirty-eight, the youngest man in the room. "They want to destroy us, and we don't want to be destroyed. What common ground does that leave?"

"That's exactly the kind of simplistic thinking that got us into this mess in the first place," said Yarkoni impatiently, looking at Reshef but addressing his words to Barzel. "There's always a diplomatic solution to every dispute."

"Peace in our time," snorted Reshef, like Yarkoni aiming his words at the prime minister. Reshef's normal arrogance was heightened, Motke understood, by the fact that he knew something the others didn't: that Barzel had already embarked upon a course of action. The Project was such a closely held secret that even the members of the Committee could not be told. As far as Motke knew, only he, Barzel and Reshef had even heard its name—and Motke was certain that the prime minister alone fully understood it. It had something to do with the United States, although Motke suspected that the U.S. president, Dewey Goldberg, was unaware of it, but Motke neither asked for nor received any details. There was no need and no point: after almost sixty years, he had learned that no one ever completely penetrated Barzel's cunning circumspection.

"What's the Mossad's assessment on this?" the prime minister asked Broun.

"Eighteen months to two years before they have ballistic delivery capability."

"Military intelligence agrees," said the chief of staff.

"Getting the bomb is one thing; using it is something else," said Foreign Minister Yarkoni. "The Cold War went on for something like forty years without anyone dropping one. The extremists know what we've got."

"Mutual deterrence only works when both sides are sane," said Reshef. "These mullahs think Allah wants them to die in a holy war. And kill everyone else while they're at it."

"That's alarmist rhetoric," snorted Yarkoni, once again glancing at the prime minister. "No one wants to die. Besides, we have the Arrow."

"Which is unproven," said Broun. The Israeli-made Arrow antimissile missile had been operational for several years but the Mossad's scientists still had grave doubts about its reliability. He turned to the chief of staff. "Am I wrong?"

"Technically, no," said the chief of staff cautiously. "Not without direct access to the Americans' Advanced Strategic Intelligence Information system.

"Which the Americans will never give us," said Reshef.

"They're afraid that providing on-line access to ASII would destabilize the strategic balance," said Yarkoni.

"How?" Reshef said with a sneer. "By enabling us to defend ourselves?"

"By giving too much power to dangerous militarists like

you," Yarkoni replied hotly. "And frankly, I don't blame them."

"Of course you don't," said Reshef. "You never blame anyone but us—"

"You didn't let me finish," said the chief of staff. "I said the Arrow is technically unproven, but the air force people are confident that it will work. Give us the budget for a crash program and we can develop our own strategic information system that will be one hundred percent foolproof within two years."

"One hundred percent?" Barzel asked mildly. "Forgive me, but the only thing I am one hundred percent certain about is that nothing is foolproof."

"It was a figure of speech," said the chief of staff, flushing slightly.

"Yes. Well, get me a proposal for supplementary funding," said Barzel. "And now, if you gentlemen have nothing more for me, I'll let you get back to your respective tasks."

Motke Vilk watched as the others hesitated, looked at one another and then silently stood and left the room. He saw the uncertainty on their faces, but he didn't share it. Toward the end of his life, Motke didn't believe in Justice or Immortality or God, but he believed in Elihu Barzel. Unlike God, Barzel never averted his eyes or shrugged his shoulders. Motke didn't know what the prime minister would do, but he was absolutely certain that he would find a way to stop the extremists. In all their years together, he had seen Barzel do many things, but never fail.

It was this confidence that had led Motke to devote his life to serving the broad-shouldered, hawk-faced old man at the head of the table; and it was what had enabled him to ponder the choice between cheddar and tuna while the others contemplated nuclear destruction. Motke had no doubt that Barzel would find a way to deal with the extremists and their bombs; what bothered him was what the hell had happened to the Bulgarian cheese.

CHAPTER TWO

CHARLIE WALKER LOOKED PAST BETH HEFFLIN'S TAN, BARE shoulder and saw Stephano the phony Italian maître d' across the room, a white cellular telephone pressed against his ear. When their eyes met, a thick-lipped smirk of cynical complicity animated Stephano's round face. Charlie shot the sleeve of his jacket and peeked at his watch, the Khomeini model he had picked up during the Iranian revolution. Nine forty-five— Dewey's call was right on time.

The watch, with a little drop of martyr's blood for a minute hand and the Ayatollah's bearded countenance glowing on the hour, was a conversation piece. When Beth noticed it earlier, Charlie had said, "The only problem with this thing is that it loses five hundred years every day." The line was delivered deadpan, in Walker's flat prairie twang. He had used it before and, as usual, it got a laugh.

Reliable witticisms made evenings like this easier. At fifty,

Charlie was single for the first time in twenty-one years, a condition that both excited and embarrassed him. He was one of America's best-known journalists and he had the syndicated column, the Pulitzer and the town house in Georgetown to prove it. He had made a career out of being observant. And yet somehow he had failed to notice that his wife, Helen, had become so bored with their marriage that she preferred living alone in Santa Fe, New Mexico, and working in an art gallery.

"I know you've seen this coming," she had said when she announced she was leaving.

"Sure," he had said. But he hadn't, not at all.

"Poor Charlie," Helen had said. "You know everybody's secrets but your own."

Some of the secrets he knew were matters of state, the kind that made headlines and, occasionally, affected the course of events. But Charlie was a compulsive collector of all sorts of information, and over the course of his career he had accumulated a mental file on thousands of people for no better reason than that they aroused his curiosity.

Stephano, now ambling toward the table with the cellular phone in his hairy, manicured hand, was an example. Not many people noticed waiters, but Charlie had seen past Stephano's unctuous professional manner and taken the trouble to find out something about him. With only four phone calls he had discovered that Stephano was, in fact, a Greek immigrant named Milos Papendopulous whose immigration to the United States, in 1959, had been illegal. Charlie suspected that a little more scratching would uncover the reason for Papendopulous's deception, but he didn't pursue it. There were limits to every investigation, and besides, the information he had was enough. One simple "Hello, Milos" had earned him years of good tables.

"Excuse me, Mr. Walker," said the maître d' in a fruity Mediterranean tone. "It is the White House on the line."

Charlie paused for just a moment, as if deliberating

whether to take the call. Then he reached for the phone and, in a matter-of-fact tone, said, "Charlie Walker here."

"Mr. Walker, please hold for the president of the United States," said the White House operator.

Charlie put a hand over the receiver and shrugged. "It's the president. I won't be too long."

"Take your time," said Beth, impressed.

Charlie nodded and winked at her. Just then a deep male voice came on the line, loud enough for Beth to overhear. "Charlie, I need to talk to you. Where are you?"

"At La Luna, Mr. President," said Charlie, smiling inwardly. It was the third time that month that Dewey Goldberg had made a prearranged call to him during a date. Charlie was a confident man, even a brash one, except when it came to women. Whatever amorous skills he had once possessed had atrophied during his years with Helen, and the thirtyish professional women he now dated—women his status and prestige entitled him to—baffled and intimidated him. Calls from the White House helped bolster his courage; in Washington, a connection to the president was a powerful aphrodisiac. "I'm having dinner with Beth Hefflin. She's an AA for Senator Briney. I'd like to switch to speaker for a minute so she can say hello." Without waiting for permission, Charlie pressed the button.

"The hell with the girl, Charlie," boomed Goldberg's disembodied voice. "This isn't a social call."

Beth Hefflin flushed as Charlie hit the off button. "Dewey, for Christ's sake keep your voice down," he hollered in a soft voice. "People can hear you."

"Sorry," Goldberg said with a laugh. "Is she still listening?"

"No," said Charlie.

"Good. Send her home. There's something I need to talk to you about."

Charlie looked at Beth Hefflin, who was running her

hands through her long dark hair in distracted embarrassment. "Ah, Mr. President, can't this wait until tomorrow?"

"Put on the speaker again," commanded Goldberg. "Beth, are you there, young lady?" he asked in an avuncular tone that he had swiped from Spencer Tracy.

"Yes sir, Mr. President, I am."

"Beth, the president of the United States needs to borrow your escort for a few hours. That all right with you?"

"Of course, Mr. President," she said.

"Now, I don't want you to hold this against Charlie," said Goldberg, a hint of a smile in his voice. "I'm sure he had high expectations for this evening."

"Don't worry, he can have a rain check," she responded lightly.

"You're a loyal American, Miss Hefflin," said Goldberg. "Come by the White House one day next week and I'll award you a medal for good citizenship. Charlie?"

"Yeah?"

"Turn off the speaker again."

"It's off," said Charlie. "Now what?"

"Meet me in an hour, at your place."

"Will you be alone?"

"Just me and the Secret Service. Do me a favor: Ask them to wrap you up an order of chicken diabla, okay?"

"Chicken diabla? Anything else I can get you?"

"A green salad," said Goldberg, ignoring the sarcasm in Charlie's voice. "The food here is lousy."

"Sorry to hear it," said Charlie. "You're the one who wanted the job."

"Like hell I did," said Goldberg.

Charlie shrugged; it was, after all, the simple truth. "Listen, what's this all about?" he asked.

"I don't want to say too much on the phone," said Goldberg. "God only knows who's listening in. Let's wait till I get to your place."

"Sure, okay," said Charlie, already more curious than annoyed. "How about giving me just the headline."

"The headline?" growled Goldberg. "Okay, sure. Here's the headline: The goddamn Jews are out to get me."

CHAPTER THREE

AS THE ARMORED LIMOUSINE SPED IN THE DIRECTION OF Georgetown, Dewey Goldberg felt the sense of relief that always accompanied his forays out of the White House. It had been eleven months since the Tragedy, when the president and vice president, on a carefree family weekend at the president's fishing camp in southwest Louisiana, had crashed their speedboats into one another, incinerating the nation's two highest elected officials in a fiery catastrophe that shocked the world and put Dewey Goldberg, first-term Speaker of the House of Representatives, into the Oval Office.

It was an elevation that Goldberg had never dreamed of. In his first few days in office, as the dazed new president stumbled through the ceremonies and routines of succession, he became starkly aware that his predecessor's staff, known in the press as the Creole Contingent, bitterly resented him. Chief of Staff Boyd French addressed him with exaggerated southern courtesy as "Mr. President Goldberg" and privately referred to him as "President Goldigger." Press Secretary Liz Yardley sniped at him with patronizing suggestions for improving his appearance and personal habits. National Security Adviser Ted Snowden spread the word all over Washington that Goldberg had mixed up Serbia and Slovakia during his first 8 A.M. briefing. And Secretary of State Mathias Pouissant, whose ancestors were once owned by the deceased president's, made his face into a hard African mask whenever he entered the Oval Office.

Goldberg understood their resentment. They were, like the late president, southerners, while he came from a blue-collar district in Michigan. More important, he was a Democrat, they were Republicans. Goldberg had tried to win them over, but his pleas for cooperation and continuity had been met by polite hostility. Even his decision to repress the findings of the Secret Service investigation that showed the cause of the Tragedy to have been drunken recklessness on the part of the late president hadn't helped.

In his first, disorienting days in office, Goldberg had turned to his oldest friend, Charlie Walker, whose advice had been direct and brutal. "These jerks are leaking stuff about you all over town," he had told Goldberg during a boozy late-night chat in the upstairs living room at the White House. "You've got less than a year to make an impression. Get your own people in right away."

"I don't have my own people. Christ, I was just getting settled in over there," Goldberg said, nodding in the direction of the Capitol. "Willis and Graff are damn good political operators, but they can't run a government."

"And you think these creeps can? Hell, a few years ago they were fixing parking tickets for each other in Noo Oawleens. Pouissant speaks French and Liz Yardley's got good tits and that just about sums up their virtues."

"She does have nice tits, doesn't she?"

"Silicone, though," said Charlie.

"You're kidding. How'd you know that?"

Charlie pinched his thin lips together in a salute to his own omniscience. "My point is, dumping these characters is no big loss. Even if your new people need a little on-the-job training."

"I can't do it," said Goldberg, shaking his head. Maybe he didn't know the difference between Serbia and Slovakia, but he knew politics. "I can't afford to rock the boat, no joke intended. People want continuity. I can't come across as some pushy usurper."

Goldberg's gaze had wandered to the picture of his predecessor, boyish and sporty in a blue blazer and khakis, that rested on a side table. "He was a drunk and the veep wasn't much better, but they were elected, not me. And you have to admit, he had the image. People look at me, they see a Jew with a broken nose and a gut."

"Go on a diet," said Charlie. "Get your schnozz fixed. But for God's sake, get rid of these Creole snakes."

"Nope," Goldberg said decisively. "I'm a caretaker and caretakers don't make waves, if that isn't mixing a metaphor."

"It is, but what the hell, you're not a poet, you're the president of the United States—"

"The accidental president," Goldberg said.

"So what? How did Johnson get in? Or Truman? The point is, you're here now, and there's an election coming up in less than a year. Why shouldn't you run?"

Goldberg ran a massive hand through his thinning, kinky black hair. "I dunno, Slim, I'm just not presidential material," he said glumly. "I never prepared myself for this. I'm a pol from Michigan, not some world leader. Half the time I feel like I'm pretending to be president, you know what I mean? Like it's some kind of gag or something."

"Didn't you ever hear of growing in the job?"

"That's the kind of crap you journalists make up. You don't grow at my age; you're either ready or you're not."

"And you're not?"

"I don't think so," said Goldberg. "I honestly don't. I'm going to tell you a secret—I don't even know how to use the goddamn nuclear button."

"What?"

"Yeah," said Goldberg sheepishly. "Right after the inauguration Snowden gave me a briefing on it, but things were so damn hectic, and you know I've never been any good with technical stuff. I thought I'd get a chance to ask again, but he's so fucking nasty I'm afraid to—it'll wind up in the *Washington Post.*"

"Jesus," said Charlie.

"Jesus is right," Goldberg agreed. "You know how it feels going to bed at night, knowing I wouldn't know what to do in a crisis? It's scary as hell."

"I already told you to get rid of Snowden," said Charlie. "If you don't want to do it right now, wait until after the election."

"You aren't giving up, are you?" said Goldberg. "I just got done telling you I'm not running."

"You'll change your mind," said Charlie confidently.

"What makes you say that?"

"I know you, Dewey. Right now you're feeling shaky—anybody who isn't an egomaniac would feel the same way. But in a few months you'll get the hang of things, and then you'll see that you're a damn sight more qualified than the alternatives. Tell me honestly, are any of the other Democrats out there better than you?"

Goldberg shrugged. "Probably not," he conceded.

"And what about Childes? He's got the Republican nomination locked up already. You want his finger on the trigger? You love this country too much for that."

"You think patriotism is going to change my mind?" said Goldberg.

Charlie grinned. "Naw, nothing that heroic."

"Then what?"

"I talked to Didi," said Charlie. "She wants you to run. And we both know you always do what she wants."

"You make me sound like a henpecked husband," said Goldberg ruefully, although he suspected that Charlie was right; Didi usually did get her way.

"It's nothing to be ashamed of," said Charlie. "You got a wife like Didi, you listen to her."

That conversation had taken place six months ago, and Goldberg replayed it in his mind as the limo sped toward Charlie's town house. Charlie had been right: Half a year in office had convinced him to run. That and the polls, which showed that he had a good chance of winning. For the past few months his approval rating had been holding around fifty-five percent—not fantastic, but not bad either—and the focus groups showed that what people most appreciated was the sense of bipartisan stability he had given the country.

By handling the transition with restraint and dignity, Goldberg had been able to maintain the national mood of solidarity that followed the Tragedy. But he had been lucky, too. The economy was strong, although he wasn't sure why and it was clear his advisers weren't, either. Still, that was how the game was played—presidents got credit for inexplicable prosperity—and he was happy to benefit.

Luckily, too, the world had been relatively quiet. Each morning Goldberg got a cold little lecture from Snowden on the status of various international trouble spots. The national security adviser goaded him in small ways—referring to "Rome, Italy" and "Ottawa, the capital of Canada" and giving him significant looks when the subject of Israel arose—but Goldberg, who had learned to hold his temper during his years in Congress, ignored the impertinences. After the election he would, as Charlie had suggested, get rid of him.

After the election. First, though, he had to win in November. The nomination was locked up—Goldberg's poll num-

bers and the party's hunger for victory had been enough to convince all seven of the other Democratic primary candidates,
known in the media as the "Seven Dwarfs," to withdraw—but
the election itself was another matter.

Republican Earl Childes's brand of right-wing populism
was scaring voters, especially in the Northeast. It was widely assumed that Goldberg, with the advantage of incumbency and
certain victory in the big-ticket electoral vote states, would beat
him easily. Goldberg himself had shared that assumption—
until a few hours ago, when his political inner circle had come
to the White House to inform him that he was in serious trouble.

"We're getting reports of slippage," said Freddy Graff
without preliminaries. Graff, a statistician from Ann Arbor,
had been Goldberg's pollster since the early campaigns in
Michigan. Except for his wife, Didi, who was in Houston dealing with details of the convention, and Charlie Walker, Graff
was Goldberg's oldest and most trusted adviser.

"The *Washington Post* had us ahead by eleven points this
morning," said Goldberg.

"Newspaper stuff," said Graff dismissively. "What I'm
seeing is a drop in the hardness of support. A lot of people
who were 'definitely' voting for you a month ago are 'proba-
blies' today."

"What's 'a lot'?"

Graff wiped his bald head with a handkerchief. "Too early
to say exactly. Varies across the country. But it's there."

"Why?" asked Ed Willis. Like Graff, Willis, a former
UAW organizer, had been with Goldberg for years.

"There could be a lot of reasons," said Jack Cassidy,
smoothly assuming control of the meeting. Cassidy was a tall,
meticulous man in his late fifties, a Chicago lawyer who had
started out with the Daley machine and gone on to bigger
things. Goldberg had known him for twenty years, but it was
only in the past few months that Cassidy had joined his politi-

cal circle. Willis, who had run Goldberg's last few campaigns in Michigan, was the nominal campaign chairman, but he was too inexperienced—and abrasive—to effectively conduct a national effort. "For one thing, Childes's Cultural Crusade is catching on, especially out West and in the Bible Belt."

"I thought it was supposed to be the Sun Belt these days," said Goldberg, but nobody smiled.

"Well, whatever kind of belt it is, it's tightening," said Cassidy. "Yesterday in Memphis, Childes called you a card-carrying member of the cultural elite."

Goldberg thought of the endless nights he had spent in grimy union halls, the hundreds of Polish and Ukrainian weddings he had danced at, the countless patriotic banalities he had spewed into the ears of graduating high school seniors over the years. He recalled the parties he had passed up, the glittering dinners he had skipped, the anniversary trip to Paris he had been forced to cancel three years ago because of a strike at a Chrysler plant in his district. "Yeah, right, I'm a regular Truman Capote," he said dryly.

"Don't laugh," said Cassidy. "You talk in real sentences. Your wife has movie-star friends. You went to a fancy law school—"

"And then there's the Goldberg factor," said the president without rancor.

"Yes, there's that," Cassidy agreed.

"But maybe not as bad as we figured," said Graff. "We've got some tough pockets, especially blacks under forty and white Catholic men in the Midwest, but a lot of people say they don't mind voting for a Jew."

"Sure they say it," said Cassidy. "This is America, people are supposed to say it. But remember what happened to Bradley in California. Nobody had a problem voting for a black candidate for governor—until they voted."

"Not the same," said Willis. "Jews ain't jigs."

"African-Americans," Goldberg corrected automatically.

He had been assured by the head of White House security that there were no recording devices in the Oval Office, but who could be sure? After the election he'd have the place checked out by someone he could trust. Until then he'd continue to play CNN in the background—the former mayor of Detroit, Coleman Young, had once told him TV noise screws up bugging devices—watch his language and hope for the best.

"Whatever," said Willis. "The thing is, we expected Jew trouble with the Yahoos and the, ah, Afro-Americans. But now it looks like we've got a problem with the Jews, too. What's Barzel got against you?"

"Barzel? Nothing, as far as I know. I've met him a few times, sat with him once or twice at state dinners. That's par for the course: The prime minister of Israel comes to town, they trot out the Jewish congressmen. That's it."

"No rough dealings with him since you got here?" asked Cassidy.

"No dealings at all. He called to congratulate me. That's the only time I've spoken to him in the last six months. He's supposed to be in Washington just after the convention. Some sort of a private visit, I think. Pouissant wants me to give him a dinner at the White House."

"*Oy,*" said Cassidy. "We need dinner with the Israeli prime minister like we need another crucifixion."

"Pouissant says the Israelis are pushing for it," said Goldberg. "They've got an election coming up, too. And evidently we want Barzel to win it. At least the State Department does."

"No chance of putting him off until after November?" asked Cassidy.

"I'm trying," said Goldberg, turning to Willis. "You started to say I had some problem with Barzel? What makes you think so?"

"I got a call from Sid Eichler today," said Willis. "Barzel's people have been spreading the word all over New York that a Childes victory would be good for the Jews."

"Childes? He's a fucking Christian chauvinist," said Goldberg, momentarily forgetting the bugging devices. "Eichler's crazy."

"I checked around," said Willis. "Apparently it's the same thing in Philly, Boston, L.A., Miami—"

"How far has it gone?"

Graff stroked his bald head. "Nothing's showing up in the polls so far," he said. "But you know how these things go—a word here, a word there, and suddenly people are talking—"

"I'm more worried about what they're writing," said Cassidy. "Specifically, checks. We're counting on big Jewish dough. So far the money's been slow, but it didn't really register until Eichler called."

"Okay, let's assume that Barzel's spreading the word," said Goldberg. "Worst-case scenario, how much does it hurt?"

Cassidy shrugged. "New York's in the bag, but California is close, and so's Florida. And without Jewish votes and money, we're in real trouble."

"In other words, this is serious?"

"Damn serious, Mr. President," said Cassidy. "We've got to find out what Barzel's problem is, and solve it."

"Well, see what you can figure out on your end," said Goldberg, standing to signal the end of the meeting. "I'll do what I can from mine."

And then he had called Charlie Walker.

Chapter Four

THE LIGHTS WERE ON IN CHARLIE'S TOWN HOUSE WHEN THE limo pulled up in front. Goldberg knew that the Secret Service had already checked the place and posted guards around the house and up and down the street. He found Charlie draped over the couch in his living room, dressed in a pair of faded jeans and a sweater. They were almost exactly the same age, but Charlie, with his sandy hair and unlined face, looked a full decade younger. He greeted Goldberg with a casual wave, motioning him to a nearby easy chair.

"It's customary to stand when the president enters the room," Goldberg remarked dryly.

"You want 'Hail to the Chief,' drop in on Ollie North," said Charlie. "How about a drink?"

"Bourbon on the rocks," said Goldberg, taking in the familiar room with envy. Charlie was a collector of international exotica and the place was full of his trophies—photographs of

Idi Amin picking his nose and Yasir Arafat shoveling chow mein into his mouth with chopsticks, lurid Nigerian election posters, a wall rug with the face of Saddam Hussein embroidered in the center and countless other reminders that Charlie Walker had been a player on the Big Stage in the years when Goldberg had been nothing but a plodding congressman from a car district in Michigan.

"Bourbon. Now, there's something worth getting up for," said Charlie, hauling his long, skinny frame off the sofa in graceful stages. He took a bottle of Jack Daniel's off the sideboard, filled two glasses with ice from a silver bucket emblazoned with the Great Seal of the Central African Republic, and placed them on the coffee table. "Pour it like you own it," he said to Goldberg, who smiled; Charlie had been using the same line ever since they shared a dorm room at South Quad in Ann Arbor, back in the sixties.

Goldberg poured two fingers, distractedly swirling the ice with his forefinger. "I'm sorry to screw up your date, but this is important," he said after a moment.

"No problem. A friend tells you the Jews are out to get him, you drop what you're doing. So what's the deal—you borrow money from Shylock or they want to use your blood to make matzos?"

"Evidently they want me out of the White House," said Goldberg.

"Who's 'they'?"

"'They' is Elihu Barzel."

"Sounds like a lucky break," said Charlie. "Getting the prime minister of Israel against you will take a lot of steam out of the Goldberg thing. You sure you didn't cook this up with Barzel, Jew style?"

"Yeah, right," said Goldberg sourly.

"I'm serious," said Charlie. "Leaking this could be your chance to clear the air, put some space between you and Jerusalem."

"Thanks for the advice," said Goldberg. He had a very high opinion of Charlie Walker's journalistic ability, but he was less impressed with his political judgment. "Anything I might pick up by dumping on Israel I'd more than lose with the Jews. Not to mention Reverend Silas."

"In the Year of our Lord 2001, the world is a-comin' to an end on the plains of Armageddon," Charlie proclaimed in a broad imitation of the Reverend Bobby Silas, head of the 2001 Club.

"He's got eight million voters in that club of his," said Goldberg. "And they all think that the Jews are god's Chosen People."

"So what are you, an Armenian?"

"No, but it's Barzel they love. I saw Silas on CNN the other day in Jerusalem practically kissing the old buzzard's ring."

"You still haven't told me what Barzel's pissed off about," said Charlie.

"That's the thing, I don't know. I sent up their aid package, same as always."

"Maybe Barzel found out about your secret pork chop addiction," said Charlie, taking a swig of bourbon.

"Laugh if you want to, but let's see if President Childes calls you up to impress your dates."

"You've got a point," said Charlie. "I can't fault you on constituent services. A change in the White House could definitely cut into my social life." He sighed theatrically. "I guess I'm going to have to do it."

"Do what?"

"Whatever it is you came over here to ask me to do."

"What I want is for you to go over there and find out what's going on. I need to know what Barzel's got against me—"

"Maybe he just doesn't like Jews," said Charlie.

Goldberg shrugged. "Who knows—my old lady doesn't.

Anyway, I have to figure out what he wants and how to call him off."

"And for this I have to drop everything and go to the Holy Land? Why not ask the ambassador over there to find out for you?"

"Starks? He's a Republican."

"Like everybody else in your administration," said Charlie. "What about the CIA? They ought to be able to do a little sleuthing for you."

Goldberg shook his head. "Those guys are the worst. The North Korean chemical weapons program?"

"What about it?"

"This is off the record, Charlie. I'm not telling you this." Charlie nodded. "A few months ago it came up in a meeting. Apparently the Japs are throwing a shit fit. So I said to Admiral Langston, maybe we can neutralize a couple of the key Korean scientists, send them a message that way."

"You said 'neutralize'?"

"Well, yeah. Look, the only thing I know about this stuff is what I see in the movies. They don't exactly have a course on it for new presidents—"

"That's what the national security adviser's for," said Charlie.

"Snowden? Get serious. Anyway, I said it and Old Man Langston gave me a look like I just drooled prune juice on the Constitution. 'The CIA doesn't operate that way,' he said. 'It's illegal.'"

"Of course it's illegal," said Charlie. "So what?"

"That's what I thought." Goldberg sighed. "What I'm saying is, I don't really know how to use the damn agency. After the election I'll get rid of Langston and put in somebody I can talk to, but in the meantime—"

"In the meantime you're asking me to go to Israel and find out what's going on," said Charlie.

"You've worked there before," said Goldberg. "You know the territory."

"Yeah, okay," said Charlie with a theatrical sigh. He took his old friend's powerful arm in his long, bony fingers and squeezed. "Don't worry, El Presidente, I'll get you what you need."

CHAPTER FIVE

SHORTLY AFTER HIS ELECTION, PRIME MINISTER ELIHU Barzel promised reporters that his office door would always be open. It was his kind of promise—literally true but completely deceptive—and although he had delivered the pledge with a straight face, it had appealed to his sense of humor: the private joke of a private and forbidding man. The punch line, as reporters soon learned, was that to reach the prime minister's open door they had to get past Motke Vilk. And nobody got past Motke unless Barzel wanted them to.

Motke was a perpetually cheerful little fellow with a round cherubic face and no ego. He and Barzel made an odd team. Motke was chatty, warm and unpretentious, the temperamental opposite of his formal, distant boss. But his affability, while genuine, was also a mask that hid his toughness, just as the sleeves of his inexpensive sports jackets concealed the blue number tattooed on his forearm.

It was easy to underestimate Motke Vilk. Journalists, politicians and diplomats who tried to pump him for information were treated to jokes, puns and long, pointless Yiddish folk tales, leading them to conclude, as Motke intended, that he was nothing more than a glorified manservant. In this they were wrong. Vilk was not an equal partner, not the prime minister's equal in any sense, but he was the only man alive whom Elihu Barzel trusted.

There were no rules limiting Motke's access to Barzel's private office, but this freedom was largely wasted on him; he preferred to stay in his own small anteroom, answering phone calls, kibitzing with the stream of old cronies who dropped by and flirting harmlessly with the middle-aged secretaries in the outer office. He had little interest in the affairs of state conducted in Barzel's inner sanctum, and he did his best to avoid the tedious discussions that took place there. There were only three occasions when he was always present: when visiting show-biz celebrities came by for a photo-op, when party politics was being discussed and when Foreign Minister David Yarkoni met with Barzel.

Yarkoni, who led the dovish faction in the coalition government, thought Motke attended the meetings because the prime minister wanted a witness to their conversations, and he was perceptibly annoyed by his inability to get Barzel alone; once he had actually requested that Motke leave the room.

"I have no secrets from Motke," Barzel had told him, blandly discounting the possibility that Yarkoni might.

In fact Barzel didn't need Motke as a witness because his office was bugged. He simply enjoyed Yarkoni's discomfort. The exprofessor's didactic, long-winded style exasperated Barzel, but he needed Yarkoni's seventeen Knesset members to form a parliamentary majority, just as he needed the eleven votes controlled by Rabbi Yehuda Bloch.

Rabbi Bloch was an easy man to deal with; all he wanted was public money and special privileges for his super-pious constituents. Barzel's transactions with him were short and, from the prime minister's point of view, not unpleasant. The press considered Rabbi Bloch a fanatic, but in all the time he had served as Minister of the Interior, Motke had never once heard Bloch hector Barzel or any of his cabinet colleagues about their religious obligations.

Yarkoni, on the other hand, never stopped lecturing. He considered himself a visionary geopolitical strategist and he used his weekly meeting with Barzel to present windy analyses of the "conflict" and proposals for resolving it. Yarkoni believed that military force was obsolete and merely perpetuated Islamic enmity, that true peace would come only when the two sides were willing to compromise and that the Moslem extremists could be brought to the bargaining table by imaginative unilateral Israeli concessions, which he called "confidence-building measures."

"Believe me," he had said in his first meeting with Barzel, "everyone wants peace. The Moslems are no different."

"Then why are they trying so hard to get nuclear weapons?"

"I can understand them," Yarkoni had said. "We've got them, after all."

"And you think it's the same thing?"

"It's not what I think," Yarkoni had replied hotly. "I'm trying to see this from their perspective. Soon they're going to have the bomb no matter what we do. That's why it's urgent to make peace now, before it's too late."

"I see you have an instinctive understanding of the extremists' position," Barzel said dryly. Motke had been amused to note that the foreign minister took it as a compliment.

That first encounter had set the tone for their subsequent meetings: Yarkoni lecturing as Barzel sat impassively, occasionally nodding or grunting, but saying little. It was a conversational arrangement that seemed to suit the foreign minister, and Barzel didn't mind, either; Motke knew he used the time to work chess problems in his head. After half an hour or so, it was Motke's duty to interrupt the flow of words by looking at his watch and announcing some urgent business. "You've given me something to think about," Barzel always said, and that seemed to be enough for Yarkoni. At any rate, it was all he got. Barzel let the foreign minister deal with the Europeans and address delegations of visiting dignitaries, but he kept him far away from serious matters—relations with Washington, secret dealings with the Moslems and, especially, the Project.

The Project was the one subject that even Motke didn't know much about and wasn't certain he'd be told about if he asked. What he did know he had learned by observation and guesswork. It took Adam Reshef back and forth to the United States on trips that were kept secret from the Israeli Embassy there. It was connected in some way with atomic bombs—several of the meetings had included Professor Haim Leshansky of the Weizmann Institute, who advised the government on unconventional weaponry—and with American politics. And the Project was evidently scheduled for sometime next year. This Motke surmised from Barzel's refusal to schedule commitments beyond December 31.

"I've got my reasons," the prime minister said without elaboration. This laconic reaction told Motke that those reasons must be the Project; he and Barzel, he was quite certain, had no other secrets.

They first met in the woods someplace in southern Germany. World War II had been over for several months and Motke was one of the many ragged Jewish refugees reeling numbly toward Italy, where they hoped to find ships that would take them to Palestine. He was fourteen years old, weighed barely eighty pounds and had spent almost a third of his life in a Nazi concentration camp.

It was just after dark on a clear winter night when Motke and three younger boys stumbled off the muddy road in the direction of a lit farm cottage tucked into a small clump of trees. Although the temperature was near freezing, the boys were so hungry that they barely noticed the cold. There wasn't much food in postwar Germany, and even less willingness to share it with Jews; but Motke, who was the informal leader of his little band, had learned that farms were a good place to steal scraps or scavenge animal fodder. After his years in the camp, eating garbage came naturally to him.

As the boys crept toward the cottage, they were surprised by the loud barking of a dog. The door opened and they found themselves staring at a large, sloppy, obviously drunk man with a shotgun in his hand.

"What do you want?" he bellowed in German. Although he was dressed in the rough peasant clothes of a farmer, Motke and the others knew what he was; the camps had made them connoisseurs.

"We're lost," said Motke. "Can you tell us how to get back to the main road?"

"Jew scum," said the man.

Suddenly one of the smaller boys keeled over in the snow. "He's starving," said Motke. It was not an appeal, merely a statement of fact.

"I'll put him out of his misery, then," said the German. He laughed uproariously, raised the shotgun to his shoulder and took aim. And then, astonishingly, he fell to the ground, red blood flowing into the white snow. In the moonlight Motke saw the glimmer of a long, jagged piece of metal sunk into the German's right eye.

"Don't waste your time on him. Get the boy into the house," said a voice from behind them in Polish. Motke turned and saw a tall, powerfully built young man dressed in an American army fatigue jacket and woolen trousers. His long blond hair hung wetly over his forehead, giving him a wild look, but as he came closer Motke could see that his eyes were calm.

"It's the Angel of Death," whispered one of the boys hoarsely in Yiddish.

"Take him into the house," the young man repeated, this time in Yiddish. Then he turned to Motke. "You, come with me."

"Where to?" asked Motke, his heart pounding. He had never seen a Jew kill like that.

"To slaughter the dog," said the young man. "Unless you'd rather eat the German."

That was how Motke Vilk first met Elihu Leibowitz, the man who came to be known as Elihu Barzel.

Adam Reshef was due to arrive for a meeting with the prime minister later that morning, but first Barzel would be spending fifteen minutes with the stars of *Doin' It*, an American film being shot at the Globus Studio near Jerusalem. Barzel considered movies a childish diversion, but Israel was trying to develop its film industry and so he accepted these photo sessions as part of the job.

When the guests arrived—producer-director Irv Stein and co-stars Tommy Malton and Barbie Swain—Motke gave them each a cup of Turkish coffee and invited them to wait in his office while he briefed the prime minister.

"Irv Stein gave two thousand dollars to the UJA last year," he said. "Malton and Swain are just actors."

"What's he worth? Stein?"

"According to the consulate in L.A., a couple of hundred million," said Motke.

"There are no small directors, just small donations," said Barzel tartly. "All right, let's get the show on the road."

Motke ushered the Hollywood guests in. Stein was a short, broad-chested, deeply suntanned man in his late fifties who radiated a kinetic authority. Malton and Swain, both obviously nervous at meeting a world leader, were tall, thin and blond; although they were playing a husband and wife in the film, they looked more like brother and sister. They held hands while Motke made the introductions.

"Mr. Prime Minister," said Stein, taking Barzel's hand in both of his and shaking it strenuously. "It's been too long."

"Not yet, but almost," said Barzel with such dignity that Stein completely missed the point.

"I'm a huge fan of yours. You're one of the giants, that's what I was telling Tommy and Barbie here. Right?" The two actors nodded shyly, willing to let Stein do the talking.

"That's quite a compliment from a man of your stature," said Barzel, straight-faced; Motke saw that the producer had, once again, missed the joke. "I trust your film is progressing well."

"It's going to be a killer," said Stein, and suddenly blanched. Evidently he knew something about Elihu Barzel's reputation. "A major success, a hit."

"A hit," said Barzel smoothly, taking the producer's elbow and steering him and the others to chairs in the corner of the small office. "That's very good news, indeed. Please sit down and tell me about it."

It was a familiar routine, one Motke had seen the prime minister perform a thousand times with visiting dignitaries and celebrities, but it never failed to amaze him. He looked at his friend and wondered: *Who is this tall, ramrod-straight old man with the impeccable American accent and polished manners? What has become of the furious, wild-haired Elihu Leibowitz I met on the road to Palestine?*

They hid in the farmhouse for two days, eating and sleeping, too exhausted to move. That first night, after devouring the emaciated German shepherd, Motke sat near Elihu Leibowitz on the rough wooden floor. "Where did you come from?" he asked.

"The woods," Leibowitz replied.

"No, before. Where did you live?"

Leibowitz shrugged his square shoulders. "A village. It's gone now."

"Your family?"

"All dead."

"Maybe someone survived," said Motke hopefully. "They say there's an office in Naples where you can look."

"No one survived," said Leibowitz with cold finality.

There was a pause and the younger boy cleared his throat. "Where did you learn to kill?" he asked quietly.

"In the woods."

"Will you teach me?"

"Yes," said Leibowitz. "Now shut up and let me sleep."

When the food was gone, they trudged back to the main road and rejoined the endless procession of refugees. Within hours the story of the Angel of Death began to spread up and down the road, and as the days passed it raced ahead and behind until it seemed that everyone knew of the mysterious young man who killed like a gentile.

Of the boys only Motke said nothing. He merely remained at Leibowitz's side, unable to lose his sense of grateful exultation. For years he had dreamed of revenge, of cold steel in German flesh, Nazi blood in the snow. Elihu Leibowitz had made that vision a reality, and for that he had won an allegiance that would last a lifetime.

Leibowitz began to attract a handful of refugees that grew as the march progressed. Nothing was said; they simply attached themselves to him, stopping where he stopped, foraging where he did, moving when he moved. He was neither welcoming nor rude, but people kept their distance, respectful of his taciturn privacy. The road to Palestine was full of people who understood that silence was the language of the unspeakable.

One day, not far from the Italian border, a young girl named Rochel nervously approached Motke Vilk. "I need your help," she confided. "There's a man named Yossl who keeps talking to me. Saying things."

"What sort of things?"

"He says he's going to marry me when we get to Naples," she said, sobbing. "He says that if I don't marry him he'll tell everyone what I did . . . there." There was no need for her to explain; Motke knew very well where "there" was and what young girls had been forced to do to survive.

"How can I help?" he asked.

"Talk to him," she said, gesturing with her eyes toward Leibowitz. "Ask him to make Yossl leave me alone."

Later that day Motke told Leibowitz about the woman's problem. Leibowitz listened impassively, and Motke interpreted his reaction as displeasure. "I shouldn't have mentioned it," he said. "It's not your problem, after all."

"No," said Leibowitz. "You did the right thing."

"I felt sorry for her. To blackmail a young girl into marriage is an *averah*," said Motke, using the Hebrew word for "immorality."

"For morality you need God," said Leibowitz in the softest tone Motke had heard him use. "There is no morality now. But there is still decency."

That night Leibowitz spoke to Yossl. The next morning Yossl was gone. Once again word spread up and down the line of marching refugees. People now knew that they could come to the Angel of Death for protection and that the way to approach him was through his friend Motke Vilk.

They reached the transit station for Palestine in early spring. The station was a crowded tent city outside Naples, run by young, suntanned Palestinian Jews who called themselves Palmachniks. They wore short khaki pants and thimble-shaped cloth hats, talked in loud confident tones, slapped one another on the back and sang Hebrew songs at the top of their lungs. They taught the songs to the refugees, too, and sometimes they slapped them on the back and called them by Hebrew nicknames, but it was clear that whatever affection they felt for the refugees was mixed with pity and contempt and an odd sort of anger.

People came back to life in the transit station. On the road they had been numb, zombielike, but now, settled in tents, fed and clothed, awaiting departure for Palestine, they thawed. Some had been driven crazy by the Nazis, and at night the tent city echoed with their cries and hysterical laughter. Others, overwhelmed by an animalistic need for sex, displayed a licentious immodesty they wouldn't have dreamed of before the war. Many ate with sickening frenzied abandon. More than a few were criminals, men and women who had been transformed by the exertions of survival into violent predators. Fights were not uncommon and occasionally there were murders, although the Palmachniks hushed them up for fear of alarming the Italian authorities. Remarkably, though, most of the refugees were not insane. The younger, healthier ones spent their time in earnest preparation for their new lives, learning Hebrew and practicing *kapap*, a form of self-defense with wooden staffs taught by the Palmachniks.

Leibowitz and Motke shared a tent with two dozen others. Leibowitz tried to remain aloof, but he was stared at and whispered after wherever he went. Soon Motke Vilk was besieged with requests. A man had stolen another man's sock—would the Angel of Death intervene? A woman had been raped near the latrines and the Palmachniks had ignored it—should such an act go unpunished? Two men had quarreled and one had threatened to push the other overboard on the voyage to Palestine—could Leibowitz convince him to retract the threat?

Motke, who had only recently celebrated his fifteenth birthday, was proud of his role as go-between, but it also embarrassed him that men old enough to be his father came to him to beg for help. To ease their humiliation he told them jokes and self-deprecating stories and implied that their requests were simple matters. Leibowitz saw this and was impressed, although he pretended not to notice. He received

Motke's list of entreaties impassively, but he seldom refused, although he did not discuss his subsequent actions. Motke heard about them later, on the camp grapevine.

They had been in the transit station a couple of weeks when Leibowitz was summoned by the camp commander, a man by the name of Navon. "We've been hearing a lot about you," he said in a dry way that was hard to interpret. "They call you the Angel of Death."

"My name's Leibowitz."

"Leibowitz is a shtetl name," said the commander.

"That's where I'm from," said Leibowitz. "The shtetl."

"Call yourself whatever you like. People say you fought back." It was a question and the Israeli stared into Elihu Leibowitz's cold pale eyes for the answer.

"In the woods, with the partisans."

"You should be proud not to be like the rest of these sheep who went peacefully."

"What do you know about it?"said Leibowitz, balling his fists in anger.

"I apologize if I offended you," said the commander. "Tell me—do you belong to a Zionist movement?"

"No."

"But you are a Zionist?"

"I am now," said Leibowitz.

"How would you like to join the Palmach?"

"I don't know much about it."

The commander gave Leibowitz a cigarette, which Leibowitz puffed in an oddly elegant manner as he listened to the Palmachnik describe his elite underground combat unit. Many of the terms were unfamiliar, but Leibowitz understood that they lived on collective farms, trained secretly and were engaged in smuggling refugees out of Italy through the British blockade off the coast of Palestine.

"So, what do you say? Are you interested in joining us?"

asked the commander in a tone that made clear the answer was a foregone conclusion.

"No," said Leibowitz. "No thank you."

"No? Why not? You don't belong to Revisionists, do you?"

Leibowitz shook his head. "I don't belong to anyone."

"Look, Leibowitz, in a few days a ship will sail with seven hundred passengers, mostly young people. Quite a few of them are hardcases. We can't afford any trouble on board—it's difficult enough already to find ships that will run the blockade. I want you to go along, help keep order."

"I've never been on a ship in my life," said Leibowitz. "And I'm not a policeman."

"That doesn't matter," said the commander, waving away the objection like a man brushing at mosquitoes. "These people look up to you."

Leibowitz stared at Navon for a moment, took a drag on the cigarette and then nodded. "All right, I'll do it. But I have two conditions. First, there's a kid named Motke Vilk I want to take along as my deputy—"

"You don't have deputies," said Navon. "My men will be in charge."

"That's the second condition," said Leibowitz calmly. "Your men can deal with the ship and the blockade, but I want total authority over the passengers."

"You've been here two weeks and you think you can give me orders?"

Leibowitz shrugged. "It was your idea."

Navon lit a cigarette and inhaled deeply. "Just for my information, why do you have to be in charge?" he asked.

"Because your soldiers are children," said Leibowitz. "And I don't like the idea of being trapped in a boat full of dangerous men that is commanded by children."

Navon stared at Leibowitz for a long moment and then nodded. "All right, we've got a deal," he said. "Move your things into my tent and I'll put you to work getting ready. Sneaking a steamer full of Jews out of Naples isn't easy. And one more thing. For this operation I want you to have a Hebrew code name. Any ideas?"

Leibowitz shook his head, and Navon dragged once more on his cigarette. "The story about you and the Nazi. Is it true?"

"It's grown, but yes, it's true."

"Good. In that case we'll call you Barzel."

"What does it mean?"

"Iron. It means iron. In honor of the piece of iron you buried in the German's brain."

". . . and *Doin' It* is just the beginning," Irv Stein was saying. "Next year I'll be back with Tom Cruise and Winona Ryder."

"Wonderful," said Barzel. "The film industry is very important to us."

"Know what I'd really like to do, Eli?" asked Stein, lowering his voice to a grainy, intimate whisper. "Your life story. The right script, the right talent, and it's a fantastic project. Not to mention the good PR for Israel."

"I'm flattered," said Barzel. He turned to the two actors, who had been silent throughout the conversation. "It's been very nice talking with you, but there's something I'd like to discuss with Mr. Stein in private. Would you mind?"

"Of course they don't mind, Eli," said Stein, nodding vigorously in the direction of the door. He waited until they were gone and then turned to the prime minister with an expectant smile.

"Mr. Stein—" Barzel began.

"Please. Irv."

"Irv. Irv, can I talk to you frankly?"

"Of course, Mr. Prime Minister. Anything."

"I've been following your career for some time," said

Barzel, holding the little man with his eyes. "You're a very impressive fellow."

"Thank you," said Stein, his thick nostrils flaring with self-regard. "Coming from you—"

"No, no; no false modesty," said Barzel easily. "Let me ask you something, and please give me an honest answer. How do you feel about this country?"

"It's the homeland," said Irv Stein, of Beverly Hills, in a reverent tone.

Barzel looked at Motke Vilk and nodded his head slightly, making sure that Stein caught the gesture. "I want to entrust you with a secret," the prime minister said gravely. "The secret of the Circle. If you agree to hear it, you must promise you'll never reveal a word."

"Of course," said Stein, leaning forward in his chair, wholly drawn into the drama that was being unfolded before him.

"Many years ago, Prime Minister David Ben Gurion personally recruited twenty men. Some were wealthy, some powerful, some exceptionally wise or well placed. They came from different countries, spoke different languages, but they had two things in common. They were all Jews and they were all prepared to help Israel in special ways. He called that group the Circle. It's been in existence ever since. It has twenty members, never more, and they are personally selected by the prime minister of Israel."

"God, what a movie that would make," breathed Stein.

"I remind you that you are being entrusted with a secret," said Barzel with great formality. "Perhaps the deepest secret of the Jewish people. It's a sacred trust."

"Of course," said Stein. "I was just thinking like a producer for a minute."

"That's inevitable, I suppose," said Barzel with a forgiving smile. "The membership of the Circle is known only to two men: myself and Mr. Vilk. None of the members knows who else belongs. But I can assure you that they are all men like yourself—great figures in their fields."

"And you're asking me to join?" said Stein in a thick voice.

"As I said, I've been following you for a long time," said Barzel. "I believe you have earned your place among the leaders of our people."

"I wouldn't have to do anything dangerous, right? I mean, we're not talking spying or something like that?"

"Certainly not," said Barzel. "You are far too valuable for such risks. I might ask you to advise us on some sensitive issue or share your insights with our senior army officers or diplomats. There might be certain professional projects in which you could be helpful—not, I might add, a film of my life. And from time to time there are special philanthropic activities that can't go through normal channels. These are funded by the Circle."

"Would I be able to say no if I don't want to do something?"

"Of course," said Barzel. "But let me emphasize this— members of the Circle assume great responsibility and must be counted on to display true dedication. I have to know that you feel such dedication. Otherwise, this conversation never took place."

"You mentioned philanthropy," said Stein. "What kind of numbers are involved here?"

"I'm tempted to say 'If you have to ask, you can't afford it,'" Barzel said with a faint smile. "But you asked a serious question and I will give you a serious answer. You are a rich man, but frankly, not nearly as rich as most of the other members of the Circle. It would be unfair not to ask you to contribute something minimal, say two million dollars. But what I am primarily interested in is your imagination and judgment. For example, we are now in the midst of sensitive negotiations with some of our neighbors. You are a man with vast experience in negotiations. Do you know Foreign Minister Yarkoni?"

Stein shook his head.

"Motke will introduce you. I want you to spend time with him, share your views. Later, I may ask to use you as a backdoor diplomatic conduit. How does that sound?"

"This is overwhelming," said Stein. "I came in here to say hello and, well, this—"

"I apologize for the abruptness, but there's no way to prepare someone for the Circle. In essence, your entire life has been your preparation."

"Two million bucks is a lot of money," mused Stein. "Would it be deductible?"

"I'm afraid not," said Barzel. He paused, gazing into Stein's eyes. "Perhaps I've been misinformed about your financial situation. I have no wish to embarrass you, Mr. Stein."

"No, no, I've got the money," said the producer hurriedly. "If the others pay up, I can, too."

"Splendid," said Barzel, rising and extending his hand. "Then you accept?"

Stein rose and took Barzel's hand. "Yes, Mr. Prime Minister," he said, his nostrils flaring once more. "Irving Stein is at your service and the service of his people."

Barzel raised his hands over the little producer's head, fingers split in the traditional priestly gesture. *"Adonai y'ten oz l'amo,"* he intoned in Hebrew. "The Lord will give strength unto his people."

"Amen," said Motke.

"Amen," echoed Stein.

"Tomorrow Motke will contact you about your meeting with the foreign minister," said Barzel briskly. "He'll also tell you where to deposit the money. Oh, and there are some documents I'd like you to look at, classified intelligence reports. Will you do that, and give your candid evaluation to Yarkoni?"

"Of course, sir," said Stein.

"Good. Well, I've kept you long enough," said Barzel, guiding the producer gently toward the door. "Your young stars are waiting for you outside."

"What if I need to get in touch with you?"

"Speak with Motke," said Barzel. "From now on, the less contact between us, the better. But when the time comes, I'll reach out to you."

"I understand," said Stein. "I won't let you down, Mr. Prime Minister. Shalom and God bless you."

Barzel waited for the door to close, sat down behind his desk and looked at Motke. "You've just witnessed a sacred ceremony," he said dryly.

"I thought I was going to crack up when you did the rabbinical blessing," said Motke, grinning. "I've never seen that one before."

"It was a spur-of-the-moment improvisation," said Barzel, still perfectly composed. "Inspired by Mr. Stein's own theatrical spirit."

"Keep this up and there *will* be twenty members in the Circle," said Motke. "What do you want to do with the money this time?"

"Rabbi Bloch needs a new yeshiva," said Barzel. "Half a million ought to cover it. Give the rest to Boroshefsky for Russian immigrant housing. Make sure he knows who it's from."

"Stein?"

"Me," said Barzel, allowing himself a faint smile. "And don't forget to introduce our newest member to Yarkoni—they were made for each other."

"What about the documents you promised him?"

"Get a stack of old briefing papers," said Barzel. "Stamp them 'Top Secret'; that should do the trick." He looked at his gold Rolex and frowned. "All right, back to business. What's holding up confirmation of my meeting with President Goldberg?"

"I spoke with the embassy yesterday," said Motke. "They're pressing the White House, but Goldberg won't give us a firm yes. He's using the convention as an excuse."

"Don't worry, he'll say yes," said Barzel. "Just get the date pinned down."

"If you say so." Motke shrugged. He knew that Barzel never made empty promises; if he said there would be a summit, there would be one. "Anything else?"

"Not for now," said Barzel. "Reshef will be here in a little while, and we'll be about an hour. Make sure we're not disturbed."

Chapter Six

THE REFUGEE SHIP, CALLED THE *SANTA CATARINA*, SLIPPED through the British blockade and docked in Haifa on April 11, 1946. As it was unloading, Barzel was introduced to a redheaded Palmach officer named Yitzhak who appeared to be about twenty years old. "You were made an offer in Naples," he said in a deep, slow baritone. "Are you interested?"

"We're interested," said Barzel.

"The offer was made to you alone. The boy is too young."

"In that case, we're not interested," said Barzel. He picked up the small canvas bag that held his possessions and motioned for Motke to do the same.

The red-haired sabra gave him a small, shy grin, almost a grimace. "I see they were right about you," he said. "Okay, at five a truck will take you both to Kibbutz Ein Harrod. In the meantime you can wander around and see the sights." Without another word he turned and walked toward the ship, which was unloading its human cargo.

"Well, what do we do now?" asked Motke.

"We get ourselves a suntan," said Barzel, unbuttoning his shirt and lowering himself onto a crate.

"A suntan? What for?"

"Because we're in the Palmach, *habibi*," said Barzel, using the Arabic term of endearment they had heard the Israelis use in Naples. "And we're going to become honest-to-God, freckle-faced Palmachniks."

In the next few months Motke Vilk watched in astonishment as Elihu Leibowitz transformed himself from a Polish Jew into a sabra. From the day he arrived at Kibbutz Ein Harrod he became Eli Barzel; few people knew his former name and those who used it were silenced by an icy look. He exchanged his tattered American army clothes for khaki shirts and shorts and replaced his scarred black leather shoes with sandals. A girl soldier named Batya cut his long, wild blond hair Palmach style—close on the sides and high on the top, with a lock falling onto the forehead—and the hot Galilee sun turned his pale skin the color of light toast.

Motke discovered that his friend had an amazing skill with languages. On the road he had heard him speak flawless Polish and German as well as Yiddish, but there was nothing unusual about that; many Jews knew several languages. In fact, Motke had been surprised that Leibowitz, who was fourteen when the war broke out, already past the age of bar mitzvah, appeared to know almost no Hebrew. But now he picked it up effortlessly, not just the words but the choppy cadences, the guttural pronunciation, even the slangy, boisterous sabra intonation that seemed so foreign to the reserved nature he had displayed in Europe. Within three months, no one would have guessed that Eli Barzel had recently arrived from Poland; within six, new recruits asked him what kibbutz he had been raised on.

The transformation of Elihu Leibowitz went far beyond clothing and language. With uncanny ease he absorbed and mimicked everything around him. By day he worked in the kibbutz fields as though he had been born on a farm. At night around the campfire he sang Hebrew tunes and gracefully executed the steps of the intricate folk dances. Most surprising of all, he took on the back-slapping pioneer heartiness of the young Palmachniks. He joined them—and in time led them—on nocturnal chicken-stealing expeditions, laughed extravagantly at their rustic practical jokes and, in more serious moments, listened without comment to their idealistic debates over the "purity of arms" and the "redemptive quality of physical toil" and the utopian society they were planning to create in the land of Israel.

In all of this, save the ideological discussions, Motke Vilk happily participated. He had the orphan's desire to belong and the victim's guilty need to please that enabled him to take on sabra trappings almost as quickly as Barzel. He learned to play the accordion, on which he accompanied the nightly campfire songfests, and entertained his new comrades with *chisbatim*, funny, exaggerated stories that won him a reputation as a raconteur. And he discovered sex. At Ein Harrod promiscuity was considered a socialist imperative, an act of liberation from the dictates of the rabbis and the values of bourgeois capitalism. It was this, more than anything else, that turned Motke Vilk into an ardent Labor Zionist.

Strangely, sex was the one Palmach activity that Eli Barzel avoided, much to the disappointment of the girls at Ein Harrod. Among themselves they giggled that he looked like a movie star, by which they meant—although they never quite put it this way—that he didn't look like a Jew. He was a compelling figure, six feet tall, with broad shoulders, a slender waist and a graceful way of carrying himself. His eyes were icy blue, his nose large and aquiline and his chin strong and cleft. In fact he did look a little like an American movie star, and a Jewish one at that—Kirk Douglas.

Barzel was friendly to the girls but aloof, and once again Motke Vilk found himself enlisted as a go-between. One day, a young woman named Galia Carmeli asked him to tell Eli Barzel that she wanted to sleep with him. It was an uncomfortable task, but Motke thought his friend might want to know, and so he told him. It was a mistake.

"This place is turning you into a pimp," Barzel said coldly. "If this girl is so wonderful, have her yourself and leave me alone."

"Your precious Eli is a homo," Galia said angrily when Motke reported his lack of success.

"No, he's not," Motke said stoutly. He knew the damage the war had done to people; it was a knowledge he couldn't begin to convey to these fresh-faced pioneer children. Perhaps, he thought, Elihu's manhood had been destroyed by the Nazis. Perhaps he was still in love with a girl who was missing or murdered. Or perhaps, underneath all the newly acquired Palmach bravado, he was simply too empty to engage in anything as joyous as sex. At any rate Motke resolved never to raise the subject again, and in fifty years of friendship, he never had.

Chapter Seven

CHARLIE WALKER SAW SARA EPSTEIN BEFORE SHE SAW HIM, which gave him a chance to look her over and react to the changes that had taken place in her appearance in the four years since their last meeting. She was at the age when four years mattered. Last time she had been a knockout, with long jet-black hair and taut, creamy skin. Now her hair was cut sensibly short and streaked with gray, and even from across the room he could see the shadow of a double chin. She was a handsome woman but no longer beautiful, and the transformation made Walker feel a little sad for himself.

It was early by Tel Aviv standards, before midnight, and the trendy little bar across the street from the Mann Auditorium that Sara had suggested was not yet crowded. When she glanced up from her drink she had an unobstructed view of Charlie standing at the door staring at her. She waved and waited for him with a small smile on her full lips. At the table they embraced. "Well, how do I look?" she demanded in her hoarse smoker's voice.

"Wonderful."

"Bullshit," said Sara with cheerful directness. "Not bad, but not wonderful. You don't look any younger, either, by the way."

"Thanks," said Charlie ruefully. He had first met Sara years before when he came to Israel on assignment. They'd had a brief affair at the time that, he soon discovered, meant even less to her than it did to him. For years now their relationship had been strictly professional, but she still allowed herself the candor of an old lover. Not that she needed an excuse—Sara Epstein was extremely direct with everyone, although Walker knew better than to confuse her plainspoken manner with ingenuousness. She was the senior political correspondent for *HaMeser*, and, although she didn't know it, a member of WIN—Walker Information Network.

WIN existed in Charlie Walker's mind and on his Rolodex; it consisted of a couple dozen journalists around the world whose information and judgment Charlie respected. He had put WIN together over years of painstaking trial and error, weeding out the recyclers of conventional wisdom, the conspiracy theorists and the experts who always had an explanation for everything. What was left were reporters like Sara—smart, well connected and willing to swap information. These were the members of WIN, and Charlie traded with them, although not on a wholly reciprocal basis. Reciprocity implied equality, and Charlie Walker made a point of always getting a little more than he gave.

There were three Israeli WINers, but Sara was the smartest and by far the best connected—especially now that she was sleeping with Amos Levran, the deputy head of the Mossad. She was a discreet woman; Walker had no illusions that she would leak him any state secrets. On the other hand he was certain that she'd tell Levran about their meeting. And since he would be poking around areas that might arouse suspicion, he wanted the Mossad to misunderstand his mission right from the start.

Sara raised her hand, caught the attention of the waiter and ordered Charlie a bourbon on the rocks. "You haven't become a health nut, I hope," she said, lighting a Kent. "Like McGreary."

Charlie shook his head admiringly. Anson McGreary was the head of naval operations at the Pentagon. Not many Americans, let alone foreigners, knew his name. Almost no one outside his family knew that he had recently been hospitalized for alcoholism. Sara had no special reason for mentioning McGreary; she was just showing off.

"Levran tell you that?" Walker asked, causing her eyes, which had clouded with enjoyment, to snap into sharp focus.

"Who's Levran?" asked Sara in her almost perfect American English.

"Nice try." Charlie laughed. "Look, I'm not here to pump you for spy stories. I need some help on something."

"What kind of something?"

"Can you keep a secret? I mean, seriously."

"Can you?"

"Me? Oh, you mean your boyfriend? No problem. That was just to show you I haven't lost my old touch."

"That'll be the day. Okay, what's the big secret?"

"I'm working on a book with an Israeli angle. A biography of Dewey Goldberg."

"What's so secret about that?"

Walker shrugged his narrow shoulders. "Nothing, really, except the publisher wants to spring it as a surprise. It's a marketing thing; secrecy's part of the deal."

"Well, I hate to disappoint you, but I don't know a damn thing about Dewey Goldberg except that he's got a big nose and a silly first name," said Sara.

"His mother was a Republican and he was born in 1948, which is the year Tom Dewey ran for president."

"Dewey ran in '44, too."

"He did, didn't he? You don't think of that, usually. Anyway, I don't need you to tell me about Goldberg. I've known him for thirty years and I'm his best friend—"

"I can see this is going to be a hard-hitting exposé," said Sara.

"They don't want an exposé, they want a serious evaluation of America's first Jewish president. And that obviously includes a chapter on his relationship with Israel."

Sara sucked on her Kent and blew the smoke out of the corner of her mouth. "There isn't that much to say, at least as far as I know. He was here a couple of times when he was in Congress, but who wasn't? As president he hasn't changed any policies. Is that what you mean?"

"But how do Israelis feel about him? A Jew in the White House? It must be a big thing, no?"

"The truth is, most people don't think about it one way or the other," said Sara. "If you mean the politicians, I'd say it makes them a little nervous."

"Scared he might bend over backwards?"

"Something like that. Maybe not quite that bad. Ever since the Moslems started blowing up buildings in New York it's pretty hard for an American president to dump on us. Even a Jewish one." The irony didn't surprise Charlie—disdain for American Jews was a common Israeli sentiment. He had heard the lecture on the hypocrisy of the diaspora many times before and the subject, like most Jewish controversies, bored him.

"You think Barzel feels the same way? That a Jewish president is bad for Israel?"

"Ask him," said Sara. "He'll talk to you. He loves famous American journalists."

"I will, but I'm interested in your take. What do you hear?"

"Nothing much," said Sara casually—maybe too casually, it seemed to Walker. "As far as I know, relations are fine. Aren't they?"

Walker recognized his cue to give something up. "There are rumors that Barzel might want the other guy," he said.

"With Barzel, anything's possible," said Sara. "I can ask around if you want."

"I'd appreciate it," said Charlie. "You know him, right?" Sara nodded. "What do you think of him?"

She paused for a moment, looking out over the restaurant. "I'm not sure what I think," she said finally.

"Sara Epstein without an opinion? That doesn't sound like you."

"You're right, it doesn't," she agreed. "But he's really not like anybody I've ever met."

"He's never been married, has he?"

Sara shook her head. "There were rumors about him when he was young, that he was gay. But they're not true."

"You speaking from personal experience?"

"You mean, did I sleep with him? No. But a woman can tell about a man."

"He's past seventy," said Charlie.

"I don't care if he's a hundred and seventy," said Sara.

"What'd he do, make a pass at you?"

Sara laughed, imagining it. "Barzel? Never. I don't think he cares much for women, but not in the way you mean it. He doesn't care much for men, either."

"A cold fish?"

"More like a lone wolf. You know how it is here: We all know each other, everybody went to the second grade with everybody else's cousin. But Barzel's not like that. He just sort of showed up here from Poland one day. Then he disappeared. Then he came back. Nobody's close to him. Except for Motke Vilk, nobody really knows him at all."

"A man of mystery," said Charlie.

"Not exactly. But he's not a regular Israeli politician, that's for sure. He's completely charming when he wants to be, but it's a sort of Olympian charm, as if he's above everyone else. I never knew Churchill or de Gaulle but that's the way I picture them. Larger than life."

"Sounds like you like the guy."

"Not 'like.' 'Admire,' maybe. 'Distrust' for sure. Have you read his book?"

Charlie nodded.

"Then you know he has scary ideas about Jewish survival. But I've got to admit, he's the only great man I've ever met personally."

"Great man? Aren't you getting a little carried away?"

Sara shrugged and blew more smoke into the restaurant. "I don't think so," she said. "Meet him and judge for yourself."

"A great man with scary ideas," repeated Walker. He wondered if Sara's opinion was shared by Amos Levran. It was an intriguing speculation, but Sara cut it short by looking at her watch.

"I've got to meet someone in twenty minutes," she said. "What else do you want to know?"

"Actually I just wanted to touch base," said Walker easily. "I'm still at the stage where I don't know exactly what I'm looking for. Who might have a good take on the Barzel-Goldberg thing?"

Sara stubbed out her Kent and rose. "Let me think about it and I'll call you tomorrow," she said. "Maybe we can have dinner one night this week."

"Just you and me?"

"And anyone you want to bring."

"I thought maybe Levran would like to join us," said Charlie lightly.

"Lavern who?" Sara replied with a smile. "Give me a call, Charlie. It's good to see you again."

"If you weren't meeting him now, I'd ask you to come back to the Sheraton for a drink," he said.

"No, you wouldn't, " said Sara flatly.

"I'm hurt," said Charlie with mock indignation. "You don't believe me."

"You're right, I don't," she said. What she didn't say was that she didn't believe he was writing a book, either.

CHAPTER EIGHT

ADAM RESHEF CAUGHT A CAB FROM KENNEDY TO LAGUARDIA, where he boarded a flight for Flagstaff, Arizona. The trip would take just under four hours, long enough for him to go over what he was planning to say to Governor Earl Childes and the Reverend Bobby Silas. Normally Reshef didn't bother planning his conversations in advance, but this one was crucial. He had to be certain that there was no misunderstanding. They had been skirting around this issue for a long time, but now that the party conventions were almost here, it was time to nail Silas and Childes down. If they were prepared to be nailed.

It had been almost two years since Reshef had first met the Reverend Silas in Jerusalem. Reshef had been at work in his small, spare office down the corridor from Barzel's when the door opened and Motke Vilk stuck his head inside. "There's somebody the Old Man wants you to meet."

Reshef repressed a scowl. He didn't like interruptions and he didn't like Motke. The little man was a court jester, full of foolish observations and practical jokes that, more than once, had been aimed at him. Still, he made an effort to be polite. Motke's relationship with Barzel was a puzzle, but it was also a fact, one he had to take into account.

"Who is it?" he asked.

"An American by the name of Silas. He has some information that falls under the heading of national security."

Reshef placed some papers in the safe, spun the combination lock and followed Motke down the hall to the conference room. "What kind of information?" he asked Motke as they walked.

"Unconventional weaponry, I think you'd say," Vilk responded. From where he stood, Reshef couldn't see the gleam in his eye.

The conference room was a large rectangle dominated by a long green-felt-covered table. As they entered, Reshef saw a youngish man, no older than thirty-five, dressed in a conservative dark suit and somber tie. His hair was light, parted neatly along the side and slightly damp, as if he had recently showered. His face, which was dominated by a long nose and quick, intelligent eyes, glowed with ruddy good health.

"Adam, I want you to meet Reverend Silas," said Vilk, his elfin face crinkling into a happy grin. "Reverend Silas, this is the prime minister's security adviser, Adam Reshef."

Reshef shot Motke a sharp look, but the little man was already retreating from the room. "You two have a good schmooze," he said over his shoulder.

"It's a pleasure to meet you, Adam," said Silas, offering his hand. His voice was a rich southern baritone.

"What can I do for you?" asked Reshef, taking the minister's hand in a limp grip. Obviously this was one of Motke's pranks, and Reshef intended to dispose of Silas as soon as possible.

"The Lord's work," said the minister. He watched Reshef's face cloud and chuckled. "In fact, you're already doing it."

"I think there's been a misunderstanding," said Reshef. "I don't deal with religious affairs—"

"Everyone in the Holy Land deals with religious affairs," said Silas. "You've been chosen for it."

"Look, I'm very busy. I don't have time—"

"Time," interrupted Silas. "Time is short. Less than a thousand days."

"Until what?"

"Until the end of the year 2001. The millennium. The final confrontation between Gog and Magog on the plains of Armageddon. What you call in Hebrew Megiddo."

"Damn, why do I have to waste my time on this shit?" Adam exclaimed in Hebrew.

"I don't know what you just said, but judging from your expression it wasn't a benediction. You think I'm crazy, don't you?"

When Reshef was at Cal Tech he had occasionally seen television evangelists on TV, grotesque, shameless con artists braying for contributions. The Reverend Silas seemed different. He sounded intelligent and the look in his cornflower-blue eyes was sincere. "I'm not a psychiatrist," said Reshef.

"Of course not," said Silas. "I understand. Prime Minister Barzel said we should meet. I simply wanted to say hello."

"And tell me the world's coming to an end?"

"On the contrary. That the world is going to be reborn. The forces of darkness will be defeated. In fact, it is already happening. The fall of Russian communism—do you think that was an accident?"

"It was the culmination of a historical process—"

"No," said Silas, raising his voice slightly and peering intently into Reshef's eyes. "Empires don't just disintegrate. It was God's hand. And now the final battle is approaching."

"Who, exactly, is the enemy?"

"Those who have declared holy war on His holy people," said Silas. "The Moslems. God will make His will manifest—and we are destined to be His instruments."

"It's been nice talking to you," said Reshef curtly. He turned on his heel and strode out of the room, certain that he had been victimized by one of Motke's stupid pranks.

Later that day, Motke stuck his head into Reshef's office again. "Did you enjoy your Bible lesson?" he chuckled.

"Don't ever do anything like that again," said Reshef tightly.

"It wasn't my idea." Motke shrugged. "The Old Man wants to see you."

Reshef found Barzel seated behind his desk, staring into space. "What did you think of Reverend Silas?" he asked.

"A lunatic," said Reshef.

"An occupational trait," observed Barzel. "Look at our own Rabbi Bloch. And yet, sometimes lunatics can be extremely useful. Without the good rabbi, for example, we wouldn't have enough votes to hold the coalition together." Reshef sat, waiting. He knew Barzel wouldn't call him in for a chat about religion. "Tell me, had you ever heard of Reverend Silas?"

"No," said Reshef. "Why would I?"

"You should broaden your horizons. He happens to be the founder and leader of the 2001 Club. There was an article about him in *Newsweek* not too long ago."

"I don't read *Newsweek*," said Reshef. "I don't have time."

"Yes, I'm lucky to have such industrious associates. It gives me the opportunity for literature and reflection," said Barzel. "The 2001 Club is an organization of born-again Christians who believe the Messiah is coming on the last day of the year 2001. And, since He's a good Jewish boy, this will be his first stop."

"Sure," said Reshef.

"*Nu*. You might think this is a crazy idea, and I might. But there are eight million Americans who happen to believe it. Eight million members of the 2001 Club."

"Eight million?"

Barzel nodded. "That's an audited figure, by the way; I checked. Reverend Silas is a powerful man. And a great friend of Israel."

"He thinks we're God's holy people," said Reshef.

"And that Islam is the enemy of Christian civilization," added Barzel. "Did he tell you that?"

"Something like that. Don't tell me you think he can be useful."

"As our Arab cousins say: 'The enemy of my enemy is my friend.' That's quite a good phrase, by the way. The Arabs have a way with words. I've often thought it was too bad that they don't make fortune cookies, like the Chinese. But, to answer your question, yes, I think that Reverend Silas can be very useful indeed."

Reshef paused, waiting. He still wasn't sure what Barzel had in mind, but he didn't want to appear lost. There were only two people in the world whose good opinion mattered to him—his mother and Elihu Barzel.

"The Project," Barzel said after a moment.

"What does this millennium nonsense have to do with the Project?" asked Reshef.

"Nothing. But it has everything to do with politics. We can't go ahead without at least the tacit support of the Americans. That means the next president, whoever he is. And ballots speak louder than words."

"You didn't tell Reverend Silas—"

"He doesn't need me to tell him anything. God talks to him. But here's what I'm telling you: When the Project begins, most of the Jews in America will run for cover. These Christians are different. They don't give a damn about the *New York Times.* They believe in God. They believe the Jews are God's chosen people. And, in all modesty, they believe that I'm God's chosen prime minister. An election is coming up in less than two years over there. Give me eight million voters and whatever Jews are still Jewish and I've got a bloc of support that provides us real leverage with both candidates."

Reshef nodded; he saw it now.

"I want you to go out and buy yourself a copy of the New Testament. Don't scrimp, get one with the colored pictures of angels and cherubs. And put together a dossier on Silas and the 2001 Club. From now on, you're going to be the point man with Reverend Silas."

"Me? He doesn't like me. I was rude to him."

"Nonsense," said Barzel wryly. "He loves you. He told Motke you remind him of a modern-day Joshua."

"Can I get you something, sir?" said a woman's voice. Reshef looked up, startled out of his reverie, and saw a trim-looking stewardess smiling at him.

"Mineral water," he said.

"Traveling on business or pleasure?" asked the stewardess. Reshef looked closely and saw a glint of interest in her eyes.

"Business," he said, accepting the drink.

"If I can get you anything else, just let me know," said the stewardess.

"Not a thing," said Reshef in an unmistakable tone of dismissal. The stewardess gave him a sharp look, began to say something and then moved down the aisle. Reshef watched her go without regret. He wasn't a passionless young man— far from it. But he had spent his life struggling to control and discipline his nature by imposing on himself a series of challenges and deprivations. Physically average as a boy, he had pushed and tortured his body until it became capable of exceptional endurance. As a candidate in flight school, he had denied himself even the slightest relaxation in his quest to become the best pilot in the Israeli air force. At twenty-eight, after doctors grounded him for diabetes, he had gone to the

United States, enrolled at Cal Tech and completed a Ph.D. in physics in four years of unremitting effort. He still allowed himself no more than four hours of sleep each night, began every day with two hundred sit-ups and strictly rationed his personal time to Friday-night dinners with his wife, Ruthie, and their five-year-old son, and Saturday lunch at his parents' villa north of Tel Aviv.

Ruthie Reshef was a nice young woman, but Adam felt no particular love for her. He had married out of a sense of duty toward his mother and a feeling that marriage would give his life an even greater discipline. Ruthie did not satisfy his strong sexual urges, but, despite countless opportunities, he never went with other women. Instead, he masturbated. For him it was an act of will, a way of asserting his independence and controlling even his most primal impulses.

The one thing that Adam Reshef never felt compelled to improve was the quality of his mind. He was, and had always known himself to be, brilliantly intelligent. In the second grade his IQ had been tested at 172. Told by his awed parents that he was considered a genius, Adam had merely shrugged; it was not news to him.

When adults asked him what he wanted to be, little Adam Reshef automatically answered, "a pilot and a scientist." He did not explain that he considered these merely means to an end, skills necessary to become what he knew he was destined to become: a hero.

Only Adam's mother, Frieda Reshef, guessed Adam's grand design. Unlike his father, a somewhat vague, very successful attorney who had immigrated to Israel in the fifties from Montreal, she had an instinctive understanding of her strange, gifted son. It was from her that he inherited his self-control and his secretive nature. Frieda Reshef had spent three years in Auschwitz, a fact she mentioned to no one. Most of her friends were unaware that she had been in the death camp. They knew her as an unexceptional housewife, warmhearted, cheerful and energetic. They did not know that she awoke almost every night shrieking in terror. She never discussed these nightmares with Adam and he never asked. He feared that bringing the night monsters into the sunlight might destroy his mother's daytime tranquillity.

Shortly after Adam's ninth birthday, in May 1967, Egypt suddenly blockaded Israel's southern shipping lanes and poured troops into the Sinai Peninsula. Adam's father was called up to his army reserve unit. His mother busied herself rolling bandages and helping clear out air-raid shelters. Teenagers dug graves in the nearby park to prepare for the casualties of the expected Egyptian onslaught.

There was no Israeli TV in 1967—Israel's flinty pioneer rulers considered it frivolous and culturally subversive—but the Reshefs, like many well-to-do families, owned a set on which, with the help of a tall antenna, they could tune in Egypt and Jordan. The night before the outbreak of war, Adam came home and found his mother sitting in the darkened living room watching a frenzied crowd of Egyptians screaming for Jewish blood.

"They're back," she said in a hollow voice.

"Who's back?"

"The Nazis."

"These aren't Nazis, they're Arabs," said Adam. At that moment he was less afraid of the Egyptian army than of the sound of his mother's voice. It was a lifeless, helpless murmur, more chilling than the shrieks in the night. He put his arms around her and awaited her embrace, but she remained frigid. "They throw the children into the fire," she mumbled.

"The army will stop them," said Adam.

"Nothing ever stops them," Frieda said. "They won't stop until every one of us is dead."

When the war was over, Adam's father came home with some empty artillery shell casings from Sinai as souvenirs, and returned to his law practice with a minimum of fuss and no war stories. Frieda used the casings as planters, bought new china, had the walls of the living room covered in pastel paper and changed her hairdo. She never spoke about the night in front of the television set. Nor did Adam. He knew she was ashamed of her breakdown.

Such sensitivity was not typical of Adam Reshef. He was an arrogant, willful boy, disliked by his classmates and teachers. The only discipline he accepted was self-imposed; attempts by outsiders to control him met with stony resistance. His lack of popularity didn't bother him; the present was meaningless, except as prologue and preparation. From the age of nine he dedicated himself to one goal: making his mother—and himself—invulnerable.

The opportunity presented itself, oddly enough, in California. At Cal Tech Adam worked part-time as a coordinator for Zionist affairs on campus. It was an undemanding job, entailing little more than making logistical arrangements for visiting Israeli dignitaries. That is how he first met Elihu Barzel.

Reshef knew very little about Barzel. He was one of those enigmatic Israelis whose names were familiar but whose deeds were somehow clouded in mystery. According to the bio forwarded by Barzel's lecture agent, he had been an officer in the Palmach, and later a very successful businessman in the United States. In 1980, after almost thirty years abroad, he had returned to Israel, where he set up a number of factories and served as a consultant to the Ministry of Defense. He had recently published a book, *When All Else Fails*, that had become a best-seller in Israel and the United States. He was in California on a promotional tour.

Reshef bought a copy of *When All Else Fails*. Twenty pages into the book he realized that he was reading his own thoughts. Reshef felt that he had finally found an intellect as keen as his, a vision of equal clarity, a bold courage that matched his own.

Elihu Barzel was not afraid to look at the world unblinkingly. "Nothing," he wrote, "not the suffering of others, not the rules of international behavior, not the law of God Himself, surpasses the right of Jews in this generation to do what is necessary to protect themselves. Better to destroy the world than to allow the blood of one single Jewish child to flow into Hitler's scarlet river."

Reshef met Barzel at the airport. He recognized him from the picture on the dust jacket, but he was unprepared for the sheer physical presence of the man. His bearing was straight but not rigid; less military than regal. Unlike most Israeli visitors, he didn't protest when Reshef offered to carry his suitcase. But, despite his age—Barzel was sixty-two at the time—it was obvious that he could have slung both Reshef and the bag over his broad shoulders and carried them through the airport without difficulty.

On the way to the campus, Adam could barely contain his excitement. "I've read your book," he said. "It's brilliant." It was rare praise from him, but Barzel, unaware, merely nodded.

"It expressed my thoughts," Reshef added.

"Did it?" said Barzel politely.

For the first time in his life, Adam Reshef experienced the fear of being thought dull by someone he admired, and it caused years of rigid reserve to come tumbling down. "Please don't patronize me," he said urgently. "It's important that you see who I am."

"What am I supposed to see?"

"Yourself," said Reshef urgently. "I'm you, thirty years ago. You're me, thirty years from now. We understand what the world is, what it's capable of. We aren't afraid of doing what needs to be done."

"I suppose I should know this, since I'm you, but what are you talking about?"

"Don't laugh," said Reshef. "What I'm trying to say is, people are too weak to face reality. They see the other side, try to bargain with evil, confuse cowardice with reason. In every generation there are just a few men who are strong enough to accept the idea that the Jewish cause is the cause of justice itself. They are the Guardians."

Barzel was staring at Reshef now. "All this you derived from my book?"

"No, I knew it before. But you put it into words."

"Words," said Barzel. "I have words and I have money. And a new thirty-year-old self, apparently. What will I do with all these riches?"

"Turn them into power," said Reshef with conviction. "*When All Else Fails* isn't a book, it's a manifesto. There's an Islamic holy war against the West, and Israel's its first target. Someone has to lead."

"I'm not a politician," said Barzel.

"Become one, then," said Reshef. "The big parties are exhausted. They have no answers. You do. People will follow a man like you."

"What did you say your name is?" asked Barzel.

"Adam Reshef."

"Are you almost finished here?"

"In California? I'll be home in a few months."

"All right," said Barzel. "When you get back, come see me. If you still feel this way, we can talk about it a little more."

It didn't happen overnight; in fact, it took years for Elihu Barzel to come to power, and for much of that time he resisted Reshef's entreaties to actively enter politics. Instead he ran his economic empire, published books and articles, gave occasional television interviews and was the subject of endless efforts by the major parties to recruit him. Even after he allowed Reshef to organize a grassroots movement, he held himself aloof from the dealings of ordinary politicians. The movement itself was less a political party than a forum for Barzel's ideas: Jewish pride, aggressive national defense, economic liberalization, free trade and social welfare.

There was nothing exceptional about these principles; what excited people was Barzel himself. He was a multimillionaire whose factories and enterprises employed eleven thousand people, and a war hero—Ben Gurion's diary referred to him as the greatest Hebrew warrior of his generation—with a mysterious past. He was at once a Polish refugee, a pseudo-sabra Palmachnik and a sophisticated man of the world, a hardheaded pragmatist and a theorist whose books—praised by some as visionary, condemned by others as dangerously chauvinistic—were taken seriously by intellectuals. Gradually, Israelis came to regard Elihu Barzel as a national asset, a man of rare gifts to be held in reserve for time of emergency.

That time arrived in the spring of 1998 when Iranian-backed Islamic fundamentalists assassinated the president of Egypt and seized power in Cairo. Two decades of diplomacy and all the painfully won gains of peacemaking were suddenly obliterated. Terrorists struck at Israeli cities and towns, turning them into deadly arenas. To make matters worse, a million Russian immigrants, many of them penniless, crowded the streets demanding work and housing.

The public wanted a strong leader, but neither of the major parties had one to offer. The prime minister, although only fifty, seemed exhausted and overwhelmed. His rival, an ex-general not much older than Adam Reshef, frightened voters with his raw ambition. In the election of 1998, Elihu Barzel, at the age of seventy-two, was chosen prime minister as a third-party candidate.

One of Barzel's first acts in office was to make Adam Reshef his security adviser. Over the strenuous objections of the intelligence community, he granted him access to every security document and top-secret contingency plan. While Barzel was setting up his coalition government and arranging his domestic and foreign agenda, Reshef burrowed through files and consulted with military and scientific experts. Then he met with the prime minister. There was no one else present. No notes were kept. No historian would ever uncover a protocol. But it was a historic event nonetheless, for at that meeting, the Project was born.

CHAPTER NINE

GOVERNOR EARL CHILDES TOOK THE STACK OF PAPERS FROM his aide, Donny Galan, glanced at it briefly and set it on the coffee table. "What's the gist?" he asked.

"Preliminary staff workups on appointments for the administration," said Galan. "Just the senior positions." There was an eagerness in his young aide's voice that amused Childes; he was willing to bet that Galan's résumé was someplace in the stack.

"Little early for that, isn't it?" he drawled amiably.

"Well sir, the way the polls are looking, it seems like we better start thinking about Washington."

"Polls this time of year are like a woman you meet in a saloon. She can give you a thrill, but it don't mean spit the next morning. Understand me, Galan?"

"Yessir."

"Get out and win me the goddamned election," he said.

"Don't worry about divvying up the spoils." Childes gestured impatiently at the pile of résumés. "I'll read these things later."

Galan knew from experience that the papers would remain unread on the coffee table until he took them away. Governor Childes was, at fifty-eight, a man of habits, and reading wasn't one of them. Childes loved to fish, to shoot animals, to play golf with famous pros and to sing hymns at the top of his lungs at the Assembly of God in Christ Church in Flagstaff. He also loved playing poker for high stakes, driving fast cars, cooking barbecue ribs for his friends and making speeches. He did not love to work, and so he rarely did. That's what his staff was for.

Galan didn't condemn his boss for his laziness, even though the brunt of the labor fell on him. In fact, he admired the way Childes lived his life. Galan's spin to the press was that the governor's light schedule enabled him to focus without distraction on the big issues. The reporters who covered Childes knew better and a few of them said so in print, but mostly they went along because Earl Childes was an easy man to like and because, in the age of homogenized politicians, he provided them with great, homespun copy.

Childes stretched, scratched himself vigorously and looked at his watch. In a little while Silas and Reshef would be arriving. He liked Reshef, even though he generally didn't much care for Jews. The ones he had met were always yipping about some damn cause or hollering because their feelings were hurt. He didn't know Dewey Goldberg very well, but he respected him because he had played football at Michigan and fought in Vietnam. But most of them were Fancy Dans or bleeding hearts, not his kind of folks.

Reshef was different. The first time Reshef had come out to Arizona, Childes had taken him hunting. It was his way of sizing up a man, and Childes had been impressed. Reshef was a natural stalker, patient and vigilant, and he knew how to handle a rifle. What Childes remembered best, though, was the look on his face when he pulled the trigger. That look told him more than all the briefing papers and strategic surveys in the world.

Still, Childes would not have agreed to this project of Reshef's if it hadn't been for General Hunter and Silas. Hunter was the man Childes trusted most on foreign policy and he thought the Israeli scheme—which Childes had initially considered insanely dangerous—was brilliant. After the election, Hunter would be Secretary of Defense, in charge of implementing the Project. Silas would get to say the prayer at the inaugural in return for his eight million voters, and then he could get the hell back to Louisiana and stay there.

As for the Israelis, Childes would do business with them, but his way. According to the almanac there were only five million of them, although they made a racket like there were fifty, and he had no intention of being led through the hoops by a pissant little country, no matter how good a shot they were. What Reshef wanted to do to the Arabs made a lot of horse sense, but, from an American point of view, it made even more sense if it got done to the Israelis at the same time. Childes wasn't sure how this could be accomplished, but he had an idea. After the election he'd get himself a smart little Jew like Henry Kissinger to help Hunter work it out. They always knew how to screw each other.

CHAPTER TEN

AS CHIEF OF STAFF TO THE PRIME MINISTER, MOTKE VILK WAS
entitled to a car and driver, but he came to work every morning
on the bus that ran past his house at seven-fifteen. It was a
twenty-minute ride from his apartment in Jerusalem's Rehavia
neighborhood to the prime minister's office and Motke enjoyed
the opportunity it afforded him to chat with the other passengers, most of them midlevel bureaucrats who worked in the
nearby government buildings of the Kirya. There was no no-
blesse oblige in this arrangement, no calculated effort to stay in
touch with the public; Motke simply liked to start off his day
with a few jokes and some gossip. Barzel, who usually arrived
by eight and with whom Motke spent most of his working
hours, wasn't much on small talk.

Most of the people who rode the bus, especially the regu-
lars, treated Motke with jocular informality, but occasionally
someone approached him for a favor. Motke listened to these

requests patiently and, when they weren't outlandish—one man wanted a street named for his mother; another asked him to tell Barzel to fire the head of the income tax—with sympathy. He extracted a little black plastic notebook from the pocket of his baggy trousers and made a note or two, promising to do what he could. More than a few of these petitioners were astonished when, a few days later, they got a phone call from Motke—he always called himself, never through a secretary—informing them that Prime Minister Elihu Barzel had personally taken an interest in their problem and solved it.

This was, in a strict sense, untrue, because Motke seldom bothered Barzel with the details of the small, everyday favors he conferred. He had, in the phrase he had learned from visiting American politicians, a "mandate" to act in the prime minister's name. There were only two conditions that he scrupulously adhered to: The requests could not be illegal and they must be things that Barzel would himself have done if he had had the time. It was an index of the absolute faith the prime minister placed in his chief of staff that he trusted Motke to know what such things would be.

Like most of their arrangements, Motke Vilk's prerogative had been bestowed tacitly. But although there had never been a formal agreement, or even a discussion, Motke knew precisely when he had first been empowered to extend favors in Elihu Barzel's name.

In the spring of 1947, Barzel was sent by the Palmach from Ein Harrod to Tel Aviv to meet with senior commanders about the allocation of arms and munitions in the eastern Galilee. Motke tagged along, claiming he needed to find a new used accordion in one of the shops on Allenby Street but actually enthralled by the opportunity to visit what passed in pre-state Palestine for the big city.

The two stayed in the cramped apartment of a man named Finerman whose three sons were all Palmachniks. During the day, while Barzel pored over figures on Sten guns and

Enfield rifles, Motke wandered up and down the beach, staring at the girls in their swimsuits, licking his first ice-cream cone and humming to himself. It was on the beach, near Trumpeldor Street, that he found Howard Grant.

There were three things about Grant that attracted Motke's attention. First, he was a giant, perhaps six-foot-six, the tallest Jew Motke had ever seen. His face was an improbable ensemble of narrow brown eyes, a huge crooked nose and plump, slightly reddish lips, topped off by a mop of curly black hair. Motke knew the man was a Jew because he was singing—loudly, obliviously and profanely—in an oddly accented Yiddish. That was the second thing that caught his attention. The third was that, at two in the afternoon, Howard Grant was dead drunk.

Motke stood in the sand staring. The tall young man eventually noticed and responded by flashing him the middle finger of his right hand. It was a gesture Motke had seen GIs make in Naples.

"You're an American," Motke said in Yiddish.

"No fucking shit," said the tall man in English.

Motke didn't understand a word. "I don't speak English," he said in Yiddish. "Why are you singing and cursing? What's the matter? Can I help?"

"You're a boy," said the American, who didn't seem much older than Motke. "What can you do to help anyone?"

"I can listen," said Motke. "And I've got enough money for a falafel if you're hungry."

"I'm starving," said the American, in fluent, heavily accented Yiddish that made him sound, to Motke, like a Jewish John Wayne. "I haven't slept in three days. I'm in love with a girl named Varda who doesn't shave under her armpits. The schmucks at the Haganah office want discharge papers which I don't have. My father disinherited me. I'm drunk. I got crabs in London. You want to hear more?"

"These you call problems?" Motke grinned. "You got

crabs in London means you've been to London. You're in love. You've even got a father. Not to mention the fact that you're an American."

"Big deal," mumbled the tall boy, smiling drunkenly. "Big fucking deal."

When Barzel came home that night, he found Howard Grant asleep on Motke Vilk's cot. "Who's this?" he asked.

"An American I found at the beach," said Motke. "He was drunk and he's in love with a girl named Varda."

"What's he doing here?"

"He wants to enlist in the Palmach, but they won't take him. He says he was an American marine. I told him you would help."

"What am I, the recruiting officer?"

Motke Vilk shrugged. "There's something about him," he said. "Wait till he wakes up, you'll see."

Howard Grant awoke the next morning with a cruel hangover and no memory whatsoever of the previous day. "Christ, where am I?" he asked thickly in English.

"You're in Tel Aviv," said Barzel, amazing Motke by replying in English. "Motke brought you home."

"Who the fuck is Motke?"

"Me," said Vilk, responding cheerily to his name. In Yiddish he said, "This is my friend I told you about—Barzel. He's the one who can get you into the Palmach."

"I don't think so," said Barzel. "Maybe you have some relatives here we could call for you—"

"My family's in the States," said Grant. "I came over here to volunteer and nobody wants me. Christ, you'd think this was the Roman fucking Empire or something—"

"There are kibbutzim where you could go," said Barzel. "They need people for farmwork."

"Farmwork my ass," snorted Grant. "I'm a soldier, not a goddamned apple picker."

"Motke says you were an American marine," said Barzel, making no effort to disguise his skepticism.

"Three years in the Pacific," said Grant. "Can you believe that? Hitler wipes out every Jew in Europe and they send me to the Pacific to kill Japs."

"Did you kill any?" asked Motke eagerly.

"Oh yeah," said Grant quietly. "I killed some."

"There are American military volunteers here," said Barzel. "They come in groups called Mahal."

"I never heard of any Mahal," said Grant. "I don't know about any groups. I heard they need Jewish soldiers, so I bought a boat ticket. And now they won't take me. How the hell did I know I had to bring my fucking diploma?"

"You want to join the Palmach," said Barzel.

"The kids in the Boy Scout uniforms, yeah," said Grant. "Or whatever else you've got."

"There's going to be a war," Barzel said. "You could get killed."

To Motke's surprise, Grant laughed, a loud, barking sound. "Forget it," he said. "If the Japs couldn't kill me, I'm sure as hell not afraid of A-rabs."

Barzel stared into the American's small brown eyes for a long moment. "Okay," he said finally. "Today I'll take you back to the kibbutz and we'll find out if you're really a soldier. If you're telling the truth, you can stay."

"Who the fuck are you, Ben Gurion?" asked Grant.

"It's pretty informal where we are," said Barzel mildly. "I think if I vouch for you they'll take you. We can worry about the paperwork later."

"Are you sure it's all right?" asked Motke, suddenly uncertain. He spoke in Hebrew so that Grant wouldn't understand.

"It's all right," said Barzel with certainty. "He's telling the truth. I see it in his eyes."

"You're a good judge of character, Ben Gurion," said

Grant in Hebrew, and he collapsed back onto the cot, holding his head.

The Palmachniks of Ein Harrod were delighted with Howard Grant. Ten minutes on the firing range made it clear that he hadn't exaggerated his combat experience and they pumped him eagerly for information about training techniques and tactics. They called him "Americanos" and "Yankee Doodle," affectionately mimicked his vowelly accent. At night around the campfire, they begged him to sing the latest American songs in his slightly off-key baritone, accompanied by Motke Vilk's accordion, and to tell stories about his life in New York before the war.

A few weeks after Grant's arrival, the bashful, redheaded Palmach officer who had met Barzel and Motke at the port in Hafia arrived at Ein Harrod. The previous night, Arabs from a nearby village had ambushed a truck carrying Jewish farmworkers. The Palmach high command wanted a reprisal raid. Elihu Barzel was their choice to lead it.

"Our intelligence has pinpointed the gunmen," said the redhead. "If we retaliate immediately, it will send a message to the other villages in the valley."

"How many are there?" asked Barzel.

"Four. They're brothers. Their house is marked on this map."

"Fine," said Barzel.

"How many men do you need?"

"Two should be enough," said Barzel. "Motke and Howard. We can go around midnight."

"I want at least a dozen men nearby, in case something goes wrong," said the redhead in his deep baritone.

"Nothing will go wrong," said Barzel. "Count on me."

That night Barzel and the others hiked the six miles to Kfar Joss under a cloudy sky. The village was set on the side of a hill, perhaps a hundred small, darkened houses clustered around a mosque. Barzel ordered the reserves to wait in a clump of woods and led Motke and Grant in the direction of the nearest building. Fifty yards from the low stone wall that surrounded the house, Barzel paused and turned to Motke. "Do you remember what I promised on the road in Germany?" he asked in a low voice.

"I remember," said Motke.

"Good. Tonight I'll teach you how to kill."

The events at Kfar Joss electrified the entire country. The four gunmen died that night, their throats slit. But the operation didn't end there. The entire population—more than four hundred people—were routed from their beds and driven at gunpoint to a stony hill half a kilometer away. From there they could see the flames and smell the smoke as their village was burned to the ground.

The incident spread panic among the Arabs of the eastern Galilee, raised cries of indignation in London and turned Elihu Barzel into an instant sabra legend.

The Palmach high command summoned Barzel, along with Motke and Grant, to an inquiry. Yigal Allon, the commander of the Palmach, was present, along with the slow-talking redheaded Yitzhak and a third officer, Avi Har-el, who had been appointed prosecutor in the informal proceedings. Har-el was a stocky man of about twenty-five who spoke with a peppery, aggressive staccato and jiggled impatiently from one foot to the other as Barzel gave his unapologetic account of the operation at Kfar Joss.

"In other words, you don't deny your orders were to kill only the gunmen," Har-el said.

"There's no need for other words," said Barzel. "I just told you I was clear about the orders."

"Which you deliberately and flagrantly violated," snapped Har-el.

"There was nothing in the orders about what to do afterward. I thought it was important for people to know the price of killing Jews."

"Tell me, do you hate Arabs?" asked Allon in a quiet, thoughtful tone. Not yet thirty, he was a national hero.

"No," said Barzel. "Until a year ago I never even saw an Arab."

"And yet you burned down their village," said Har-el. "You're a fast learner."

"This is a war. The Arabs are the enemy. In wars you kill the enemy before he kills you. Infantile babble about the 'purity of arms' doesn't change that."

"We know all about your heroic exploits in Europe," said Har-el angrily. "Maybe you learned your military ethics from the Nazis."

Allon reddened with embarrassment at the suggestion and even the unflappable Yitzhak shifted uncomfortably in his chair, but Barzel was unruffled. "It was the Americans who dropped atomic bombs on civilians," he said. "It was the Allies who destroyed Dresden. In a war, men fight and leave the philosophy to cowards and simpletons."

Now it was Har-el's turn to redden. "I don't give a damn what the Americans did or the British or anyone else. I'm a socialist and a Zionist; we have our own code of ethics. We're through imitating the goyim."

"Goyim is just another word for the rest of humanity, the tiny minority that doesn't happen to be Jewish," said Barzel with naked sarcasm. "You want to fight without killing, kill without blood on your hands. You judge Jews by an inhuman standard. Maybe it's you who learned from the Nazis."

"I don't have any more questions to ask this piece of shit," said Har-el. "This is an open-and-shut case."

"Leaving aside the moral issue, we have a practical reason for showing restraint," said Allon in his mild, thoughtful voice. "After the war we're going to have to live with the Arabs. Brutality creates hatred. That's why what you did at Kfar Joss is so serious."

"I disagree," said Barzel. "The Arabs hate you already. You think they'll hate you less if you only kill four of their sons instead of forty?"

"You just said you never even saw an Arab until last year," said Har-el, unable to remain silent. "Now you're an expert."

"So what's the answer?" asked Allon quietly. "Kill them all? Drive them out?"

"There's no need for that," said Barzel. "What we should do is defeat them and then swallow them up."

"What do you mean, swallow them up?"

"Turn them into Jews," said Barzel.

"Into Jews? Convert them? It can't be done."

"Of course it can be done. How do you think they got to be Arabs in the first place? A few hundred Saudi bedouins rode in a thousand years ago and forced everybody to speak Arabic and worship Allah. Probably in the beginning they didn't like it, but they got used to it. They can again."

"This is insane," said Har-el. "This man doesn't belong in the Palmach, he belongs in an asylum."

"Is it more insane than trying to turn Polish Jews into biblical Hebrews? You'd see the logic of it if you weren't such a racist."

"Racist?" sputtered Har-el, gathering up his papers. "I don't have to listen to any more of this bullshit." He stormed out of the room, leaving a composed Barzel facing the two senior Palmach officers.

Allon cleared his throat. "That's quite a theory," he said. "Just out of curiosity, how would you go about carrying it out?"

"By force," said Barzel. "The same force that turned Arabs into Arabs or Romans into Romans or Greeks into Greeks."

"That all happened a long time ago," said Allon. "Times are different."

"Human nature doesn't change."

"I've lived among the Arabs all my life," said Allon. "They're tough, stubborn people. Force would only breed resistance."

"A little force breeds resistance," countered Barzel, "but overwhelming force overwhelms. Up to a point force strengthens the enemy's resolve; beyond that point it breaks him. And then you put the pieces back together in a way that suits you."

"You've thought about this a lot," said Allon.

"Yes," said Barzel. "I've had time to think about it."

The red-haired officer coughed loudly and stood up. "I don't know about all this palaver," he said. "What I know is that you got an order and you disobeyed it. What I want to know is, would you disobey again?"

"We can't have you fighting a private war," added Allon. "No matter what you think we should be doing."

"If you don't trust my judgment I'll find some other way to fight," said Barzel. "I wasn't born in the Palmach."

"Go back to Ein Harrod," said Allon. "We'll let you know what we decide."

The decision to allow Barzel to stay was made by Ben Gurion himself. With independence only a few months off, it was clear to him that there would be all-out war with the Arabs. The Jewish forces were tiny and untested; men like Barzel, who knew how to fight, were a rare and important asset. Ben Gurion found Barzel's insubordination and eccentric political views troubling, but he feared that expelling him from the Palmach would drive him into the hands of the rival Irgun, or even the Stern Gang. Those groups would have to be disarmed after independence, and Ben Gurion didn't want a man of Barzel's ruthlessness and charisma to contend with.

And so, over the objection of the Palmach high command,

he ruled that Barzel be given a slap on the wrists and reinstated. "This man is a cannon," he told Allon. "Do your best to keep him pointed in the right direction."

"I'll make sure Yitzhak stays on top of him," said Allon grimly. "I don't want another Kfar Joss."

"If I were you I wouldn't keep too tight a rein on him," said Ben Gurion in his high-pitched mumble. "He may do things you'd rather not know about. If you don't know—"

"You mean if he goes wild again and burns down another village? Is that what you want?"

"No," said Ben Gurion. He picked up his eyeglasses and scanned some papers on his desk, a sign of dismissal. Allon stood for a moment looking at the little man behind the desk, swallowed his protest and turned to leave. He was at the door when Ben Gurion called his name. He turned and saw the old man gazing at him mildly.

"Yes?" he said.

"But if he does, make sure it's a village that deserves burning," Ben Gurion said, and returned to his reading.

Chapter Eleven

CHARLIE WALKER TOOK A LITTLE EXTRA CARE DRESSING FOR dinner, sending his unwrinkled blue blazer and gray slacks down to the hotel valet for a touch-up and changing his shirt twice before settling on the pale blue button-down that accented his flat stomach. Sara had told him on the phone that she was bringing a friend to dinner, someone she was certain he'd find interesting.

Charlie liked Israeli women, especially Sara's friends, who tended to be brainy and intense. He recalled one in particular named Dorit, a thin redhead with sparkling brown eyes, long legs and a nasty sense of humor. When they met five years before, Charlie had been in a faithful phase of his marriage, but he had definitely felt a charge between them. Now he had a premonition that she was the guest Sara was bringing. Just before leaving the room he slipped a pack of breath mints into his jacket pocket and strapped on his Khomeini watch.

Charlie walked the few blocks from his hotel to the Shangri-la, a Thai restaurant near the beach. Tel Aviv had changed over the years, he reflected, as he walked past the crowded pubs along HaYarkon Street. When he had first visited Israel, it had been a sort of kosher Salt Lake City, dull and lifeless, and the food had been awful. Now there seemed to be interesting restaurants on every block and the streets near the hotel were alive with neon and music and the teeming energy of laughing young people. *Something good's happened here*, he thought to himself, and resolved to mention it at dinner. It was the sort of observation that was certain to get a rise out of Sara, who, like most westernized Israelis, was thoroughly ashamed of her patriotism and resented the compliments of foreigners almost as much as their criticism.

Shangri-la was almost empty when Charlie arrived. He sat at a table in the rear of the room, facing the entrance, and sipped a Jack Daniel's while he waited for Sara and Dorit. After fifteen minutes, just as he was beginning to wonder if he had come to the right place, the glass door opened and he saw Sara accompanied by a medium-sized man with thin gray hair combed back on his head and a neatly trimmed salt-and-pepper mustache.

"Hello, Charlie," Sara said brightly. "You're looking very handsome tonight."

"And you look beautiful," he replied automatically. Walker's good manners were instinctive, but they couldn't quite hide his disappointment.

"This is the friend I was telling you about," said Sara, leaving it to the man to introduce himself, Israeli style.

"Amos," he said, taking Charlie's hand in a strong grip, and suddenly Charlie was no longer disappointed.

"I thought the two of you would enjoy getting to know each other," said Sara with a mischievous grin.

"I've heard a lot about you," said the man in a friendly tone. His voice was light, vaguely nasal, and there were little laugh lines in the corners of his warm brown eyes. The most striking thing about him was his smile. Charlie had been smiled at all his life, but he had never before been charmed by the smile of a man.

"I've heard about you, too," said Charlie. He had, too; Amos Levran was a legend.

They ate pad thai and drank Goldstar Beer and talked movie trivia. Charlie was good and so was Sara, but neither could compete with the deputy head of the Mossad. "I can't believe you know all this stuff," Charlie said with a laugh after Levran successfully named—and sang a few bars of—every song in *Going My Way*. "You must have a photographic memory."

"More like phonographic," said Sara, who liked showing off her ability to perform word games in English.

"Neither," said Levran, flashing the smile. "My uncle owned the movie theater in Tiberius. If a movie ran for six nights, I saw it six times."

"Sometimes explanations are simpler than you think," said Charlie.

Levran nodded. "That's one of the hardest things to learn," he said.

Charlie was warmed by the acknowledgment. Over the years he had met plenty of spooks. As a group he found them arrogant and aloof. They were willing enough to trade favors, but it was clear that they considered him a lesser member in the fraternity of inside information, like diamond dealers looking down on a salesman of costume jewelry.

Levran was different. There was something open and un-affected in his attitude that proclaimed their equality and in-vited friendship without soliciting it. Charlie reminded himself that he was almost certainly being seduced, but he couldn't help responding.

"You two think you're so smart," said Sara. "Things aren't always what they seem. A couple of geniuses."

"That's not quite what Charlie said," Levran corrected her. "He said explanations are often more simple than you think."

"Very profound," said Sara, adroitly scooping up noodles with her chopsticks. Charlie noticed that Levran ate his food with a fork and spoon, the way it was done in Thailand.

"Have you spent a lot of time in the Far East?" he asked.

"Oh, some," said Levran. "It's a strange part of the world. Hard to understand. I prefer Africa. They make up the rules as they go along, but you can't find any place with more amazing characters."

"I know what you mean," said Charlie. "I covered Bukassa's coronation. The Napoleon of Central Africa. And I interviewed Idi Amin. What a loony he was."

"My favorite was Sergeant Doe of Liberia," said Levran. "Years ago he came here on a state visit and then skipped his meeting with the prime minister because he was busy playing football across the street from his hotel. He told his foreign minister, 'You go.'"

"You go?" Charlie laughed. "Jesus."

"Another time we were trying to sell military communications equipment to this African country," continued Levran with the relish of a skilled raconteur. "Radios, walkie-talkies, listening devices, things like that. We flew in a whole team of technicians and set up a demonstration. All their generals were gathered around, acting very impressed. When we finished, the chief of staff said, 'I have only one question: How do you kill with it?'"

"How do you kill with it?" repeated Charlie. "That's funny. What country was it?"

"I forget," said Levran with a slight wink.

"Sounds like Uganda," said Charlie. "I remember the last time I was there, I saw a whole unit of soldiers training with poison darts—"

"Fascinating as it is to sit around listening to your war stories," interrupted Sara, "I'm ready for a change of subject."

"Listen, I've got an idea," Levran said, slapping his hand on the table. "Charlie, I want to show you something special, a part of Israel you've probably never seen. Do you have time?"

"Sure," said Charlie. "Let's go."

They went in Sara's white Subaru, Levran next to her and Charlie in the back. As they drove, Levran sang a song with Hebrew words and a Russian-sounding melody. He had a sweet tenor, richer than his speaking voice. Charlie was taken by the simple ease with which he sang, unself-consciously, the way a man would sing with his family on a driving trip. After a while Sara joined in and Charlie, who hadn't sung out loud since seventh-grade glee club, found himself wishing he knew the words so that he could sing along as well.

They drove for about ten minutes and then pulled into a crowded parking lot. In front of them was what appeared to be a brightly lit basketball court. Accordion music blared over a tinny loudspeaker. Several hundred people of varying ages, dressed in T-shirts, shorts and jeans and sandals, moved to the music in wavy concentric circles.

"This is it," Levran said happily. He leaped from the car and walked quickly toward the dancers, joined hands with two teenage girls and effortlessly picked up the step. Within seconds he was gone, twirling toward the far corner of the concrete dance floor. Charlie and Sara watched him go.

"What is this, a bar mitzvah?" asked Charlie.

"Folk dancing," said Sara.

"You're kidding. I didn't know anybody really did this stuff anymore, except for tourists."

"Actually it's pretty popular," said Sara. "It's not my favorite activity, but Amos loves it. He comes all the time. How do you like him, by the way?"

"He seems like a terrific guy," said Charlie. "What made him agree to come to dinner?"

"As a matter of fact, it was his idea," said Sara. "He likes meeting new people. And I think maybe he was a little jealous."

On his next swing around, Levran gestured vigorously for Sara and Charlie to join him. "Feel like dancing?" she asked.

"We didn't do too many horas in Fargo, North Dakota," said Charlie.

"It's not hard," said Sara. "I'll teach you."

"I don't think so," said Charlie.

"Amos won't give up," she said, taking his hand and leading him toward the dancers. "Come on, be an Israeli for a few minutes."

Levran caught Charlie by the hand and gracefully slid him into the whirling circle. At first Charlie felt ridiculous in his polished loafers and sports jacket as he awkwardly aped the twisting, leaping steps. "You're doing fine," said Levran encouragingly, pulling him ahead as Charlie finally caught the rhythm and began to move more confidently.

The tempo slowed and the dance changed, people flowing gently now toward the center, coming together with their arms raised, meeting with a shouted "Ho" and then retreating backward. Once again Charlie felt Levran's powerful grip leading him, and he began to relax as he moved to the music. He couldn't wait to describe the scene to Goldberg. He wished he had a camera to record the picture of himself dancing hand in hand with one of the world's legendary spies.

After half an hour, a sweating Amos Levran led them out of the circle of dancers. *"Nu?"* he said to Charlie. "What do you think?"

"Fun," said Charlie. He, too, was soaked in sweat. "Hot, though."

"What do you say we go to Avatichim for some water-melon?" Levran suggested. "It'll be cool there by the beach."

"Not me," said Sara. "I've got to go home and write. You go ahead."

"Well, it's just you and me," said Levran to Charlie. "What about it?"

"Are you kidding? It's my dream date." Charlie Walker grinned.

Avatichim turned out to be a huge outdoor area packed with Israelis eating watermelon, drinking beer and calling out to one another in loud, happy voices. Half a dozen people stopped Levran on the way to the table and he greeted each one by name, kissing the women on the cheek and slapping the men on the back.

"Everybody seems to know you," said Charlie, surprised.

"Why not? I've lived here all my life and it's a small country."

"Well, I just thought—"

"What?" Levran grinned. "That I walk around Tel Aviv in disguise? Don't tell me you never see the heads of the CIA out in Washington. You've probably had dinner with them in restaurants."

"Is that a question or are you quoting from my file?" asked Charlie, returning Levran's grin.

"Just a supposition," he said. "Although I should say I'm quoting from the file, just to make you nervous. People think we have a file on everyone."

"You mean I don't? Have a file?"

Levran shrugged. "Probably not. I wouldn't be surprised if your name was in Dewey Goldberg's, though. I know how close you are."

"You're telling me that the Mossad keeps a file on the president of the United States?"

"Of course," said Levran. "Just like the CIA has one on Barzel. It's standard."

"That's a file I'd be interested in seeing," said Charlie.

"Which one? Goldberg's? Or Barzel's?"

"Both, but I meant Dewey's. I don't suppose there's a chance of taking a peek?"

"You probably wouldn't find it very interesting," teased Levran. "It's just a collection of old press clippings and speeches. And evaluations."

"Evaluations," mused Charlie. "You know, as a matter of fact I'd be kind of interested in knowing how the Mossad evaluates Dewey."

"For your book," said Levran dryly.

"Will you let me see the file?"

"I can't do that," said Levran. "But I don't mind answering a few questions. Providing that what I tell you is all the way off the record."

"Why?"

"You mean, what's in it for me? Nothing, except that you're a friend of Sara's and I like you. Besides, there's nothing top secret. People overestimate us. Our evaluation of President Goldberg probably isn't too different from yours—well, maybe not yours, you're his best friend, but most others. We don't have any Deep Throats in the White House feeding us information—"

"And if you did, you wouldn't tell me."

"No, obviously not. But we don't. Our relationship with America is much too important to jeopardize with espionage. We learned that lesson with Pollard."

Charlie paused, considering Levran's offer. Throughout his career he had made a point of scrupulously honoring his agreements with sources—it was one of his strengths as a reporter. And, integrity aside, he liked Levran. On the other hand, all he was being asked to promise was that he wouldn't publish the information; the Israeli hadn't said anything about not telling Goldberg personally.

"Okay," said Charlie. "Totally off the record."

"Fine," said Levran. "What would you like to know?"

"Dewey's the first Jewish president. How does that affect your view of him?"

Levran cut himself a large piece of seedless watermelon and chewed it thoughtfully. "It doesn't," he said. "Not per se. Jewish in America is not the same as Jewish here. For us, it's a nationality. But for most American Jews it's just a religion, or a kind of hobby. The fact that somebody's Jewish doesn't give us any information. We have to look at specifics."

"Okay, specifically."

"Well, President Goldberg comes from an assimilated family. He has no real Jewish education. He doesn't speak Hebrew or Yiddish. He has no relatives here and he's never made a private visit, only congressional delegations. He's a wealthy man, or at least he comes from a wealthy family, but he gives five hundred dollars a year to the UJA. He belongs to a reform temple for political reasons but isn't a member of any Jewish group. His wife, his closest political associates, Graff and Willis, and his best friend are all not Jewish. His son wasn't bar mitzvahed and his daughter's married to an Irish Catholic. How am I doing so far?"

"Sounds right," said Charlie. "I never asked him about the UJA thing, but otherwise . . ."

"So, the first thing I'd surmise is that being a Jew is not so important to President Goldberg personally."

"A lot of people over here think that his being Jewish is a bad thing for Israel. That it might cause him to bend over backwards."

"There are Jews like that, but I don't think Goldberg's one of them. His voting record in Congress was excellent, almost perfect from our point of view. This is a good period for U.S.–Israeli relations, and he hasn't done anything to change it. And it seems that he understands the issues that concern us. He's not an expert on international affairs, or the Middle East, but he knows that we're on the same side in the fight against the extremists. So far, if we put him on a scale of one to ten, as you Americans like to say, I would give him a nine."

"Who's a ten?" asked Charlie.

"There is no such thing as a ten." Levran smiled. "You know we Israelis are never satisfied."

"What about his personality?" asked Charlie. "What do your analysts say about that?"

"Here I wouldn't like to get into any official views," said Levran. "Not because it's negative, but personalities are a somewhat touchy matter. But if you ask me my own private opinion—"

Charlie nodded.

"—I think he's a good man. So far he's been very cautious. Probably that will change if he is elected, but not so much. I believe he is a cautious man by nature."

Once more Charlie nodded. "I think that's right."

"He is also smarter than he appears," Levran continued. "He likes to be underrated." He looked at Charlie for confirmation, but this time the journalist kept his face expressionless. Levran's assessment was shrewdly accurate, but Walker didn't want to start trading information, at least not yet. "The one thing I wonder about is whether he is tough enough for his job," Levran added. "For instance, I was surprised when he didn't change his staff, pick assistants from his own party."

"He wanted continuity," said Charlie.

"A president has to be able to count on the loyalty of his advisers," said Levran.

"I've known Dewey a long time," said Charlie. "He's tough when he needs to be. Maybe tougher than some people here are counting on."

Amos Levran looked at Charlie blankly. "What people do you mean?"

"Come on, Amos," Charlie said. "You know what I'm talking about."

Levran shook his head.

"It's all over the Jewish community that the Israelis are down on Dewey," said Charlie.

"I haven't heard that," said Levran. "It would be foolish to get involved in an American election."

"Rabin did, when he was ambassador to the U.S."

"That was against McGovern," said Levran. "And even that didn't justify it. But at least there was a reason—McGovern would have been a disaster. Goldberg's not a problem for us. Why would we want to do something so stupid?"

"That's what I was wondering," said Charlie.

"Of course there is another possibility," said Levran with a teasing smile. "Just suppose, for the sake of argument, that a presidential candidate, let's call him X, wants our support. Now, this is completely hypothetical, but maybe X sends an emissary over here to tell us he knows we're supporting his opponent. Then, to prove we aren't, we support X. Quietly, of course."

"That's ridiculous," said Charlie. "Nobody would do something that convoluted."

"Politicians do more Machiavellian things every day," said Levran. "We both know that."

"Dewey doesn't operate that way," said Charlie. "Of course, he isn't a retired Mossad agent."

"I'm not retired," said Levran pleasantly. "Unless you know something I don't."

"I meant Barzel," said Charlie. "It's his people who are spreading the word in the States."

"I doubt it," said Levran. "I'm not involved in these things, but I know a little about Israeli thinking, and what you're saying doesn't make sense. Maybe somebody said something that was misinterpreted. That happens in elections. Or maybe it's disinformation—there are Republican Jews in America, too, you know."

"You're telling me you know for certain that Barzel isn't out to get Dewey? You're positive?"

Levran smiled his charming smile. "How many buttons are there on the front of your shirt?" he asked.

"Huh?"

"How many? You put on a shirt like this almost every day and take it off at night. How many buttons does it have? Without looking down."

"Ah, six," said Charlie after a moment's thought.

"Six. Are you sure?"

"Yes," said Charlie. "Six."

"But are you positive? Would you bet a thousand dollars on it?"

"I, ah . . ."

Levran was still smiling, but his eyes were serious now. "*Positive* is an easy word to use," he said. "I don't want to say positive, but I'm as sure that you're wrong about Barzel as you are that there are six buttons on your shirt. Now, let's finish our coffee. I've got an early day tomorrow."

It was a balmy night and Charlie walked back alone to his hotel along the seaside promenade. The evening had been, by turns, disappointing, fascinating and confusing. Thirty years of experience argued that he should not believe Levran's denial. But those years had also taught him to trust his instincts and, illogical as it seemed, Charlie's instinct was that the Mossad man had been telling the truth.

A leggy, well-built young woman in a loose-fitting halter sauntered past and Charlie felt a momentary pang of regret over Dorit. It would have been nice to be walking with her now in the direction of the Sheraton. Still, he wasn't sorry that Sara had brought Amos instead. If he hadn't learned any secrets, he hadn't given up any, either, and that was a good feeling. After all, it wasn't every day that you matched wits with a man like Levran and came out even.

There were no messages at the hotel, and the lobby and bar were quiet. Feeling suddenly exhausted, Charlie went up to his room, took a quick shower, put on his pajamas and climbed between the fresh sheets. He was almost asleep when he remembered something. He slid out of bed, picked up the shirt he had tossed over the chair and examined it. There were slightly damp sweat stains on the armpits, a small brownish drop of dried sauce he hadn't noticed before on the left cuff. And, down the front of the pale blue shirt, seven little white buttons.

CHAPTER TWELVE

CHARLIE WAS AWAKENED BY THE TELEPHONE. IT WAS SARA Epstein. "You still looking for dirt on Barzel and Goldberg?" she asked without preliminaries.

"Information," Charlie corrected with a yawn.

"Whatever. Avi Har-el will see you this morning at ten, at his office."

"Who's Avi Har-el?"

"The world's leading Barzologist," said Sara. "I just spoke with him and he's dying to meet you."

"Are they close?"

"Like a nose and a boil," said Sara with a wheezy laugh. "If there's something bad to say about Elihu Barzel, Avi knows it. He's nuts on the subject."

"What's he got against Barzel?"

"He wasn't in the right youth movement," said Sara.

At precisely ten, Charlie arrived at Har-el's well-appointed office in the Asia Building. Although the little lawyer was past seventy, he greeted Walker with a boyishly eager intensity. He guided Charlie to a padded leather chair, took the seat across from him and regarded him with animated curiosity. "Mr. Walker, what can I do for you?"

"Sara probably told you that I'm working on a book about Dewey Goldberg. She said you might be able to help on a couple of things."

"I've had the honor of meeting President Goldberg several times," said Har-el. "I remember one dinner years ago in Washington. We talked about the Palestinians. I think he learned a lot. He was very appreciative."

"Yes, he mentioned that," Charlie lied.

"Well," said Har-el, beaming.

"And I was hoping you could do the same for me," said Charlie.

Har-el cleared his throat and his eyes took on a distant focus that Walker recognized as the gaze of the compulsive lecturer. "The Palestinian dynamic has changed of course but—"

"No," said Charlie quickly. "What I was hoping you'd do is fill me in on Elihu Barzel's feelings about President Goldberg." The little lawyer's face clouded at the mention of the prime minister, and Charlie quickly added: "I understand you're an expert on Israeli politics."

The word "expert" had the intended effect. "I wouldn't bother about Barzel," said Har-el. "He won't be in office by the time your book is published. Our election is next year and he will be thrown from the job."

"Really? I thought he was popular—"

"Ahhh," declared Har-el in a throat-clearing scrape of negation. "Popular with Russian immigrants he gives money to and Moroccan riffraff in the development towns. Popular with the *haridim*—"

"*Haridim?*"

"The ultra-orthodox, the rabbis. He buys them off with

army deferments for their children and money, so they support his coalition. But the real Israelis know what this man is, believe me. We see right through him."

"This is interesting," said Charlie avidly, producing a notepad. "Do you mind if I take some notes?"

"No problem," said Har-el expansively.

"Thanks," said Charlie dryly. "You say people can see through him—what is it they see?"

"That Elihu Leibowitz—that's his real name, you know, Leibowitz—is a fraud. An empty balloon full of nationalistic slogans. 'Jewish pride.' 'National security.' 'Free enterprise.' Slogans."

"He's got a pretty impressive track record," said Charlie evenly. "Some people think he's a hero."

"Hero? For what? Killing innocent people during the war? Flying around the world assassinating harmless old men? Making a fortune selling weapons to dictators?"

"Ben Gurion wrote that he was the greatest soldier in the War of Independence," said Charlie mildly.

"Ben Gurion. To you Americans he's some great leader with white hair like Napoleon or George Washington. I knew Ben Gurion personally and this I can tell you: He was a terrible judge of character. He had a Russian spy for a military adviser, did you know that?"

Charlie nodded. "I've read it, uh-huh."

"Ben Gurion in some ways was a genius, but he was also a fool and a coward. He was afraid that Jews couldn't fight because he himself was a Polish shtetl Jew. That's why he loved Leibowitz. Believe me, any one of us was worth ten Leibowitzes."

"Us?"

"The sabras," said Har-el with a vehemence that made his eyes water. "The real heroes of the war were the sabras—people like Allon and Dayan and Laskov who were born here and raised here. We won the war and we did it without compromising the purity of our cause."

Charlie pretended to listen, idly scribbling in his notebook, as Har-el lectured about who did what in the War of Independence. Israelis were always setting the historical record straight, usually at the expense of someone else's reputation. It was a prelude to conversation, like coffee and insincere compliments among the Arabs.

"What you're saying is that Barzel isn't a real Israeli," said Charlie. "He's more a diaspora type."

"Precisely," said Har-el, pleased to have made his point. "A ghetto Jew. Always worried that the world is against us. A Jewish chauvinist."

"You'd think that he'd love Goldberg, in that case," said Charlie.

"That's what you don't understand," said Har-el. "Until now Leibowitz was King of the Jews. But with a Goldberg in the White House, who's the king now? It makes him look small, and this, believe me, Elihu Leibowitz cannot stand."

"So you think he'd like to see Childes elected?"

"Childes, Schmildes, what does he care? As long as it isn't Goldberg."

"That's hard to believe," said Charlie, leading Har-el a bit more firmly now. "Childes is a right-wing isolationist. That can't be good for Israel."

"And it's good for Israel to have a government that depends on crazy rabbis and Russian immigrants?" demanded Har-el in a high, angry voice. "It's good to destroy the kibbutzim and the welfare system we built here for a hundred years and replace them with greed? It's good to teach our children that the Moslems are Nazis? Since when does Elihu Leibowitz give a damn about what's good for Israel?"

"You're saying he's not a patriot?"

"Patriotism is the last refuge of scoundrels," declared Har-el, as if he had just coined the phrase.

"So you think Barzel might really be supporting Childes?"

Har-el shrugged. "Who knows? He'll do what he thinks is good for Elihu Leibowitz, this I am certain about."

"How about the people around him? Do they feel the same way? About Goldberg, I mean."

"There are no people around him," said Har-el. "Just stooges and yes-men, like Motke Vilk. The great Elihu Leibowitz listens only to himself."

"Sara mentioned someone named Howard Grant. What about him?"

Once again Har-el's face mottled with anger. "Leibowitz's partner in crime," he snapped. "He lives in Herzliya Pituah now with a young girl the age of his granddaughter. Go talk to him, by all means. You'll see what kind of mafia bum is the friend of the great Elihu Leibowitz."

"I will," said Charlie, closing his notebook and rising. "I want to thank you for giving me so much of your time. I know how busy you are."

"Not at all, not at all," said Har-el. "Before you go, I have a little present for you. Something I think you'll find very valuable." He went to his desk and returned with two copies of a thin volume. It was titled, *Avi Har-el: A Man and His Generation.*

"It's my autobiography," said Har-el solemnly. "The true story of what this country once was, and what it could have been. What it was like here before the Leibowitzes ruined it. Keep one for yourself and give the other one to my friend President Goldberg."

"I know he'll appreciate it," said Charlie.

"Yes," said Har-el, shaking Charlie's hand with a moist weak grip. "I'm sure he will."

CHAPTER THIRTEEN

CHARLIE RETURNED TO THE TEL AVIV SHERATON AND FOUND two messages: a terse note from Howard Grant—"Sorry, no dice"—and a request to call Mr. Joseph Textile at home. Walker smiled with the pleasure that secret information always gave him. He was the only person in the world who knew that Joseph Textile was the president of the United States of America.

The nickname—now a code name—went back almost thirty years, to the day when Charlie, dressed in his best madras shirt, khaki pants and loafers going-to-college ensemble, walked into the pungent little dorm room at South Quad and found a hairy, muscular young man lying naked on a narrow bed, playing air guitar and singing along, off-key, to a record about a woman who was marrying somebody's best friend. The music was so loud that Charlie had been forced to shout. "Hey, are you Goldberg?"

The boy on the bed opened his brown eyes and looked at Charlie without embarrassment. "All I could do was cry, cry, cry, cry, cry," he sang, nodding his head. Charlie couldn't tell if the nod was affirmation or rhythm.

"If that's a yes, I'm your roommate," he said. "My name's Charlie Walker." He hoped Goldberg wouldn't get up; the idea of shaking hands with a naked stranger didn't appeal to him.

Charlie had nothing to worry about. Goldberg looked at him narrowly, said "Hey," and went back to his singing.

"Mind if I turn down this noise?"

"Noise? Joe Tex?"

"I've never heard of him," said Charlie, turning the volume knob in the direction of zero.

"You never heard of Joe Tex," said Goldberg. "What are you, a foreign exchange student?"

"I'm from Fargo. North Dakota."

"You're shitting me. Fargo? Like Wells Fargo? Jesus, Slim, no wonder you never heard of Joe Tex. Sittin' around the campfire, singing them ole Roy Rogers tunes."

Charlie sat down heavily on the unoccupied bed and looked at his new roommate. "Damn," he said quietly.

"What's your problem?"

"We're supposed to live together in this cell," Charlie said in a flat voice. "And I can't do that if I have to listen to idiotic jokes about cowboys all year."

"You're not too sensitive or anything," said Goldberg.

"I'm sensitive to morons," said Charlie without rancor. "Fargo's full of them. College was supposed to be different."

"For a skinny guy, you've got a big mouth," Goldberg said amiably, sitting up for the first time. The movement was at once graceful and threatening; Goldberg had the body of a young heavyweight boxer.

"I'm not calling you a moron," said Charlie. "I'm just stating a fact. Some people are allergic to tuna fish, I'm allergic to corny stupidity. That doesn't mean there's anything wrong with tuna fish—"

"You say your name was Charlie?" asked Goldberg in a Fred Flintstone voice. "Ooh, now I get it, you're Charlie Tuna, chicken of the sea. You know that ad on TV? They do have TV out on the prairie, right? 'Charlie Tuna, how you doin'?" Goldberg saw a look of disgust come over Charlie Walker's pale, even features and burst into laughter. "Hey, be cool. I'm just kidding," he said. "I just felt like confusing you."

"What's confusing about acting like a moron?"

"Because I'm not one," said Goldberg reasonably. "Ask you a question: What did you think when you found out my name? What popped into your mind?"

"Nothing much."

"Bullshit," said Goldberg. "You came in here expecting some squirrely little guy with glasses and a violin. Don't bother answering, I can see it on your face. Then you get here and find this fucking monster. I mean, look at me." He scanned his own body approvingly. "So you forget the violinist and you say to yourself—dumb jock. Skinny guys like you always do, it makes you feel superior. Lemme ask you this—what'd you get on your SATs?"

"Seven forty on the verbal, seven ten on the math," said Charlie.

"Well, that's better than I did," conceded Goldberg, slightly abashed. "But not all that much better. Scores like that, what are you doing here?"

"Scholarship," said Charlie. "My dad's dead and my mom doesn't have much money. Besides, Michigan's a good school."

"My folks have nothing but money," said Goldberg with a grin. "My old man's Fat Fred Goldberg, the King of Scrap. You're rooming with royalty, Slim."

"Charlie. If your scores were so good, how come you're here?"

"Politics," said Goldberg. "When I get out of school I'm

going into politics, and Ann Arbor's the place to get started. You can make contacts here up the ass, not to mention the reputation you get playing football."

"You're a football star?"

"Not a star, but I'll start junior year, maybe even sophomore. Linebacker."

"How come you aren't rooming with one of the other players?"

"I didn't feel like it," said Goldberg. "I didn't want to hear 'Jew this' and 'Jew that' for the next four years."

"I thought dumb jocks were a stereotype," said Charlie, suddenly enjoying the conversation.

"Don't make it wrong." Goldberg grinned. "Besides, you want to get ahead in politics, you've got to learn how to relate to normal people. Living in a regular dorm with regular people is a good way to practice."

"You a Democrat or a Republican?"

"Democrat," said Goldberg. "Despite my name."

"Dewey's strange," agreed Charlie.

"You gotta know my mother," said Goldberg. "Her old man, my grandfather, is a socialist and a big-time Zionist. And she hates his ass. So naturally she's a Republican and she pretends to be some kind of Episcopalian."

"But you're a Democrat?"

"Republicans don't get elected around here. This ain't Fargo."

"Why do you want to be a politician?"

Goldberg shrugged his massive shoulders. "I'm good at it," he said. "I was president of the senior class at Mumford."

"You don't want to save the world or anything?"

"That, too," said Goldberg. It took Charlie a moment to catch the facetiousness in his new roommate's voice.

"Can I ask you another question?"

"You're a one-man quiz show," said Goldberg, but he was smiling. "Yeah, go ahead, what?"

"Am I going to have to listen to that music all year?"

"Fuckin' A," said Goldberg. "Whatever that means. You know what the A stands for?"

"Never thought about it," said Charlie. "Maybe it means 'affirmative' in astronaut talk."

"Probably," said Goldberg. "Don't sweat the music, you'll get to like it. That's why you came to Michigan, right, for diverse cultural experiences? Joe Tex, man. He's so cool."

"Working on the Negro vote?"

"Joe Tex is for real," said Goldberg. "Sometimes I listen to him and I wish I *was* Joe Tex."

"Textile," said Charlie Walker.

"Huh?"

"That's what Joe Tex's name would be if he was Jewish. Joe Textile."

"Joe Textile. That's great," Goldberg laughed. "You're cool, Slim. My kind of roommate." He climbed out of bed and, still naked, enveloped Charlie Walker in a powerful bear hug.

"Hey, Textile, calm down," said Charlie, at once embarrassed and warmed by the hug.

"I'm calm," said Goldberg. He went to the closet and took out a pair of white gym shorts. "What are you majoring in?"

"English. I want to be a writer."

"Fan-fucking-tastic," said Goldberg. "We've got to get your ass on the *Daily*."

"They don't take freshmen," said Charlie.

"I know the editor," said Goldberg. "I'll fix it."

"Can you?"

"Damn straight," said Goldberg, extending his huge hand. "From now on, we're a team. You take care of me, I take care of you. Partners?"

Charlie looked for a long moment at the semi-naked stranger standing in front of him with his hand outstretched. Eighteen years of midwestern Lutheran reticence told him to

go to the dean's office and ask for a different room assignment. But something he didn't quite understand—and had
never, in all the years that followed, fully understood—compelled him to take Dewey Goldberg's hand. "Partners," he
said. And, ever since, they had been.

At Michigan, Goldberg and Charlie became campus
celebrities—Goldberg as a starting linebacker and student government leader, Charlie as a reporter and later managing editor
of the *Daily*. The bottom floor of an old house they rented on
State Street was the one spot in Ann Arbor where jocks and
radicals met to talk politics and sports, smoke dope, drink beer
and meet each other's girls.

Goldberg presided over the activities at the "hou" with
energetic conviviality. His allowance was more than ample to
keep the place stocked with cases of Schlitz and boxes of
Domino's pizza, which formed the heart of Ann Arbor's cuisine. Charlie's friends usually brought grass and while most of
the football jocks smoked it, Goldberg didn't. "Someday I'll be
running for something and a reporter like you is going to get
up in a press conference and ask if I ever smoked dope," he explained to Charlie. "It isn't worth the risk."

At the start of his third year, Dewey Goldberg was elected
president of the student body, the first junior ever to be chosen
for the job. Given the radical antiwar winds sweeping over the
University of Michigan, a jock candidate wouldn't normally
have had a chance. But, thanks to Charlie, Goldberg had the endorsement of the *Daily* and the goodwill of the hippies, and
that tipped the scales. "I owe you for this," he told Charlie over
victory beers at the P-Bell.

"Forget it," said Charlie. "That's what friends are for. Besides, I think you'll do a good job."

"You don't understand politics. The first rule is to always
pay back favors, especially to friends. Don't worry, you won't
have to ask—I'll know when the time comes."

It came that April. Acting on a tip from a disaffected assistant professor, Charlie discovered that Malcolm H. Melrose, the esteemed dean of the School of Humanities, was receiving kickbacks from several local bookstores. When he approached the dean for a reaction, he was informed that the story was a slanderous lie. Half an hour later the president of the university, James Lindsay, called to remind Charlie that the administration had the final say about the *Daily's* content. "And my say is no," Lindsay said. "We're not going to ruin a distinguished career over some undergraduate rumor."

"What are you going to do?" Goldberg asked Charlie that night.

"I dunno," said Charlie glumly. He had no doubt that the story was good—students who worked in three of the bookstores had confirmed it—but he was still on scholarship. "What would you do?"

"Me? I'd let it slide," said Goldberg. "But I'm not you. You're a reporter, and this is a hell of a story."

"I guess," said Charlie. "You think Fat Fred will give me a job in the scrap business if they boot me out of here?"

"Probably," said Goldberg. "He'd love to have a nice white boy to boss around. Listen, hold the story for a day, can you?"

The next morning Goldberg drove down to Detroit, to the office of a lawyer named A. S. Shapiro. Shapiro was a childhood friend of his father's and an ardent fan of Michigan football. It was his boast that in the twenty-nine years since his graduation he had never missed a game, at home or away. He was also a member of the university's Board of Regents.

"Dewey, Dewey, Dewey," said Shapiro, grabbing the young linebacker by his powerful shoulders and shaking him. "What brings you down here in the middle of the week when you should be in school?"

"I got a situation, Uncle Abe. I'm not going to play next season."

"What are you talking about? You're All-Big-Ten, you

could be All-American next year. You got money problems, girl troubles, grades, what?"

"Nothing like that," Goldberg said. Quickly he ran down the details of Charlie's confrontation with the authorities. "He's going to print the story. If they screw him, I quit. And so will half a dozen other players, the guys with any conscience at all." It was a lie—Goldberg knew that there wasn't a single player on the Wolverines team, himself included, who would miss a practice, much less a season, on account of Charlie Walker's conscience. But it was the kind of lie that, in the supercharged atmosphere of the time, men like A. S. Shapiro believed about undergraduates.

"That would be a disaster," he said. "I'll have a word with President Lindsay."

"That's a conversation I'd love to hear, Uncle Abe," said Goldberg. "Mind if I listen in?"

The lawyer looked at him through hooded eyes. "You're a shrewd bastard," he said approvingly. "Sure, listen away."

That night Goldberg came home to find Charlie bent over a pizza. Six empty Schlitz bottles and the look on his face told Goldberg that his friend was fairly drunk and very worried.

"Charlie? Print your story," Goldberg said. "And remember—we're even."

The *Daily's* Melrose exposé was picked up on the AP wire out of Detroit and flashed around the country. It was just the kind of thing people were looking for, an example of idealistic student radicalism successfully confronting the establishment. The story forced Dean Melrose's retirement and won Charlie a summer internship at the *Detroit Free Press* and the promise of a job when he graduated.

"How'd you do it?" Charlie asked.

"Politics," said Goldberg. "I told you it's a great profession."

In his senior year, Dewey Goldberg was injured in the

Purdue game and didn't make All-American. Secretly he was relieved when his gridiron career ended; he had never really enjoyed the game. He grew a beard, made a few anti-Vietnam speeches at rallies on the Diag and, in the spring, a week after graduation, got his draft notice.

"We've got to figure a way to get you out," said Charlie, whose mild asthma and status as sole son of a widowed mother ensured his deferment. "There's a weight limit, you could go for that. Or maybe Fat Fred can find a shrink—"

"Forget it," said Goldberg stoically. "I'm going."

"What are you, crazy? Nobody goes to Vietnam."

"You ever hear Joe Tex's song on the war?" asked Goldberg. He closed his eyes and began to sing: "When I got your letter ba-by, I was in a foxhole on my knees. And your letter brought me so much strength, I reached up and got me two more enemies."

"Oh, well, now I understand. Joe Tex says go, you gotta go. Jesus, Dewey, guys are getting killed over there."

"American guys."

"Not guys like you. Not guys with a way out."

"Listen, Slim, you think I want my ass shot off in Vietnam? The thing is, this war's going to get over someday and guys who dodged the draft are going to have zero future in politics. Don't worry about me; I'll ace the war. I'm too lucky to die."

That night Charlie came into Goldberg's darkened room and sat on the foot of the bed. "Tell me something," he said in a soft voice. "When you said you're too lucky to die—I was just wondering, ah, whether you believe—"

"What, in God?" Goldberg groaned. "Shit, I thought we were going to get through four years without having this conversation."

"Don't be an asshole," said Charlie. "I want to know."

There was a long silence in the dark and finally Goldberg said, "Okay, as a matter of fact, I don't."

"I do," Charlie said. "I think I do. Don't tell anybody, okay?"

"Good," said Goldberg. "In that case you can pray for my ass. Just don't tell Jesus that my name's Goldberg."

"What's it like to be a Jew?" blurted Charlie.

"You've been living with one for four years—you tell me."

"I dunno," said Charlie. His voice was more tentative than usual; talks this personal between them were rare. "Usually you act like it's no big thing. But sometimes I get the feeling that it makes you different somehow—"

"Ah, you want to hear the secrets of the Jews," said Goldberg in a mock conspiratorial whisper. "You know what it's like? It's like inheriting a bad stock you can't ever sell. You may not give a shit about the company, maybe you don't even know what it does, but your future's tied up in it. And so you have to keep checking the listings to see how it's going."

"You said a bad stock," said Charlie. "Why bad?"

" 'Cause it never goes up," Goldberg said with a laugh. "It's just a question of how far down it is."

"You mean, like the Holocaust?"

"Actually I was thinking about the fact that I can't be president. Congress, yeah, maybe even the Senate, or governor. But I know in advance that I won't ever get to the top. Because of this stock I can't get rid of."

"Things are changing," said Charlie. "Someday America will elect a Jewish president."

"Not in your lifetime," said Dewey without bitterness. "And, what's worse, not in mine."

Charlie recalled that conversation as he dialed the number on the Sheraton's little pink message sheet. The American Embassy was right down the street and he could have gone there to call Goldberg, but he didn't want anyone to know he was in contact with the White House.

The call went to the direct line in the upstairs apartment,

theoretically bypassing the White House switchboard. Only Didi, Willis, Graff and Charlie knew the number. It rang three times before Goldberg answered.

"Hey, Textile, how's it going?" said Charlie.

"Good, Slim. What's the deal?"

"Too early to say yet. Right now all I'm getting is speculation. I need a few more days at least. Didi back yet?"

"Day after tomorrow. You see Mr. Redding?" Before leaving, Dewey had given Charlie a list of names. Starks, the American ambassador, was Aretha. The Mossad was Sam and Dave. Barzel himself was Otis Redding. The code was really unnecessary, but Goldberg got a kick out of it and so did Charlie.

"Tomorrow," said Charlie.

"Good," said Goldberg. "I need to know soon. We've got to decide if Otis is coming to dinner or not."

CHAPTER FOURTEEN

MOSSAD HEADQUARTERS WAS LOCATED IN AN ORDINARY TEL
Aviv office building on an ordinary street. The lobby was pleasant but simple and the security arrangements, at least to the
naked eye, practically nonexistent. There were medium-sized
police departments in the United States with far more impressive headquarters.

Amos Levran's private office was a small, well-lit room appointed with the government furniture issued to senior officials. Its white walls were decorated with inexpensive Israeli
landscapes. On his desk, which was free of papers, sat a normal-
looking white telephone. Along the wall across from the desk
was a narrow, backless couch that doubled as a cot. And on the
couch sat the bulky figure of Marcus Broun, daintily sipping
coffee from a mug.

Broun was only a few years older than Levran, but he
seemed to belong to another generation. Partly it was his

looks—the large, bald head flecked with liver spots, the hearing aid in his prominent right ear, his smooth, beardless skin, the thick glasses that hid his eyes. And then there was his accent. Although he had been brought to Palestine from Berlin as a young boy, his precise Hebrew was still German-inflected, making him seem not merely old but somehow foreign.

Levran had long since ceased to notice Broun's strange appearance. They had known one another for almost thirty years. It was Broun who had insisted on appointing Levran his deputy, despite a feeling among some of the senior people that, while Levran was a wonderful fellow and a terrific field operator, he was slightly too convivial and lighthearted for the uppermost level.

Broun himself could never be accused of frivolity. He was a dour man, a collector of coins and German first editions, famous throughout the Israeli intelligence community for the fastidiousness of his work and his demanding nature. They called him the "Yekke," a not altogether affectionate sabra nickname for the Jews of Germany, but one that connoted respect. There weren't many Yekkes left these days, and the younger agents, most of them native-born recruited from the army's elite units, considered him a relic.

Broun was aware of his forbidding image and cultivated it. He was a genuine introvert who was uncomfortable with informality sabra-style, and his chilly demeanor kept the hearty back-slappers at a distance. He referred to people by their last names and encouraged them to reciprocate, never attended the social functions of the insular intelligence community and kept face-to-face contact with his agents to an absolute minimum. He had a wife and a dog and a hobby—playing cello twice a week with three German-born musicians from the Israel Philharmonic Orchestra. And one friend—Amos Levran.

It was a friendship that Levran had initiated long ago, and for many years Broun had mistrusted it. He was a believer in logic, and he couldn't find a logical explanation why the popular, lighthearted sabra would want to be his friend. And so he had kept a wary distance, certain that Levran was playing some nasty psychological game with him, or trying to extract a professional advantage. He had scrutinized the relationship like a suspicious bank examiner searching for counterfeit bills, until finally he had been forced to accept the improbable truth: that Amos Levran simply liked him.

This realization had led to no great moment of intimacy, no sudden embrace or exchange of confidences. Broun had simply begun calling Levran by his first name. He trusted Amos to interpret the change, and when he began calling Broun "Marco"—not merely a first name, but a nickname—Broun saw that he was right.

Theirs was not a social friendship. Once Broun had tentatively asked Levran if he ever attended the philharmonic, but when Levran simply shrugged, Broun hadn't pursued it. On Broun's fiftieth birthday, Levran had taken him to dinner at a Yemenite restaurant in Jaffa, but the occasion hadn't gone well; Levran's date had giggled when Broun formally scooped his humus with a spoon. Since then they almost never saw one another outside the office, and even at headquarters they seldom talked about anything other than work. It was there that their friendship found its real expression, in a bond that went beyond professional rapport to an instinctive harmony of thought.

Broun made a point of staying in his private office as much as possible. He disliked meeting underlings in the hall or on the elevator, where someone might buttonhole him with a request or, worse, engage in small talk. People who wanted to speak to him made an appointment. The one exception was Levran; Broun dropped by his office from time to time. It was a small act of informality, but, like the first names, it expressed the regard that Broun could not articulate in words.

". . . and so it looks to me like Sara was right," Levran was saying, coming to the end of his account of his meeting with

Charlie Walker. "He's not here to write a book. Goldberg sent him. He thinks Barzel's out to get him. And you know something? He's right."

"What makes you say that?" asked Broun. He took a sip of tea and peered at Levran through steam-fogged glasses.

"I checked in Washington," he said. "The word's out."

"Politics," said Broun unhappily. "Well, supposing it's true: What business is it of ours?"

"There was something Walker said last night that lit a bulb. He said 'Barzel's people' have been spreading the word. Not 'the embassy' or 'AIPAC,' but 'Barzel's people.' That stuck with me. I wondered who he could mean."

"And you found out," said Broun.

Levran nodded.

"Motke Vilk?"

"Nope. It's Adam Reshef."

"Reshef? Since when does he have anything to do with American politics?"

"Since now, I guess," said Levran with a shrug.

Broun was silent for a long moment. "Well, I still don't see that it's our problem," he said. "He's Barzel's adviser. If he wants to use him to run political errands, that's up to him."

"If that's all this is," said Levran. "It could be a lot more."

"Yes," said Broun. There was no need for him to put it into words; he knew that Levran was referring to the Project.

The Mossad had no file on the Project. There was nothing in writing because there was almost nothing to write; the little they knew could be easily carried in the heads of Broun and Levran.

"It's time to use Chanele," said Levran.

Broun frowned. Chanele was Adam Reshef's secretary. Reshef knew that she was on loan to him from the Mossad— not an unusual arrangement for government secretaries in supersensitive jobs. What he didn't know was that she was also the daughter of Amos Levran's stepbrother. The little that the

Mossad knew about the Project came from information she had gleaned. "Reshef doesn't trust me," she had told Levran shortly after going to work for him. "He won't let me place calls for him or give me the combination to his safe."

"What's he keep in there, do you know?"

"Mostly tapes, I think," said Chanele. "I walked in on him one time and got a peek."

"Tapes of what?"

Chanele shrugged. "I think he may be taping his conversations with the prime minister," she said. "He usually goes into the safe after their meetings."

Levran looked at his stepniece steadily. "Since when do you need a combination to open a safe?" he asked.

"I don't," Chanele said. "What I need is authorization. I can't do something like that on my own."

"Neither can I," Levran had said. Broun was a stickler for principle, especially the principle of civilian control of the Mossad. He had reluctantly agreed to plant Chanele in Reshef's office, but he would never permit her to rifle the safe of the prime minister's security adviser without a very compelling reason.

Now, thought Levran, they had such a reason.

"If Barzel's trying to intervene in the American election, this thing must be very big," said Levran. "We have to find out what is going on."

"No," said Broun.

"Reshef's taping his conversations with Barzel," said Levran. "That could be a security problem."

"No," said Broun. They both knew that internal security was the province of Shin Bet, not the Mossad. "Besides, why shouldn't he record his conversations? Barzel does."

"That's not the point. I think you should go to Barzel and demand to know what this Project of his is."

"No," said Broun. "I don't make demands of the prime minister."

"What if Reshef's acting on his own? You know him—he's capable of it. At least let's find out that much."

"No," said Broun. He took a sip of tea, removed his thick glasses and wiped away the steam. "Not yet."

CHAPTER FIFTEEN

CHARLIE WALKER HAD BEEN WRONG WHEN HE HAD CALLED Elihu Barzel a retired Mossad agent, although it was an understandable mistake. It was the way Barzel was invariably described in press biographies, and the prime minister himself had never done anything to set the record straight. "Mossad agent" sounded official, self-explanatory and, in Israeli politics, sexy. Whereas there was no simple way to describe what Barzel had really been, what he had done, and why, in the end, he had been forced to stop.

When the War of Independence ended in 1949, Israel had been faced with a multitude of problems. New immigrants, many of them ill and destitute, flooded into the country. They had no common culture or language and, in many cases, no desire to be there—they were simply stateless and unwanted Jews. Jobs had to be created, food rationed, tent cities constructed to put a roof over their heads. An army had to be maintained to protect them from their predatory Arab neighbors. These were the urgent tasks that faced Prime Minister David Ben Gurion.

There was also the unfinished business of the Holocaust. Ben Gurion's critics claimed that during World War II he had virtually ignored the slaughter of Europe's Jews, concentrating instead on developing the tiny Jewish community of Palestine. Now, they said, he was once again shirking his duty by failing to put revenge at the top of the new nation's agenda.

Ben Gurion felt no guilt for his inaction during the Holocaust. He was a supremely practical man and not much given to self-doubt. A year after Hitler's rise to power he had warned the Jews of Europe, calling on them to flee to Palestine and help build a pioneering society in the ancient homeland. That call had gone unheeded and the Jews had died. There was nothing he could have done to stop it, and nothing, now that the war was over, that could bring its victims back to life. History had entrusted him with the role of reinventing Jewish sovereignty after two thousand years, and that was job enough. His responsibility was to the present and the future, not the past. Revenge was a luxury he could not afford.

And so it had not been revenge that had prompted him to send for Elihu Barzel in the spring of 1950. A mighty nation had devoted its energies to the killing of Jews. That nation had been defeated, and a few of its leaders tried and punished, but there were still millions of Germans who hated Jews. The vast majority were unarmed and harmless, but there were among them a number of men with dangerous skills. The top scientists had been whisked away by the Americans and the Russians to build bombs and rockets, but there were others—experienced combat leaders, experts in intelligence and sabotage, munitions manufacturers—who had been of no use to the Allies and were now unemployed.

There was one obvious market for Jew-haters with such skills. The Arabs, Ben Gurion believed, had the temperament for mass murder. What they lacked was the training and technology that the Germans could provide. World War II had been over barely five years and already ex-Nazis were turning up in Egypt, Syria and elsewhere. America needed German support in the Cold War; it had no appetite for a confrontation over something so trivial as Israeli paranoia. And so Ben Gurion had resolved to act alone.

Much of this he explained to Elihu Barzel as they sat in the prime minister's untidy, book-lined office in Tel Aviv. It was their first face-to-face meeting and their last, but Ben Gurion felt no compunction about sharing his fears with the tanned, broad-shouldered young man. He had followed him closely since the incident at Kfar Joss, and the reports had been encouraging. Throughout almost two years of fighting, Barzel had been consistently bold, imaginative and ruthless.

"I need someone to stop the Germans," the prime minister said in his high-pitched mumble. "I think you are the right one."

"You want me to join the Mossad?" asked Barzel.

"The Mossad has nothing to do with this," said Ben Gurion. "The Mossad is an official body, responsible to the state of Israel. There are things it cannot do, places it cannot operate. You would be on your own. Completely alone. If you are caught, you are a private *messugenah*, taking revenge for the death of his family. If you are killed, you will be buried where you die. If you succeed, no one will know except you and me."

"How will I know what to do, where to go?" asked Barzel. "Where will I get my orders?"

"You speak German, Polish and English," said Ben Gurion. "Papers will be arranged for you and a list of people we are concerned about. Go to Germany. Nazis are not so hard to find there." He permitted himself a fleeting smile. "Ingratiate yourself, become an anti-Semite. Find out who is selling himself and who is buying. Follow where your nose leads you."

"And when I find someone?"

The prime minister shrugged. "Use your judgment. You are an experienced fighter, you have an appreciation of who could be dangerous. Choose your targets. After all, you can't stop everyone."

"You are giving me permission to kill them?"

Ben Gurion looked out the window of his small office for a moment. "A sum of money will be deposited in a German bank. The account number will be sent to you along with your other papers. Also, the name of a businessman in New York, who should know how to reach you in case of emergency. Keep him informed of changes in your address, but do not, under any circumstances, try to contact me or any Israeli official."

"How long will this take?" asked Barzel.

"As long as it takes," said Ben Gurion. "Come home when you feel you are finished."

"It could take a lifetime," said Barzel.

"It could," said the prime minister.

"You didn't answer my question," said Barzel. "I asked if you are giving me permission to kill."

"Yes, I heard you," said Ben Gurion. "I am giving you permission to kill, but not to murder. It is a terrible permission. Always remember that there is a difference."

In the fall of 1950, Eli Barzel, who had once been Elihu Leibowitz, became Ernst Hoffmann. The money he found waiting for him in Germany was more than enough to set up a travel agency, Deutsche Tours. It turned out to be a good business move—Germans were beginning to venture abroad for the first time since the war—and it enabled him to make his own travel arrangements without unwelcome supervision.

Barzel hired an experienced man named Kurt to run the day-to-day operation. "Germans are ashamed to travel," he told Kurt. "Our job is to give them confidence, make them feel they have a right to go anywhere. Perhaps Hitler went too far, but this is not a reason for Germans to feel guilty. Don't you agree?"

"Of course," said Kurt, whose family had been living on the edge of starvation since the war. For a job, he would agree to anything.

"I have only one rule," said Barzel. "This company will not book trips to Israel. If someone wants to visit the Jews, let him go someplace else. Is that clear?"

"Yes," said Kurt. "Perfectly clear."

It was several months before an American theological student stopped by the agency to make arrangements for a Christmas holiday in the Holy Land. "I am sorry," Kurt said stiffly. "We do not book tours there."

"Why not?"

"Orders," said Kurt. "Company policy."

"You people never learn," said the incensed young American. He told the story to a journalist, who visited the agency, confirmed the story and wrote an outraged article about the *Judenrein* travel agency.

Public reaction was swift. Throughout the country Ernst Hoffmann was denounced as a Nazi. The state prosecutor threatened to bring charges on the country's new antiracism laws. A group of young Germans picketed the agency. Hoffmann's only comment was that he was free to do business where and with whom he chose.

At first the number of customers dwindled to almost nothing. Kurt was alarmed, but his boss reassured him. "There are plenty of good Germans who will be happy to do business with a patriotic company," he said.

Herr Hoffmann was right. Slowly the agency developed a new kind of clientele, middle-aged people, mostly men, interested in traveling to South America or to the Middle East. They were respectfully treated, and the news spread throughout Dusseldorf and beyond that if you wanted a sympathetic, discreet, like-minded travel agent, Ernst Hoffmann was your man.

One day a tall, sparse fellow in his late fifties entered the agency and asked for Hoffmann. He introduced himself formally as Dr. Adrian Schnell. "I am planning a business trip to Egypt, and I have a small problem," he said. "I am a biologist and I would like to take some laboratory samples with me. But I would prefer that they not go through the regular route. I am afraid, you see, that they could be damaged if they are handled by clumsy people."

"I can make a request for special handling at the airport," said Hoffmann. "We have friends there."

"I would prefer that it not go through the airport at all," said Schnell in a conspiratorial voice. "I would rather pick it up in Cairo. Perhaps you have some means of arranging for this?"

"I see," Hoffmann said. "Yes, I believe it would be possible."

"I would be willing to pay whatever it costs," said Schnell. "Money is not the object."

"The cost will be small," said Hoffmann. "I am a great admirer of the Egyptians. Perhaps what you are selling will be of benefit to them. Besides, I would like for you to become a regular customer."

Over the next two years, Adrian Schnell flew twice more to Cairo and three times to Damascus. Each time he asked Deutsche Tours to make special arrangements. Each time he was gratified by the agency's efficiency. After returning from his sixth Middle Eastern trip he invited his travel agent to lunch.

"Your business is going satisfactorily?" Hoffmann asked circumspectly.

"As well as can be expected," said Schnell. "Unfortunately,

I am forced to deal with idiots. I know you admire the Egyptians, but they are very stupid people. And the Syrians are worse. It takes them a very long time to understand."

"What?" asked Hoffmann blankly.

"What I am trying to sell them," said Schnell. "Tell me, Ernst, haven't you wondered about my business?"

"It is not my concern."

"I have my own product," said Schnell. "My own invention. It is something I worked on during the war."

"Perhaps it is better not to say more," Hoffmann whispered.

"I trust you," said Schnell. "I have a very good sense of whom to trust."

"It is better to trust no one," said Hoffmann. "The Jews have spies all over Germany."

"The Jews are a diseased people," said Schnell. Suddenly he smiled bleakly. "That is why they need to take their medicine."

"I see," said Hoffmann. "Yes, I quite agree."

Adrian Schnell was the first man Elihu Barzel killed in Europe after the war. He did it by hanging him in his own apartment. He hung him slowly, by degrees, forcing the names of four other Nazis active in the Arab world from Schnell's thin, trembling lips before allowing the rope to snap his neck. The police ruled it a suicide.

For the next few years Ernst Hoffmann built a thriving tourist agency, opening branches in Munich, Hamburg and Vienna. He found that he had a real aptitude for business and he was becoming a rich man. Whilst Ernst Hoffmann prospered, Elihu Barzel went about his work methodically. As Ben Gurion had observed, it was easy to find Nazis in Germany. Many became Ernst Hoffmann's friends. With some he drank beer and gossiped. With others he did business. Nine, he assassinated.

During these years, Elihu Barzel kept a strict distance

from Israel. All he knew was what he read in the papers. As a result, he had no way of realizing that, in 1952, Ben Gurion had changed his mind about hunting war criminals. The Holocaust was becoming a political problem; some survivors claimed that his party, Mapai, had made deals with the Nazis during the war to save its own supporters in Europe while abandoning the others to their fate. This, they said, was the real reason that Ben Gurion didn't want to catch Nazi criminals. To put this rumor to rest, the prime minister ordered the Mossad to hunt down several prominent mass murderers, including Adolf Eichmann and Dr. Joseph Mengele.

Finding Adolf Eichmann was not part of Barzel's assignment; as far as he knew, Himmler's former deputy posed no threat to Israel. But Barzel had been in Germany a long time and he was sick of it. At a drunken card party, he heard someone whisper that Eichmann was in Argentina, and a scenario began to take root in his mind. He would go to Buenos Aires, hunt down Eichmann, kill him and then return to Israel. It was the way to end his exile; no one could reasonably ask for more.

He arrived in Argentina in early 1958, at the height of the summer, and immediately began to make friends. Ernst Hoffmann was young, wealthy, unattached and well connected, and the German community of Buenos Aires greeted him warmly. He talked of opening a travel agency and, perhaps, a seaside resort with German food and entertainment. "Somewhere for our kind of people," he told his new friends. "A place we are free to be ourselves."

During his first months in Argentina, Barzel talked and talked about his plans, but he listened, too; listened for a whisper of the name Eichmann. The hunt invigorated him, snapped him out of the homesickness he had felt in Germany. He had a sense that Eichmann was someplace close by, watching him, perhaps, and that it was only a matter of time before their paths crossed.

One morning as he sat sipping coffee at an outdoor café, he noticed a stout, balding young man at the next table. The man had a copy of *Der Spiegel*, which was not unusual—it was a coffeehouse frequented by Germans—but Barzel had the feeling that he was being sized up. He gave the young man a polite smile and said, "Good morning."

"Good morning to you," the man answered in German. "I have regards for you from Mr. Vilk."

Barzel kept his face expressionless. "You must have me confused with someone else," he said. "I don't know a Mr. Vilk."

"Will you take a walk with me?" asked the man.

Barzel left some money on the table and stood up. "We can walk in the park," he said.

Wordlessly they crossed the wide boulevard and entered a small, grassy park where old people sat on benches feeding the birds. "Well, what can I do for you?" asked Barzel.

"You've done enough," said the man. "It's time for you to go home."

It took Elihu Barzel a split second to realize that the man had spoken in Hebrew. He hadn't heard the language in years. "I beg your pardon," he said in German.

"It's all right," said the bald fellow in Hebrew. "I have a message from Ben Gurion. He said to tell you, he was right to trust your judgment."

Barzel looked around the park and saw that they were alone. "Who are you?" he asked in Hebrew, the unaccustomed words feeling rough and heavy in his mouth.

"Broun," said the man. "I work for the prime minister's office."

It was a euphemism for the Mossad that had become current while Barzel was away. He looked at the squat man quizzically. "What are you doing here?"

"The same thing you are. Looking for Eichmann."

"Stay out of my way," said Barzel.

"We want him alive."

"I don't take orders from clerks in the prime minister's office," said Barzel.

"It is not my order," replied Broun with stiff formality. "It comes directly from Ben Gurion."

"What if I refuse?"

"You may not refuse."

Barzel peered into the eyes of the squat, bald man, who returned his stare without emotion. "You're threatening me," he said, a note of wonder in his voice.

"I am delivering a message," said Broun. "Between us, I don't like it, either. But it is an order."

"You sound like one of them," said Barzel.

He expected the young man to flush with anger, but he merely said, "There are certain things they are very good at."

"Give me one month," said Barzel.

"You leave tomorrow," said Broun. "Go by way of Germany and settle your affairs. What you have earned in the travel business is yours to keep. When you get home, go to Ein Harrod. Someone will be in touch with you."

"Just like that," said Barzel.

"For what it's worth, I think you're a hero," said the young man.

"It's worth nothing," said Barzel. He turned and walked away, leaving Broun standing alone.

That night Elihu Barzel took his last trip as Ernst Hoffmann. His destination, however, was not Germany. Instead, he went to New York City, to see Howard Grant.

After Elihu Barzel had left Kibbutz Ein Harrod for Germany, Grant had returned to America and gone into the shipping business. Motke Vilk spent two lonely years on the kibbutz and then moved to Tel Aviv, where he opened a small restaurant on Allenby Street, not far from the shops where he had once searched for a new used accordion. The restaurant was called simply Motke's Place and it became a popular hangout for the Palmach old boys, many of whom were slowly making their way up the ladder in the army and the government bureaucracy. Through them Motke tried to keep track of Barzel, but no one seemed to know where he had vanished.

And then, late in the summer of 1960, Elihu Barzel walked into Motke's Place. It was lunchtime, the restaurant was crowded, and it took Motke a moment to recognize the dapper man with slicked-back hair, dressed in an elegantly tailored blue pin-striped suit and a red silk tie.

"It's good to see you, Motke," said Barzel in Hebrew. "You've become a businessman, I see." He gestured at the packed little restaurant. "I'm impressed."

"It's a living," said Vilk. "You've changed. You look like a real European gentleman. Smell like one, too."

Barzel shrugged. "You can't do what I've been doing dressed in khaki shorts and sandals," he said. "Anyway, it's finished."

"Can I ask?"

"What for?" asked Barzel. "You don't need to know. Tell me, are you happy here? At Motke's Place?" The question was straightforward, but Motke detected a thin irony in his friend's voice.

"Make me a better offer."

"I'm working with Howard in America now," said Barzel. "He's a big shot."

"I know," said Motke. "He writes. Not like you."

"I'm going there in a week," said Barzel. "Are you coming?"

"A week? How can I find a buyer in a week?"

"What's the place worth? Don't be conservative, exaggerate."

"Thirty thousand lira," said Motke. "Maybe thirty-five."

"Sold," said Barzel. "To Grant Enterprises. For fifty thousand lira."

"Make it fifty-five," said Motke. "Just so I don't feel like a schmuck."

"Sixty," said Barzel. "Find me a manager and start packing."

CHAPTER SIXTEEN

ZION AMRANI TOOK ONE LOOK AT CHARLIE WALKER AND
fell in love. Charlie was everything Amrani looked for in a passenger. The suitcase he was carrying indicated that he was
going to the airport—an eighteen-dollar fare. The bag looked
light, too; Amrani had a bad back, but his professional pride
required him to personally hoist luggage into the trunk of his
Mercedes cab. Best of all, the tall, thin man was obviously an
American, which meant a ten percent gratuity. Tipping cabbies
was not a local custom, and while Amrani was a fervent patriot, he felt that this was one area where foreigners had something to teach Israelis.

"What time is your flight?" Amrani asked.

"Not till nine," said Charlie. "First I want to go to the
Accadia Hotel in Herzliya, then Jerusalem and then the airport. Can you handle that?"

"Of course. For sure."

"Good. I'll pay you two hundred dollars for the day, how's that?"

"One fifty," said Amrani.

"Two hundred's more than one fifty," said Charlie, certain that the cabby had misunderstood.

"Two hundred is too much," said Amrani. "Maybe on the plane you will tell somebody, 'I pay two hundred dollars for a taxi,' and he will tell you, 'You got ripped off.' Then you will say, 'Damn Israelis, always cheating tourists.' This way, instead you will say, 'In Tel Aviv I met the honest cab driver Zion Amrani.'"

"Okay," said Charlie, "one fifty."

"One twenty-five," said Amrani, and then quickly burst into laughter. "No, I am making a joke. One hundred and fifty dollars."

"It's a pleasure to meet an honest man," said Charlie as he slid into the backseat of the cab. "I don't run into many in my business."

"You are a journalist, no?"

"How did you know that?"

"I am driving a taxi twenty years," said Amrani. "I know who is what." He didn't mention that he had been told by his cousin Moshe, the Sheraton concierge who had steered Charlie to his cab. He also didn't mention that the correct price for the day was ninety dollars. Amrani had his professional ethics, but full disclosure wasn't among them.

When they reached the Accadia Hotel, Amrani accompanied Charlie into the air-conditioned lobby. "Wait here," he told the driver. "I want to look around for someone."

"You know where he is?"

Charlie shrugged. "He lives here. Maybe he's in one of the dining rooms or the coffee shop."

"What is his name?"

"Why?"

"I will find him maybe. I am Temani, Yemenite," said Amrani, as if that explained everything.

"Do Yemenites have ESP?"

"No." Amrani smiled. "Yemenites have big families. My cousin is working here. In security. What is the name of your friend?"

"Howard Grant," said Charlie.

"Take five," said Amrani, who had learned the phrase, like much of his English, from the movies. "I come right back."

Charlie watched the thin, curly-haired cabbie walk with determined strides toward the bank of house phones, place a call and then return with a triumphant grin. "Your friend is at the swimming pool," he said. "Playing cards."

"The price just went back up to two hundred dollars," said Charlie. "Thanks."

"Never mind," said Amrani grandly. "Yemenite mafia."

Charlie walked through the hotel to the swimming pool. There, sitting at a small table shaded by a beach umbrella, he saw an old man in a straw hat playing solitaire. There was a tall, frosty glass at his elbow and, across the table, a young woman in a skimpy bikini. A Hebrew magazine hid her face, but Walker could see as he approached that she had a terrific body.

"Mr. Grant?"

"Who wants to know?" snapped the old man, not looking up from his cards.

"My name is Charlie Walker. I've been calling you."

"I told you no dice," said Grant, still looking at the cards.

"I'm a reporter—"

"I know who you are, I read the papers," said Grant brusquely. "I don't give interviews."

Charlie glanced at the woman, who was still engrossed in the magazine, and back to Grant. "This isn't an interview," he said. "I'm here on behalf of the president of the United States."

"That's nice," said Grant. His tone was pure apathy, but he looked up from the cards. He had cynical, sunken brown eyes set over dark, droopy bags; large, hairy ears; a tubular, veiny nose; and plump, rubbery, slightly tremulous lips. The overall effect was one of a corrupt bloodhound.

"The reason I'm here is that President Goldberg's interested in American-Israeli, uh, bilateral relations and I wanted to hear your views—"

"You mean he wants you to pump me about Barzel."

"Something like that," said Charlie with a crooked smile.

"Well, it so happens that I don't want to talk about Barzel. I got nothing special to say."

"You two were partners," said Charlie.

"Yeah, we were. Once. Not anymore."

"But you're still in touch."

"He's not exactly the kind of guy who drops around for a hand of pinochle, but I talk to him from time to time."

"The two of you made a fortune together," Charlie said.

"Correction: *I* made the fortune. Barzel turned up in New York with his dick in his hand and I took him in. I'm not saying he didn't do his part. He's a hell of a deal maker, I'll give him that. Credit where credit's due. But all this stuff about him being a self-made millionaire is a lot of crap. You can't make millions unless you got millions, and I was the one with the dough. I staked him to a place at the table."

"What happened between you? Why did you stop working together?"

"He wanted to be a politician," said Grant. Suddenly he looked at Charlie as though he were seeing him for the first time. "You're a real smoothie," he said admiringly. "I tell you I don't wanna talk and here I am, yakking away like we went to *cheder* together. No wonder Goldberg sent you. You're good."

"Do you mind if I sit down?" asked Charlie. "I mean, since we're old school chums and all—"

"Yeah, what the hell," Grant said. "Honey, take a hike." The woman in the bikini lowered the magazine for the first time, gathered her drink and suntan lotion and wordlessly left the table. Grant and Charlie watched her walk away.

"Twenty-six years old," said Grant.

"She's lovely. You're a lucky man."

"A rich man," Grant said. "You know how I got so rich?" Charlie shook his head. "By not giving something for nothing. You understand what I'm saying?"

"What could I possibly do for you?"

"You personally, nothing," said Grant. "But those crumbs at the IRS are poking around my asshole like a bunch of proctologists—"

"I can't make any promises," said Charlie quickly. "And I can tell you right now, neither would President Goldberg."

"President Goldberg." Grant snorted. "What kind of name is that for a president? A president is Adams, Jefferson, Washington. Good goyish names. President Goldberg sounds like the name of a sandwich at the Carnegie Deli."

"You forgot President Grant," said Charlie.

"Yeah, Ulysses S. He was my uncle on my zayde's side. Anyway, if President Goldberg wants my help on his bilateral problems, he can goddamn good and well give me a little hand with mine. That's the way it's done, boychick."

"I suppose I could mention it to him," said Charlie. He had dealt with enough men like Grant to know that their pride required them to extract something, even an empty promise, from any transaction. Charlie understood the impulse; he didn't like giving things away, either.

The ploy didn't work on Grant, though. "Suppose

away," he said. "When you got an answer, come back and we'll talk."

"How do I know you'll have something to say that's worth talking about?"

"Listen, boychick. I know more about Elihu Barzel than the whole CIA. We stole horses together for twenty years, all over the goddamned world. I know things about him he don't know about himself. I'm an expert, believe you me."

"There's all sorts of information," said Charlie neutrally. "I'm not really interested in stories from the old days."

"Bullcrap," said Grant. A gleam came into his hooded brown eyes. "Okay, I'll make you a deal. A special introductory offer. One question, just to sample the goods. You like the answer, talk to Goldberg. You don't, you're one answer ahead."

"I can't promise you anything."

"A Boy Scout," said Grant. "I admire your honesty. Go ahead, take a shot. One question."

"All right. Barzel's put out the word in the Jewish community to hold off support for Dewey. Dewey's fine on Israel—a lot better than Childes. There's no particular tensions between the two governments—"

"This sounds like one of those story problems we used to get in arithmetic," said Grant. "If St. Louis is one hundred miles away and you go forty miles an hour, how much gas does it take to get there?"

"I want to know why Barzel is giving Dewey a hard time," said Charlie. "That's the question."

"A piece of cake," said Grant. "He wants something and when he wants something, that's how he works. Some people, when they need a favor, they're nice to the guy they need the favor from. With Barzel, it's just the opposite. Causes a problem, then solves it in exchange for the favor. That's him all over. I seen him do it a hundred times."

"You don't think it could have something to do with

Goldberg being a Jew? Maybe Barzel doesn't trust Jews in power? Or maybe he doesn't like sharing the stage with a Jewish president?"

"Hey, I said one question," said Grant. "Besides, I'm not through with my answer. There's one thing that doesn't add up."

"What's that?"

"You," said Grant.

"Me?"

"Yeah. If you're here, it's because Goldberg knows that Barzel's behind this. That's not the way he works. Usually the other guy never knows who caused the problem, he just needs Barzel to solve it."

"Maybe Dewey's sources are a little better than the people you did business with," said Charlie. "He is the president of the United States, after all."

"I don't care if he's the president of the fucking universe," said Grant dismissively. "If Barzel didn't want him to know, he wouldn't know. Period."

"Will you answer just one more question?"

"Jesus, you're a real schnorrer, you know that?" said Grant, but he was grinning. Whatever he thought of Barzel these days, he obviously enjoyed talking about him. "Yeah, okay, one more. But make it a quickie."

"What happens when it doesn't work?" asked Charlie. "When the guy says no anyway?"

Grant took a sip of his drink and looked at Charlie through narrowed eyes. "I couldn't tell you," he said. "Nobody ever says no to Elihu Barzel. Not in the end."

"Not even you?" asked Charlie, but Grant was already shuffling his cards. The discussion was over.

"It's been nice talking with you," said Charlie. "Educational."

"Good," said Grant, putting a three on a four. "You want more classes, get the IRS off my ass. Tell President Sandwich."

*   *   *

On the way to Jerusalem, Charlie asked Zion Amrani what he thought of Prime Minister Barzel.

"He is a great man," said Amrani without hesitation. He had driven enough reporters to know that they always asked about politics. Several times over the years he had been interviewed, although the real media star of the family was his cousin Baruch, whose tailor shop was next door to the *New York Times* bureau in Jerusalem and whose opinions were constantly cropping up in the paper. Baruch couldn't read English and he brought the clippings to Zion for translation. The Amranis referred to the shy little tailor as "the pundit."

"I've heard that," said Charlie, remembering that Sara Epstein had used the same adjective to describe Barzel. "What makes him so great?"

"He is not afraid."

"Of the Moslem extremists, you mean?"

"Of nothing. Not the Moslems, not the politicians, not nothing. He is a real man. One of us."

"What do you mean, 'us'?"

"A Yemenite," said Amrani proudly.

Charlie laughed. "He was born in Poland."

"So he is a Polish Yemenite," Amrani said with a chuckle. "I'm on my way to see him right now."

"Tell him Zion Amrani says hello."

"He knows you? Personally?"

"Of course. My cousin Rachamim is a good friend of his. He is a political man in the market in Tel Aviv."

"And he supports Barzel?"

"All Yemenites are supporting him," said the driver flatly.

"Why?"

"The other politicians think they are better than us. But for Barzel, all Jews are the same."

"A man of the people," said Charlie.

"He is not the man of the people," the driver replied. "He is a special man. Like a king. He takes care of us, and we love him very much."

There was nothing regal about Barzel's office, Charlie thought. It had a businesslike simplicity that was, in itself, a statement; clearly, the prime minister didn't feel the need to impress his visitors with external trappings.

Motke Vilk ushered Charlie into the room, announced him and then plopped down on the sofa. Barzel greeted the reporter with a pleasant nod. "So," he said with a faint smile on his thin lips, "you are here to interview me for your book on President Goldberg. I'm always delighted to be able to cooperate with a famous writer on a literary project." The old man's tone made it clear that he was well aware that the book was a subterfuge. Charlie briefly wondered who it was who had tipped Barzel off, Levran or Grant. It really didn't matter; since he had decided to play his cards face up, there was no further need for a cover story.

"There is no book," said Charlie. "I came to Israel because President Goldberg sent me."

"President Goldberg is a lucky man," said Barzel. "I wish our journalists were as cooperative."

"I'm not here as a journalist."

"No? Then how are you here?" asked Barzel, his blue eyes twinkling.

"As an emissary. To find out why you're trying to get Dewey defeated."

"What on earth gives you that impression?" asked Barzel, sounding genuinely surprised. Charlie had expected a denial, but he was nonetheless impressed by the sincere tone. He had been lied to often in his professional career, but rarely with such convincing disingenuousness.

"Dewey knows you've been putting out word to hold off

on contributions," he said. "What's more, you want him to know. At least, that's what Howard Grant thinks."

"Does he?" said Barzel neutrally.

"Yes, he does," Charlie replied, determined not to be taken in by Barzel's suave self-assurance. "He said Dewey'd never know what you were doing if you didn't want him to."

Barzel sighed. "I'm afraid Howard overestimates me," he said. "The truth is, I have no reason to wish President Goldberg anything but success. Although the feeling doesn't appear to be mutual."

"What do you mean?"

"Well, since you are the president's envoy, I suppose I can confess to you that I've been rather disappointed by his unwillingless to receive me in Washington."

"It's an election year," said Charlie.

"In both our countries. A cordial reception at the White House is an important electoral asset here. Perhaps it shouldn't be, but we are, unfortunately, a small and somewhat provincial country. Our relationship with the United States is extremely significant."

"You're saying that an invitation to the White House would square things?"

"Square things?" mused Barzel, as if he were hearing the expression for the first time. "I don't know about that, but it is always an honor to visit the White House. And I believe it would go a long way toward reassuring our friends in the U.S. that President Goldberg is a sincere supporter of Israel."

"I see," said Charlie.

"Do you?" asked Barzel. "I am not surprised. You have a reputation for clear vision."

"That's flattering," said Charlie, allowing himself to succumb momentarily to the compliment.

"Not really," said Barzel. "Merely the truth. President

Goldberg is fortunate to have such a talented and devoted friend. It speaks well for his character."

"I'll be going back to Washington in a few hours," said Charlie, rising. "Is there any sort of message you'd like me to convey?"

"Yes," said Barzel, rising as well and taking Charlie's hand in a powerful grip. "Please tell him that if I have a chance to see him before the election, I'd be happy to dispel any mistaken notion he has—or perhaps others have—that I feel anything but friendly toward him."

Mokte accompanied Charlie to his waiting cab and then returned to Barzel's office. "What was that all about?" he asked.

"The answer to a message," said Barzel. "I want you to go to Washington personally to set up the visit. Make sure there's a dinner as well as a meeting. Sometime in late summer, after Goldberg gets the nomination."

"You're sure he's going to invite you?"

"I told you he would," said Barzel.

"This should be some visit," said Motke, shaking his head.

"What makes you say that?"

"Play innocent with Charlie Walker; this is me, Motke. You don't need a meeting with Goldberg for political reasons. This has something to do with the Project, doesn't it?"

"I'm hurt that you would question my sincerity," said Barzel with a small smile.

"You didn't answer my question, though."

"No, I didn't, did I?" Barzel said, a hint of annoyance in his voice.

"This is a new thing, secrets," said Motke.

Barzel looked at the little man and suddenly softened. "Don't be upset," he said gently, "there's nothing you need to know about now. When there is, I'll tell you. I always have. But in the meantime, don't push me."

"When did anyone ever push you?" grumbled Motke, but Barzel could see he was already suppressing a grin.

"They push me all the time, little brother," said Barzel. "All I do is push back."

CHAPTER SEVENTEEN

WHEN DIDI GOLDBERG GOT BACK FROM HOUSTON EARLY
Friday evening, she and Dewey did what they always did when
one of them returned from a trip—they went to bed. After
ten years of marriage, absence still generated sexual heat, and
the presidency hadn't done anything to cool their ardor. In
fact, it turned them on. On their first night in the White
House, after performing oral sex, Didi lit a cigarette and said,
"You think Eleanor ever did that to FDR?" Dewey had burst
out laughing: He had been wondering the same thing about
Abe and Mary Todd Lincoln.

Like a couple of naughty kids, they invented lewd stories
about their predecessors. One day, after staring at a portrait
of James Madison, Dewey decided that the fourth president
had actually been a transvestite. A couple weeks later, on a
trip to California, Didi bought her husband a powdered wig
at a costume store and laughed hysterically when he wore it to

bed. Another time they made love wearing JFK and Jackie masks that Goldberg had been given as a gift by a group of high school students from Pine Bluffs, Arkansas. Dewey had a kinky side and he was grateful that his wife shared it. Over the years it kept him faithful and saved him from one of the great political pitfalls of the media age: making a fool of himself with women.

As president, sex had taken on new importance for Goldberg. It was no longer merely recreation and release but a refuge as well. In bed with Didi was the one place he could be completely his old, comfortable self. Didi understood this because she was a very smart woman who had spent years studying Dewey Goldberg. He could still occasionally surprise himself, but never her.

Didi Travers Goldberg was Dewey's third wife. After coming home from Vietnam he had married Abby Fineberg, a former U of M cheerleader whose father, Ruby, was a crony of Fat Fred's. The marriage lasted three years—just long enough for Dewey to get through Harvard Law School—and produced no children, no repercussions and practically no memories. When, a few years ago, Dewey had bumped into Abby at a fund-raiser in suburban Detroit, he had fumbled momentarily for her name. It had been an embarrassing incident, especially since Goldberg prided himself on his politician's recall of faces and names.

Goldberg's second wife, Jan Garber, was a young political consultant from Detroit who came on board for his first congressional campaign and stayed to run his office in Washington. Theirs was a political collaboration that led to matrimony; it was in political time that Dewey measured their union. They were married during his first term in Congress. During his second, Jan gave birth to a son, Daniel; during the third, to a daughter, Susan, called Sissy. During his fourth term Jan was diagnosed with breast cancer. She died two days before the election of 1986.

A year later, an article in the *Washington Post* listed Goldberg as one of the capital's Most Eligible Bachelors. It didn't seem that way to him. He was close to forty and constantly drained from the exertions of his legislative duties in Washington, weekend fence-mending trips to Michigan and the strain of raising two young kids. There was little time left for socializing. In the year following Jan's death, Dewey's sex life consisted of a few hollow one-night stands.

Charlie Walker was living in New York then, but he came down to Washington often. On one of his trips Charlie mentioned that a colleague, Diane Travers, wanted to meet with him. "She'll call sometime this week," he said. "Do me a favor, give her an hour."

"What's she working on?"

"I'm not quite sure. But whatever it is, it's serious. She's still a kid, but she's going to be a star. You'll like her."

Diane Travers called the next day. "I can't see you till late next week," Goldberg told her. "Tomorrow I'm flying out to Detroit."

"Why don't I fly out with you? That way we can talk on the plane."

They met at the Northwest counter at National Airport. "Hello, Congressman," she said, giving his hand a good shake. "I'm Didi Travers."

Goldberg stared at her for a long moment. "Charlie didn't warn me," he said.

"Maybe he wanted to surprise you."

"I'm surprised." When she said nothing, he added, "You know why."

Didi nodded. "I hope you'll be able to see past it," she said in a matter-of-fact tone.

"I'll try," said Goldberg. "Jesus."

As a Congressman, Goldberg was used to being noticed in public, especially on the D.C. flight to Detroit. But as they sat waiting in the passenger lounge he was aware that people were staring in an unfamiliar way. "Do people always gawk at you like this?" he asked.

"You get used to it," she said.

"I admire your detachment."

Didi shrugged. "I was born this way. It's like being seven feet tall. I once heard Wilt Chamberlain say that strangers always ask him the same things. 'How did you get so tall?' and 'What's the weather like up there?'"

"And what do they say to you?"

"That I'm the most beautiful woman they ever saw," said Didi Travers, without the slightest hint of ego or apology.

"... want to do is a profile of you," said Didi, sipping her Bloody Mary. They were in first class, talking over the din of the engine. "Longish, about five thousand words. For the *New Yorker.*"

"I don't think so," said Goldberg. "Five thousand words about me, some of them are bound to be unflattering."

"I don't blame you for being cautious. In fact, I expected it. You're known as a cautious man."

"I'm not so sure that's a compliment," said Goldberg. "Where did you get that impression?"

"From the clips. I've read just about everything that's been written on you. I know your life story, at least the public part, backwards and forwards."

"I'm not so sure I like the sound of that, either," said Goldberg with a smile.

"Born in Detroit, 1948," Didi recited. "Wealthy parents, father a big-time scrap dealer, mother a Republican, which explains the first name. Class president in high school and college. All-Big-Ten linebacker—"

"Second team," said Goldberg.

"Second team, AP; first team, Coaches Poll. Squad leader in Vietnam, 1971. Graduated Harvard Law. Elected to Congress in 1976 from a heavily Catholic district. Liberal domestic voting record, strong on civil rights despite the constituency, very tough on trade issues, moderate to hawkish on defense. Well liked by colleagues. Member of Ways and Means and Judiciary, chairman of the subcommittee on foreign trade. Extremely popular at home, electoral majorities in the high seventies."

"I got eighty-three percent last time out."

"I'm talking about the average," she said. "Two children, a boy and a girl, six and four, looked after by a housekeeper named Estelle Franklin—"

"Looked after by me," said Goldberg. "Estelle helps, but I'm raising my own kids."

"I stand corrected," said Didi. "Want to hear more?"

"Sure," said Goldberg. "This is fun. What else do you know?"

"Well, you belong to Temple Israel in West Bloomfield, but you only go on the holidays. You're a moderate bourbon drinker. You play squash twice a week and you're a bad loser. You sing off-key, you sometimes practice Temptations moves naked in front of the mirror, you snore like a bastard—"

"Hey," Goldberg said with a laugh. "What kind of clips have you been reading?"

"Charlie told me," said Didi with a grin. "He talks about you so much I feel like I've known you all my life."

"I didn't realize you two were so close."

"If that means are we sleeping together, we're not," said Didi. "He's married. If he wasn't, it might be different, he's a fantastic man, but he is."

"You're right about that," said Goldberg. "I mean about him being a great guy."

"He really loves you."

"I hope so. He's been my best friend for twenty years."

"That's what got me interested in doing the profile," said Didi. "Charlie's so cynical about politicians, but he admires you—"

"He uses that word? 'Admire'?"

"It doesn't sound like him, does it? He did, though. Are you surprised?"

"Flattered," said Goldberg.

"Why? Don't you admire him?"

"Sure, but that's different. He's a superstar. You can hardly turn on a talk show these days without seeing him pontificate about something. I'm just a fifth-term congressman from Michigan."

"You're still young," said Didi. "You could wind up as Speaker someday, or run for the Senate. You might even be president, who knows?"

"President Goldberg? That'll be the day."

"Maybe that's my angle," mused Didi. "Why can't this man be president?"

"Do me a favor," said Goldberg. "I don't want to be the Great Jewish Hope."

"Why not?"

"Is this on the record?"

"No," said Didi. "I'll tell you when we go on the record. All right?"

Goldberg nodded. "The truth is, I don't need it. When I first ran, being Jewish was a disability, but the district's used to me now. I think they're even a little proud of it. For them it's a status symbol, like having a Jewish doctor."

"What about you? Are you proud of it?"

"I'm not ashamed, if that's what you're asking. I was born that way. What are you?"

"Religion? An Episcopalian, I suppose. At least my parents are. More or less."

A bell sounded and the loudspeaker switched on. "Ladies and gentlemen, we are beginning our descent into Detroit's Metropolitan Airport," said the flight attendant. "Please fasten your seat belts."

"That was quick," said Goldberg, looking at his watch. "Seems like we just took off."

"Where are you going from here?"

"Give a speech at the Knights of Columbus Man of the Year banquet," said Goldberg. "Honoring Mr. Ralph Traggiano, the Motown Mogul of Mid-range Ve-hicles."

"Can I tag along? It would be interesting to see you in action."

"This isn't going to be the Gettysburg Address," said Goldberg. "Besides, I don't think you're the K of C type. I'll meet you afterwards, though, if you like. Around ten."

"I'm staying at the Pontchartrain. Is that far?"

"It's downtown," said Goldberg. "I'll get there."

"We can talk about the profile then," said Didi, but Goldberg shook his head.

"No," he said, "I don't want you to write about me. It might cause problems later on."

"Later on?" asked Didi Travers, but from the look on her face, Goldberg could see that she understood exactly what he meant.

They were married the following September in a civil service in Detroit. Charlie was the best man. The wedding party consisted of Charlie's wife, Helen, who seemed relieved that Didi Travers was going out of circulation; Didi's parents, a mild blond couple who flew in from San Diego and called Dewey "Congressman"; Fat Fred, who slapped the judge on the back and said, "Make it stick this time, the kid's costing me a fortune in wedding presents"; Millie Goldberg, who didn't try to hide her satisfaction that her son was finally marrying an Episcopalian; and Estelle Franklin, who held Daniel's and Susan's hand throughout the brief ceremony and cried.

Goldberg's political advisers reacted to his marriage with concern. Willis, especially, feared the effect a dazzling young third wife would have on the voters. Goldberg was unimpressed by their jitters. He had a lock on his district, but he would have married Didi no matter what kind of professional liability she might have been. In fact, though, she turned out to be an asset.

Didi couldn't be said to possess the common touch, but she was no snob, and when she accompanied Goldberg on his weekend excursions to Michigan she did reasonably well. It helped that people knew she was raising Dewy's kids, a fact Willis aggressively publicized throughout the district. It was in the capital, though, that she made a real contribution to her husband's career. Before her, he had been a well-liked congressman on a slow upward trajectory, but his marriage turned him into half of one of Washington's most glamorous couples—a status that was ratified when *People* magazine put them on the cover. Hostesses added them to the A-list, congressional leaders included them in their intimate little dinners and even the Republican president saw to it that they were invited to White House social functions.

Didi's greatest political value, however, came late at night, after the dinner parties were over, when she and Dewey sat in their oak-paneled, toy-strewn den and dissected the people and events of the evening. Powerful men became talkative in her presence, and she had the reporter's knack for asking the right questions and remembering the answers. Didi was young and she didn't always get things right—she sometimes mistook sardonic Washington humor for hypocrisy and she tended to be overly cynical in attributing motives—but most often her observations were shrewd and accurate.

Within a short time, Didi Travers Goldberg learned a great deal about politics, particularly the politics of the House of Representatives. She became, along with Willis, Graff and Charlie Walker, Dewey's adviser; and in 1990, when she single-handedly dissuaded him from running for the Senate, she emerged as first among equals.

"There are four hundred thirty-five representatives and

only a hundred senators," Willis had argued. "The Republican's a weak sister and the recession's hurting him. This could be your best shot, maybe the only one. We got the dough, we got the name recognition, we got the nomination if we want it. I say, let's go."

"The polls look good," added Graff. "Upstate you're weak, but the tri-county area and the Saginaw Valley ought to be enough. I think you can win."

It was Didi who made the case for staying in the House. "You've got fourteen years of equity built up," she pointed out. "In the Senate you start all over again with no seniority. If you were shooting for president, maybe it would make sense, but you're not. Besides, there may be a hundred senators, but there's just one Speaker."

"Last time I looked we had a Speaker," said Goldberg.

"One step at a time," said Didi. "You've got a good chance to get elected majority leader next session. The Speaker's sixty-seven; he's not going to be around forever."

In the end he took her advice, won the leader's job easily and used it to accumulate IOUs. He was careful not to offend the prickly Speaker, and this punctiliousness was rewarded when the old man announced his retirement and endorsed Goldberg. In March 1998, at the age of fifty, Congressman Dewey Goldberg of Michigan became the Speaker of the House of Representatives.

As Speaker, Goldberg became the most important and visible Democrat in Washington, a status enhanced by the fact that he was not running for president. The Republicans didn't mind cooperating with him because they didn't fear his electoral potential. In his own party, he became an honest broker among undistinguished presidential hopefuls. If there was a consensus in Washington, it was that Speaker Dewey Goldberg was the right man in the right job.

Goldberg himself was satisfied. He had gone as high as he could have reasonably expected, and gotten there faster. He had a beautiful, loving wife, healthy, well-adjusted kids, plenty of money and a great job. He was, in short, a happy man.

And then along came the Tragedy, and he became what he had known all his life he could never be: president of the United States. Suddenly he was forced to cope with the fears and phobias of an increasingly edgy nation. Violent crime was at an all-time high—a recent Gallup poll showed that there were three times more firearms than people in America. Overseas, the Japanese were building an army to protect their money, Russia kept splintering into ever more unstable republics and Iran-based Islamic extremists, who had already taken over Egypt and Iraq, were now threatening Turkey, Israel and, worst, Saudi-Arabia. It was widely (and, Goldberg knew from his CIA briefings, correctly) assumed that the Iranian mullahs had three or four atomic warheads and, thanks to North Korean missiles, the capacity to fire them as far as Southern Europe.

These problems were compounded by the fact that America was gripped by millennialist fever. The 2001 Club claimed eight million members, with more joining every day. Satellites beamed the Reverend Bobby Silas's message about the impending clash of Good and Evil on the plains of Armageddon into fifty million homes. According to Silas, the Great Battle would take place before the end of 2001; his broadcasts featured a Good News Clock that counted down the days. On the morning Charlie Walker returned from Israel and met with Goldberg and Didi, there were 511 days left.

Goldberg and Didi sat holding hands on the couch in their upstairs living room as they listened to Charlie's account of his trip to Israel. When he described his meeting with Barzel, Didi interrupted him for the first time. "Sounds like he impressed you," she said.

Charlie nodded. "He's a chameleon; everyone you talk to has a different take on him. Some think he's a hero, others say he's a dangerous nationalist. I talked to people who consider him a Jewish Robin Hood, and people who called him a crook. The only thing everybody agrees on is that he's a formidable old bastard. And he is, too. Extremely formidable."

"What makes you say that?" asked Goldberg.

"It's a feeling," said Charlie. "I've met a lot of heads of state, but this guy's special. Obviously he's very smart and very tough, we already knew that. But there's something more. He radiates a kind of authority. I know that sounds vague, but I really can't explain it any better than that. You'll see what I mean if you meet him."

"Should I? Do you trust him?" asked Goldberg.

"Trust him? No. But I think I believe him. He doesn't have any obvious reason for opposing you. None of the explanations I heard sounded plausible, really. Sara Epstein said he doesn't like American Jews—"

"I can't say I blame him there," said Goldberg with mock ruefulness.

"—and Avi Har-el told me his vanity is hurt sharing the limelight with a Jewish president. But I don't buy that."

"I don't, either," said Didi. "He doesn't sound like the hurt-feelings type."

"The most interesting theory was Howard Grant's. He's rough-hewn, reminds me a little of Fat Fred, as a matter of fact. He wants you to help him with an IRS problem."

"That's all I need," said Goldberg.

"Right. But he's smart and he knows Barzel. He says that putting pressure on you is Barzel's way of getting something. And I think the something is an invitation to the White House."

"That's all this is about?"

"Can you think of anything else? Anything he might want?"

"Not really, no."

"But he could surprise you," said Didi. "And it's too

close to the election for surprises. Would he go to all this trouble for a photo-op?"

"He hasn't really gone to much trouble," said Charlie. "Just a couple of phone calls. And I believe him when he says a White House visit would help him politically. But I think there's something else, too. My guess is, he's looking for some reassurance. After all, he's right about you putting him off."

"Willis and Cassidy didn't like the idea of my being seen with the prime minister of Israel this close to November."

"That's his point," said Charlie.

"Well, yeah, but Christ, Charlie, the man's a politician. He should understand."

"Barzel isn't famous for being understanding."

"So, you think I should see him."

Charlie bit his lip, considering. "Yep," he said finally. "Especially since you need Jewish campaign money."

"You don't need it that much," said Didi. "You're ahead in the polls now, there's no reason to gamble. Charlie's probably right, but who knows—maybe Barzel's going to ask you for something you can't give him that will cause some sort of ruckus. And even if he doesn't, Cassidy and Willis could be right about the negative impact of a meeting with him this close to November."

Goldberg looked at his wife for a long moment and then, in a soft tone, said, "You don't think I can handle this guy, do you?"

"It's not that," said Didi, touched by her husband's vulnerability. "All I'm saying is, why take chances?"

Goldberg looked at Charlie and then back at Didi. "I'm going to see him," he said. "The party needs the money."

"You're sure your ego's not getting in the way of your judgment?" Didi asked.

"It probably is," said Goldberg. "I am the president of the United States, after all; I'm entitled to a little goddamn ego. But I honestly think I can deal with this guy, and I don't like the idea of ducking him. I've had enough of that this past year. If I'm going to be president, I ought to act like one. Yeah, I'll see him, right after the convention."

"In that case, lay on something big," said Didi. "This isn't a state visit, but we should have some kind of a formal dinner. If you're going to meet with him, it shouldn't look like you're ashamed of it. Let's turn it into a plus."

"Cassidy and Willis won't like it, but you're right," said Goldberg.

"Good. Now that you've decided, I'm sort of looking forward to it," said Didi. "Barzel's going to be a fascinating dinner partner."

"You think so, do you?" said Goldberg. "Well, for your information, this administration's policy is one fascinating Jewish partner per shiksa."

"Sara Epstein says he's not interested in women," said Charlie.

"Maybe he's just not interested in her," said Didi. "No, I think an hour or two with Mr. Barzel might be fun."

"So everybody's happy," Goldberg said, rubbing his huge hands together. "Didi's got a date and Charlie's got a scoop."

"And you've got a historic summit," said Charlie. "The first Jewish president and the prime minister of Israel."

"Yeah," said Goldberg. "A summit. I'll tell Boyd French to set it up. After all, what's the worst that can happen?"

CHAPTER EIGHTEEN

MOTKE VILK ARRIVED AT THE WHITE HOUSE CARRYING A leather briefcase and dressed in a tan sports jacket that barely covered his small paunch and a pair of wrinkled corduroy trousers. He was accompanied by the Israeli chargé, a man as dapper as Motke was disheveled. When he picked up Motke at the Madison Hotel, he had diplomatically suggested that a dark suit might be more appropriate, but Motke had merely pushed his wire-rim bifocals higher on his pug nose, grinned and said, "Never mind, you look nice enough for both of us."

The White House was quiet that morning. The president was in Houston, and most of the Creole Contingent were taking advantage of his absence to do a little midsummer malingering. The meeting was chaired by Chief of Staff Boyd French and, on the American side, included Press Secretary Liz Yardly; Ike Griffith, the deputy head of the Secret

Service; and, at Motke's request, Edward Mirello, the White House chef. Willis was supposed to be there, too, to look out for Goldberg's political interests, but a last-minute hitch in Houston over the selection of the vice president had forced him to stay in Texas. That morning he had called and cautioned French not to make any major changes or commitments without his approval.

Motke shook hands all around as everyone took their places at the table. When coffee was served, he popped open his briefcase and produced a stained brown paper bag. "Bourekas," he said happily. "I bought them in Tel Aviv on the way to the airport. Cheese, potato and, ah"—he peered into the bag and poked with his finger—"good, there's some spinach ones left. Help yourselves." He handed the bag across the table to Liz Yardley and, from the corner of his eye, saw the pained expression on the charge's face.

"Mine's potato," said Yardley, chewing happily. "It's delicious."

"America's a great country, but you can't get real bourekas," said Motke. "I lived here twenty years and I missed them like hell."

"I see what you mean," said Griffith. "These are tasty."

"How about you?" said Motke to the stiff young chief of staff. "You're not eating."

"No thanks," said French. He had a golf date in two hours at Burning Tree and he wasn't in the mood for a coffee klatch.

"Dieting," said Motke with a sympathetic sigh. "I've got the same problem." He watched French automatically check his taut stomach for flab and passed the bag to Mirello. "Chef, give me your expert opinion."

Mirello took a small bite and nodded. "Very good," he said. "Perhaps the crust is a bit heavy—"

"That's because they were in my bag the whole flight,"

said Motke. "They got a little soggy. You should taste them when they're fresh."

"Let's talk while we eat," said French. "Mr. Vilk—"

"Motke. Mr. Vilk was my father," said the little man cheerfully.

"Motke. I understand you have some questions about the arrangements for Prime Minister Barzel's meeting with the president."

"A couple little things," said Motke. "The embassy could deal with them, but I decided to come to the States. I wanted to see a couple Broadway shows and I thought as long as I was going to be in New York, I might as well come down here first and be a nudnik. You know what I mean by *nudnik?*"

"A pest," said French.

"Exactly. A pest. Anyway, one thing I want to talk about is the television. I noticed on the schedule that there isn't any coverage by the networks at the dinner. Usually there are cameras for the toast at the end."

"Mr. Willis thought that the prime minister might prefer a low-key evening," said Liz Yardley.

"Nah, we want the cameras," said Motke. "President Goldberg is a very popular man in Israel. And, to be honest, we've got an election coming, too. You know what I mean?"

"Willis was quite clear about this," said Yardley.

"How would it look if there's no television?" said Motke. "The people in Israel would think that the prime minister maybe didn't even come to Washington. Or that the president was ashamed to be seen with him—"

"I'm sure President Goldberg would be delighted to have coverage of the speeches," said French smoothly. "I'll take it up with Willis, Liz." He didn't give a damn about Goldberg. Win or lose, after November French would be out of a job. There was no point in antagonizing anyone now, especially the networks. If there was going to be fallout from the television people or the Israelis, let it fall on Willis.

"Excellent," said Motke. "Now, about the guest list."

"Yes?" said French.

"It's fine," said Motke.

There was a puzzled silence that was finally broken by French. "But?"

"No buts," said Motke. "Just an end. We have a few last-minute additions to the prime minister's party. Rabbi Yehuda Bloch, the Minister of the Interior, will be accompanying him. And Mrs. Bloch. And their two sons, who are also rabbis, and their wives. Six, altogether."

"That's not a problem," said French. He turned to Mirello. "How many are invited?"

"Sixty-four, eight tables of eight," said the chef. "Adding another table is simple. We'll need two more guests, I suppose."

"All right, fine," said French briskly. It was beginning to look like he'd make the first tee with time to spare.

"Excellent," said Motke. He turned to Mirello. "Tomorrow one of the rabbi's people will be in touch with you about the menu."

"The menu? It's already set."

"There's a small problem with kashrut," said Motke. "What you call here keeping kosher."

"Dinners for Israeli dignitaries are always strictly kosher. I've served dozens of them. There's a rabbi in Washington who supervises."

"Well, there's kosher and then there's kosher," said Motke with a small shrug. "Take me, for example. My definition includes bacon and eggs. But a Jew like Rabbi Bloch, it's very important to him that things be just exactly right."

"I assure you we've never had any complaints before," said French.

"You've never had a guest like Rabbi Bloch before," said Motke. "You know what kind of government we have?"

French scowled; he wasn't in the mood for an Israeli civics lesson. "A democracy, of course," he said. "The only democracy in the entire Middle—"

"A coalition," said Vilk. "To govern, you need sixty-one votes in the Knesset. Prime Minister Barzel's party has forty-one. The left-wingers have seventeen and they don't eat kosher, but it doesn't matter because they won't be here. Rabbi Bloch's party has eleven votes. And for them, kosher food is very, very important. One wrong spoon and the government could collapse."

"Fanatic," muttered the chargé under his breath, but loud enough for the Americans to understand that he had nothing to do with the medieval political rabbis. The chargé was a graduate of Princeton.

"I wouldn't use the word 'fanatic,'" said Motke mildly. "I would say, 'extremely pious.'"

"Yes, well, what are the culinary implications of this piety?" asked French.

"The rabbi would like to have his own menu and his own kosher supervisor," said Motke. "That way there are no misunderstandings."

"We don't let strangers in the White House kitchen," said Griffith, the security man.

"I'm afraid it's not negotiable," said Motke. "I love saying that—it makes me feel like a diplomat. Anyway, if Rabbi Bloch can't have his own kosher food, he won't come. And if he doesn't come, the prime minister won't be able to come, either. It wouldn't look good if he visited the White House after you refused to honor Jewish religious commandments."

"I see what you mean," said French. "Mirello?"

"What does the rabbi want to eat?" asked the chef with a deep sigh. He had been cooking for foreigners long enough to resent them all. The Moslems didn't eat pork or drink alcohol, at least not in public. The Hindus wouldn't touch beef. The Israelis couldn't eat seafood. At times it seemed to him that the world's great religions were nothing more than a dietary conspiracy to make his job impossible.

"Gefilte fish is always a good starter," said Motke. "Personally I love it with white horseradish, the really strong kind that gets up your nose and makes you sneeze. Maybe some herring or boiled fish. No scales. Fruit and vegetables, you can't go wrong. A nice piece of sponge cake for dessert."

"You want me to serve gefilte fish and herring at a White House dinner?" asked Mirello.

"What's the difference, nobody ever notices the food at these things anyway," said Motke. He turned to the Secret Service man. "For security problems, talk to one of the boys at the embassy. They'll work with you on this."

"So be it," said French, trying to bring the meeting to an end. "I'm sure the president will have no objection. Is there anything else?"

"Yes, one more thing," said Motke. "Prime Minister Barzel would like the meeting to take place just between the two of them. No aides."

"Fine," said French. "Just one person on each side to record a protocol."

"No, he'd prefer it if it was just the two of them. No note takers. So that they can schmooze, so to speak."

"Schmooze," said French, letting the Yiddish word roll slowly through his lips. "Yes, I see." He looked at Liz Yardley and saw that she was sharing his thought—two Jews alone in the Oval Office, schmoozing away about God knows what, three months before the election. Liz was smiling; she was a Republican, too. "I'll raise it with the president," French promised, "but I don't see it as a problem. In fact, I'm certain he'll be delighted to have a little schmooze with

Prime Minister Barzel." He knew that Willis and the others would have a fit, but it wasn't his problem; if they wanted a crisis with the prime minister of Israel, who was he to interfere?

CHAPTER NINETEEN

WITH MOTKE VILK IN WASHINGTON, THE PRIME MINISTER'S office was quieter than usual. There was no loud kidding in the anteroom, there were no supplicants crowded around Motke's desk and there was no raucous laughter. This was the way Adam Reshef preferred it: quiet, dignified, businesslike. It seemed more appropriate for the conduct of serious matters. Especially today.

Reshef's secretary, Chanele, was sitting in for Motke, and she waved her boss into Barzel's office with a smile. The prime minister was, as usual, seated behind his gleaming desk. Although Jerusalem was in the middle of a July heat wave, Barzel was wearing a dark suit whose expensive tailoring accentuated his broad shoulders and deep chest. Reshef, who did two hundred sit-ups each morning, had never heard of the Old Man doing any form of exercise, and he briefly wondered how he maintained his physique.

"You're back," said Barzel. "And from the look on your face, you've got good news."

"Very good," said Reshef, flushing with annoyance. He prided himself on being inscrutable, but Barzel read his moods easily. "Yesterday afternoon I had my last meeting with Childes." He paused for dramatic effect, then added simply, "He's in."

"Tell me exactly what was said and how it was said. Take your time, don't leave anything out. I've got to be certain that he knows what he agreed to."

"He knows," said Reshef. "We've talked about it enough."

"Humor me," said Barzel.

"Okay. There were four of us, same as last time—Silas, Childes, General Hunter and me. Childes referred to Hunter as 'the next Secretary of Defense,' by the way."

"Interesting," said Barzel. "The man is an optimist. I like that about him."

"Anyway, Silas talked about the Project for a while, putting his own spin on it as usual. Then he told Childes it was time to make a final decision."

"What were his exact words?"

"He said, 'Governor, it's nut-cracking time.'"

"Future historians will puzzle over that phrase," said Barzel dryly. "And then?"

"I've got the whole thing on tape," said Reshef. "Why don't I just play it for you?"

"Put the tape in your safe," said Barzel. "I don't need to listen to it. Just give me your description."

"Okay. Childes said to Silas, 'I want to make it perfectly clear that there is absolutely no connection between the plan Mr. Reshef has presented and any political arrangement we might reach. Is that understood?'"

"He said this with a straight face?"

"Absolutely. And Silas said, 'Of course, Governor. But we

can't save the world if we don't get you in the White House first, can we?'"

"How did Childes react to that?"

"I don't remember his exact words, but it was something like, 'Reverend, together we're going to do God's will.' I have the feeling that Childes doesn't really buy all this millennium crap. Not like Silas, that's for sure. Childes is supposed to be a born-again Christian, and maybe he is, but he's a politician first. And Hunter thinks Silas is crazy."

"Will that be a problem?"

Reshef shook his head. "Hunter is a military man. He sees what the Project can mean for the United States."

"Get back to Childes," said Barzel. "What else did he say?"

"There was more of that fundamentalist stuff, and then Silas said, 'Does that mean you are prepared to commit yourself and your administration to Operation Armageddon?'"

"Operation Armageddon," said Barzel. "That's a name the press would love."

"That's exactly what Childes thought. He said, 'Reverend let's just refer to it as the Project, if you don't mind.' So Silas said, 'As long as we all know what it involves.' Then we went over the whole thing again, point by point. This time Hunter did most of the talking. And then Childes said, 'Reverend, I am prepared to commit my administration to the Project. In my judgement it is in the national interest of the United States.'"

"You think he means it?"

Reshef shrugged. "He knows he can't get elected without Silas's support, that's for sure. But I'm not sure he would agree to something this big and this dangerous if he didn't believe in it. Maybe I'm naive, but I don't think he's that much of an op-portunist. In my opinion, he really thinks the Project is good for American interests."

"Well, it so happens he's right," said Barzel. "For that

matter, even Silas is right—there is an element of salvation in all this. What does the Talmud say? He who saves one life saves the entire world."

"One Jewish life," Reshef corrected him.

"Yes, of course," said Barzel mildly. "But I don't think the rabbis would mind if we save a few hundred million gentiles along the way, do you?"

"I've had enough religion lately," said Reshef with a shrug.

"Well, as you get older you may find yourself feeling differently," said Barzel dryly. "As I myself approach the twilight, I find religion a source of ever-increasing comfort. Speaking of which, I want you to spend time with Rabbi Bloch on our trip to Washington. Sit with him on the plane, get to know him. Swap a few tales in Yiddish. Do you speak Yiddish?"

"Not a word," said Reshef proudly.

"Ah, well, speak to him in Hebrew, then. I'm afraid he's not always intelligible in the Holy Tongue and he has a tendency to spit when he gets excited, so don't get too close. But I want you to establish a rapport. We're going to need him."

"What for?"

"The Project," said Barzel. "When the time comes, Yarkoni and his peaceniks are going to scream bloody murder. Needless to say, they'll quit the government."

"So what? The hawks have twenty-two votes, and they'll back this all the way. We'll still have a majority in the Knesset."

"Not without Rabbi Bloch's eleven," said Barzel.

"You think he won't go along?"

"No, I think he will go along—for a price. It'll be a high price—Rabbi Bloch regards coalition crises as a sort of supermarket sweepstakes. Did you ever see that program when you were in America?"

Reshef shook his head. Sometimes he wondered if Barzel took him seriously.

"No? Pity. It's a fascinating study in human greed. It ought to be required viewing for any aspiring politician. Anyway, under normal conditions, a few new yeshivas and maybe a sabbath blue law or two would do the trick. But this time there's a complicating factor."

"What's that?"

"Reverend Silas and the millennium," said Barzel. "Rabbi Bloch is not a great admirer of Christianity. In fact, he considers it an abomination. When things get going, there will inevitably be a lot of Armageddon talk from Reverend Silas."

"So far he's been discreet."

"Yes, but once the Project is under way, he'll be less reticent. A man who believes he has just saved humanity in partnership with God might be unable to resist the temptation to share the news with mankind. He might even be inclined to portray the Chosen People as the instrument of Christ."

"Who cares what Silas says?"

"I'm afraid Rabbi Bloch will care very much. You don't know him as well as I do. He's an extortionist and a political whore, but it so happens that he's actually sincere in his religious beliefs. Fanatical might not be putting it too strongly. Now, I can't stop Silas from talking and I certainly can't afford to get into a public fight with him over what God wants, but I don't want Rabbi Bloch to interpret my silence as agreement."

"So what do I tell him?"

"For now, nothing. Merely get to know him, open a channel of communication. When the time comes, you'll explain to him that Silas is delusional. Don't worry, it won't be hard to convince him; he already has a low opinion of gentiles."

"Why me? Why don't you explain it to him?"

The prime minister leaned forward in his chair and looked directly into Adam Reshef's eyes. "There are two reasons. First, I'm not going to live forever, unfortunately." He saw the alarm in Reshef's eyes and smiled. "Don't worry, I'm not going yet. But when the Project is completed, three or four years from now, I'll be ready to retire. Naturally, I've been giving a lot of thought to what comes after me. It's not easy for a man to contemplate the world without him, but I don't have the luxury of simply walking away. I suppose the thought of my successor has crossed your mind from time to time."

"Yes, it has," admitted Reshef.

"That's perfectly reasonable, you're young and ambitious," said Barzel. And obvious, he thought wryly. He had noticed that in his conversations with Childes, Reshef never invoked Barzel's name. Clearly he already thought of himself as a major player, not merely an aide. That was fine with Barzel; in fact, it was more than fine, it was exactly what he wanted. "You once said that you were me, thirty years younger. I agree—there are similarities between us. That's why I can tell you that when I was your age, I wasn't ready to be prime minister of Israel. And neither are you. Yet."

Adam Reshef felt his palms sweat as he squirmed under Barzel's steady, blue-eyed scrutiny. "I don't really think that this is a conversation we need to have now," he said.

"Indulge me," said Barzel. "To do this job, you need a number of attributes. You have to be extremely smart, for one thing. Jews won't follow a stupid leader, at least not for long. You also have to be very tough. I don't mean to sound melodramatic, but not even the Project will make Israel totally secure. If history teaches us anything, it's that the world doesn't leave Jews alone for long. Belgium can afford a weak leader, Italy can, even America. But Israel cannot."

"You don't think I'm tough enough?" asked Reshef, unable to keep the wounded indignation from his voice.

"No, I think you are," said Barzel. "Tough enough and smart enough. Those are necessary qualities but not sufficient. A good prime minister also has to be able to work with others, bend them to his will. For better or worse, this is a democracy, and the people you deal with aren't always to your liking. Take

Yarkoni, for example. He's an idiot, but he controls a bloc of votes, and the votes of idiots count as much as yours or mine. And so I have an idiot for a foreign minister. He wants to come with me to Washington, to take part in the talks with Goldberg. What would you do in my place?"

"Tell him no," said Reshef. "That's what you did. His name's not on the list."

"Ah, but it's how you say no. This morning I informed Professor Yarkoni that he can't go to Washington because I need him here, as acting prime minister. He'll get to chair the cabinet meeting, take a ride in my helicopter, even sit at my desk if he wants. I also told him he'll have to appear on television to brief the nation on my talks in Washington. Believe me, he walked out of here happy as a lark."

"I know how those things are done," said Reshef. "I've seen you do them often enough."

"Seen me, yes; until now you've had the luxury of observing. Now you're going to get some hands-on experience in the fine art of political management, courtesy of Rabbi Yehuda Bloch. Believe me, he'll teach you all you need to know about tolerance and self-control."

"So this is a sort of test?"

"Not a test," said Barzel softly. "I've known you too long for tests. You're my heir—my political heir, that is—and with luck you'll be the next prime minister. I want you to be a great one. That's why I'm assigning Rabbi Bloch to you."

"I wasn't expecting this," said Reshef. "I don't know what to say."

"It's time," Barzel said solemnly. He rose from his chair and extended his hand to Reshef. "Will you handle Bloch for me?"

"Yes, of course," said his young aide, returning the handshake. Suddenly he remembered something. "You said there were two reasons you want Bloch to deal with me instead of you."

"Did I?"

"Yes, you did. What's the other one?"

"Ah, yes. Well, the second reason," said Barzel with the shadow of a smile, "is that it will keep Rabbi Yehuda Bloch from spraying spit all over my suitcoats."

Chapter Twenty

AT THE PHOENIX AIRPORT, AN EXCITED CROWD GATHERED around the Reverend Bobby Silas, dozens of people reaching out to touch him and receive his blessing. Silas smiled and nodded, briefly holding the hands that were extended to him, offering words of Christian fellowship to the crowd. It was a scene that repeated itself wherever he went and he accepted it gracefully. He felt that his popularity was not of his own making but God's. Years ago he had been given three gifts by the Lord. Charisma was one of them, but not the first. First had come the gift of tongues.

Young Bobby Silas had never expected such a gift. He was a Louisiana boy with a conventionally Christian upbringing but no special spiritual leanings. At Acadiana High School in Lafayette he had been known for his debating skills and a pretty good curveball. At the University of Southwestern Louisiana, where he was a B-minus engineering student, he spent his spare time working on his vintage '65 Mustang. He was in the Mustang, on the way back from Spanish Lake near New Iberia one afternoon during his sophomore year, when a sudden cloud of mist seemed to envelop him. Feeling light-headed, he pulled off the road. And there, just outside Broussard, Louisiana, twenty-year-old Bobby Silas heard himself barking strange words in an unknown language.

The experience lasted only a few moments, but it left him exhausted and overwhelmed. There could be no mistake: God had spoken holy words through his lips. Silas was a practical young man, not given to fantasies; but there was no denying the Divine reality of what had occurred. In that moment of realization, Bobby Silas was born again.

The following Sunday he went to a small pentecostal church near his home. He had no idea what made him choose that particular church from among the hundreds in Lafayette, but he entered the sanctuary confidently, as if he had been there many times before.

In the midst of a rollicking hymn, Bobby Silas rose from his seat and walked to the pulpit. He was not in a trance, but he felt directed by the Lord's hand. The minister looked at him quizzically. Silas said, "I've come to testify."

"Go ahead, son," said the minister. He signaled to the choir for silence and the song died as the congregation stared at the young man.

"This young brother has something to say to us," said the minister. "What's your name, son?"

"Bobby Silas," he said haltingly. "Something happened to me on the road near Broussard the other day. The Lord spoke through my mouth."

"Amen," the congregation murmured.

Silas raised his voice. "He spoke holy words."

"Amen, praise God," chorused the congregation.

Silas broke into a smile. "I don't know what He was saying, but it sure felt wonderful!" he shouted, and the congregation burst into frenzied applause. Suddenly he was preaching, the words flowing through him as he talked and hollered and whispered for an hour. When it was over and the weeping people gathered around to shyly touch his hand, he knew that he would never be a petroleum engineer. God had blessed him with a calling and given him the gift of charisma to pursue it.

Word of Bobby Silas spread quickly through the Evangelical community of southwest Louisiana. He was invited to speak at local churches and, since he refused to take any part of the offering, invited back. When people called him "Reverend" he protested that he was unordained and untutored, but his modesty merely confirmed the general opinion that he was a sincere and exceptional young man.

It was the mideighties and many born-again Christians had been badly disillusioned by self-promoting flakes like Jim Bakker and Jimmy Swaggart. But Bobby Silas inspired confidence. A group of Lafayette businessmen collected money to buy him airtime on KATC, and the Sunday morning program became an immediate success.

Silas refused to solicit money from his television audience. He returned the checks people sent in with a note suggesting they give the money to charity. He lived simply in a small frame house that needed paint, sold the Mustang and replaced it with a used Chevy station wagon and spent his time preaching and studying the Bible. The syndicate of born-again businessmen donated enough to pay him a small salary, which he accepted without protest or thanks. At the end of each year, he returned the balance.

In 1991, Reverend Bobby Silas went to the Holy Land for the first time. In Jerusalem, at the Christian Consulate, an outreach center run by American Evangelicals, he met Reverend Enos Throne of Decatur, Alabama. Throne was a fiery man in his sixties who took an immediate liking to the young television preacher. "There's a place you need to go before you leave," he said. "I don't know why, but I feel the Lord wants me to take you there."

They drove to the Galilee in Throne's Land Rover. Along the way they talked about God's plan for the Holy Land. The state of Israel, they agreed, was the fulfillment of prophecy, and the Jews, God's Chosen People. "A lot of Israelis think we're crazy for loving this country and this people," said Throne. "They say, 'We're just like ever'body else.' I reckon they feel that way, but come the Great Day they're in for a surprise. When the Lord gets ready, you gotta move, ain't that so?"

"Amen," said Silas.

They drove along a green rural road until they came to a junction with a sign that read: MEGIDDO, 7 KMS.

"We're coming up on it," said Throne. "Megiddo's the Hebrew name for Armageddon. You feel something special?"

Silas shrugged. "This whole trip has been a blessing," he said. "But nothing special here, no. Why?"

"I just felt like I needed to bring you here. Heck, maybe I'm wrong. It's a fine drive, one way or the other."

That night, back in Jerusalem, the Lord woke Bobby Silas out of a sound sleep at four in the morning and spoke to him. Silas had never been spoken to directly before, but he knew immediately that he was hearing God's voice. The message was clear. In the year 2001, the Great Battle would be fought between righteousness and evil. The people of Israel would be on the verge of destruction, but a mighty Christian army would come to the rescue. And at the head of that army would be the Reverend Bobby Silas. "Go forth and sound the call," said the Lord. "This is my third gift to you. The gift of prophecy."

And it had come to pass. When Silas returned to America he began to preach the coming of the millennium and the Great Battle that would presage it. Letters and love offerings arrived by the thousands. This time Silas kept the checks and used them to buy more and more TV airtime. His broadcasts reached millions and soon Silas was flooded by requests from people who wanted to join the great Christian army he spoke of.

"This thing is getting too big," said one of his Evangelical supporters, a born-again lawyer named Bret Damon. "You need an organization."

"I'll leave that to you," said Silas. "On one condition: I want the money audited by an outside source."

"Don't you trust me?"

"Of course I do," said Silas. "But I don't want either of us to face temptation. This isn't some TV preacher swindle. This is something God told me to do."

As the 2001 Club flourished, Silas took it as a sign that he was proceeding correctly. He made no plans of his own beyond preaching the Word and traveling the country to recruit new members. He was confident that God would let him know what to do next.

After the Tragedy, when Dewey Goldberg became president, Silas had believed that a new stage of the plan was unfolding. One of the Chosen People was in the White House as the year 2000 began; it couldn't be mere coincidence.

And then, on a visit to Jerusalem, he had met Elihu Barzel. Barzel didn't scoff at him the way other Jews did. He listened intently and sympathetically as Silas explained his vision of the coming Kingdom. "I'm an old man," Barzel had said with a sigh, "and like Moses, I am a sinner. I don't imagine I'll enter the Kingdom. But Adam Reshef is a Joshua. He will lead the struggle. He'll be your, ah, evangelical liaison."

When Barzel referred to himself as Moses, Silas felt a tremendous shiver go through his body. The Israeli leader seemed to be a truly biblical figure. And so, when Barzel, through Reshef, had revealed his Project, and said that it couldn't come to pass without Earl Childes in the White House, Silas had accepted it unquestioningly. Perhaps Dewey

Goldberg was a false Jew. Perhaps God wanted only one Jewish leader. It didn't matter—he was prepared to follow Elihu Barzel. He would help him make Earl Childes the next president—and then let the Lord lead from there to the mighty battle.

CHAPTER TWENTY-ONE

DEWEY GOLDBERG NEVER THOUGHT HE'D ENJOY WASHINGton in August, but after Houston the steamy capital seemed almost pleasant. In Texas he had been forced outside, into the midsummer humidity, to shake hands with the damp-palmed crowds in front of his hotel and take a much-publicized jog through the streets. The Secret Service hadn't liked it—Texas still spooked them after all these years—but Cassidy had insisted that he needed to be seen on television with real people. "This is the big leagues, Mr. President," he said. "I've been here before. Trust me."

Implicit in this remark was the fact that Goldberg, despite a lifetime in politics, had comparatively little campaign experience. It had been twenty years since his last serious challenge in his district, and his recent electioneering had been conducted mainly at senior citizen picnics, factory gates and ethnic festivals. The presidential campaign, which would officially be kicked off in Detroit on Labor Day, would be his baptism in national politics.

The maneuvering over the vice presidential nomination, which took place in his suite at the newly remodeled Astrodome Hilton, had been a different matter. Backroom dealing was a familiar art, and Goldberg enjoyed ramming Larry Livingstone down Cassidy's throat. Never before, not even as Speaker, had he been in a position of such strength. It made infighting fun, reminding him of why he had gone into politics in the first place.

Livingstone, the junior senator from New Jersey, had been Goldberg's choice for vice president from the beginning. "He's the WASPiest WASP man in America," he explained to Willis. "If anybody can balance the Goldberg factor, it's him. Besides, he's smart. If something happened to me, I'd trust him."

Cassidy, representing the party leaders, had resisted. "He's only thirty-eight," he objected. "That's way too young. I can see the bumper stickers now: DEMOCRATS 2000—THE YID AND THE KID. And he's too liberal. Steve Ridgeway's your guy. He's strong where you're weak, in the South and West, he's a terrific campaigner and he'll bring in a lot of money. Frankly, we're still concerned about the financial situation."

"Don't worry, I'll get Barzel to open the tap," said Goldberg. "But no Ridgeway. His dentures are too big for his mouth and his hair looks like a toupee."

"It's his real hair," said Cassidy defensively.

"Just kidding," said Goldberg. "But I've got a problem with Ridgeway. Five, six years ago he got pissed off during a conference on the health bill and called me a fucking kike intellectual. There were half a dozen people there."

"Come on, Dewey. Steve's a little rough, but he's no more of an anti-Semite than I am," said Cassidy.

"You're probably right about that," said Goldberg dryly. "Anyway, you're missing the point. Nobody calls me an intellectual and gets away with it."

"Well," said Cassidy, "the nomination's your call, but you've got to think about November. No one can win without a united party."

"That sounds like a threat," said Goldberg.

"Not at all," said Cassidy. "I'm just telling you the facts of life. This is a national campaign and it has its own rules. One of them is, keep everybody happy."

"The facts of life," mused Dewey. "You ever meet my old man?"

Cassidy shook his head.

"Too bad. He's a real character, my dad. I remember when I was, oh, twelve or thirteen, he sat me down and gave me his version of the facts of life. 'Dewey,' he said, 'in every situation there's always a fucker and a fuckee. The rest is just jerking off.'"

"I don't see what it's got to do with—"

"My not letting you guys screw me into taking Ridgeway? Okay, I'll spell it out. For the last year I've been going around on my tippy-toes, taking crap from Creoles, laying low with Congress, even listening to insulting little lectures from the so-called leaders of this party. I had to because of who I am and how I got here. But that's over now—it ended last night when the party nominated me. I'm the candidate and I'm going to get elected president this fall. Which means that as of now, I am the fucker."

"Mr. President, I—"

"So much for the facts of life," Goldberg continued, ignoring Cassidy's interruption. "Now for the facts of politics. You've got a major interest in National Oil through your sister's husband. The oil guys want Ridgeway out of the Senate, because he's against the offshore depletion bill. So you want to palm him off on me in the name of party unity."

"Jesus—" said Cassidy indignantly, but Goldberg cut him off with a gesture.

"I don't hold it against you," he said mildly. "Despite

what you think, I'm a big boy. I still want you on the campaign—the Goldberg-Livingstone campaign. After the election, if the oil guys want to push the bill, I'm ready to listen. Hell, I'm for the goddamned thing anyway."

"Where did you get that stuff about National Oil?" asked Cassidy. His voice was tight, but Goldberg could see that he was impressed.

"A little bird," he said. "You remember the birds and the bees—they're right in there with the facts of life." The bird had been Charlie Walker.

"All right, you win," said Cassidy. "I'll sell it to the others. But Jesus, Mr. President, get Livingstone to grow a mustache at least. He looks like a damn choir boy."

"Thanks, Jack," said Goldberg in his old, amiable tone. "I knew I could count on you."

Cassidy rose, keeping his eyes fixed on Goldberg. "You surprised me," he said. "I don't get surprised often."

After the convention, Goldberg and Didi spent a week at their summer place on Michigan's Upper Peninsula before returning to Washington. Goldberg would have liked to stay longer, but the Barzel visit was coming up and he needed time to prepare. For three days he immersed himself in briefing papers on Israel and the Middle East, reread Barzel's CIA file and met with Snowden and Secretary of State Pouissant to discuss bilateral issues. By summit day, Goldberg was confident that whatever the old Jew threw at him he'd be able to handle.

Barzel, accompanied by Motke Vilk, the Israeli ambassador and Israeli and American security guards, arrived at the White House by limousine promptly at four. The rest of the entourage was invited for cocktails and dinner at six. Goldberg stood under the portico to greet his guest, who, despite the steam-bath heat and humidity, emerged elegantly unwrinkled from the armored Lincoln.

"Mr. Prime Minister, welcome to Washington," said

Goldberg, careful not to bow his head even slightly. There were camera crews behind a red plush rope, and Goldberg wanted to make sure that his greeting was warm enough for New York without being too intimate for Mississippi.

"Mr. President," said Barzel, taking his hand. The prime minister's grip was as dry as his collar, and very firm. Goldberg was impressed by the Old Man's sheer animal presence; Goldberg would have thought twice about arm-wrestling him in public.

"I want to thank you for taking time from your busy schedule to meet with me," Barzel continued, his eyes sparkling with an ingenuous sincerity that held no hint of the pressure he had applied. He gestured to the round, sweaty leprechaun at his side. "Please meet my associate, Mr. Vilk. Of course you already know our ambassador."

"Mr. Vilk, I heard you did the impossible. You convinced our chef to change his menu."

"A *groise glick*," said Motke.

Goldberg recognized the phrase from his boyhood—it was one of his father's favorites—and scowled slightly. He didn't want to exchange Yiddish pleasantries in front of the camera crews. "I beg your pardon?"

"It means, 'a big deal,'" said Motke. "Don't tell me you don't speak Yiddish."

"I'm afraid not," said Goldberg, loud enough for the reporters to hear.

"You have to excuse Motke," Barzel said. "He thinks everybody speaks Yiddish. He even tried it on Prime Minister Mitzakowa last year in Tokyo."

"Let's go inside," said Goldberg, more abruptly than he intended.

"Thank God," said Motke, wiping his brow with the sleeve of his jacket. "I'm *schvitzing* out here."

Goldberg led them into the Oval Office, where Larry Livingstone and Didi were waiting. The Israelis had won on the culinary front and achieved a partial victory on the television issue—cameras were to be allowed at the welcoming ceremony, although they would be banned from the dinner—but Willis and Cassidy had absolutely insisted that there be witnesses present at the discussion. "No offense, boss," Willis said in his blunt way, "but we can't afford any private Jew-talk this close to November." A compromise had been struck: Didi and Livingstone on the American side, Vilk for the Israelis. The ambassador was shuttled off to French's office, and no official protocol was recorded.

Goldberg began the meeting by inviting Barzel to give an account of current Israeli concerns. For half an hour, as the Old Man described his domestic scene with mordant wit, Goldberg waited for some hint of a problem, some suggestion of a request. But there was none. He began to think that Charlie had been right: Barzel had come to the White House with no agenda greater than a political rubdown.

"You haven't mentioned your security situation," said Goldberg. "Can I assume that things are satisfactory?"

"It is the unhappy fate of small countries to be satisfied with small margins of safety," Barzel replied pleasantly. "Well, perhaps not satisfied—"

"What do you mean by that?" asked Livingstone. He and Goldberg had agreed that he would ask any pointed questions.

"Only that Israel is vulnerable, as you know, to an unconventional strike by the Islamic extremists."

"We have no information that they have unconventional weapons," Goldberg lied. "Believe me, we're watching very closely."

"Watching . . ." said Barzel, letting the word hang in the air.

"Yes," said Goldberg. "Not just the CIA. Your people, too."

"My people?" said Barzel, looking bewildered for a moment.

"The Mossad," said Goldberg sharply. "What did you think I meant?"

"Oh, I see. Forgive me," said Barzel. "My accent is unfortunately better than my comprehension. I'm afraid my English is a bit deceptive."

"*Deception* is a word that comes up about you," said Didi boldly. "People say you're a devious man."

"Like all public people, I am reputed to be many things," said Barzel easily.

"But you're not?" she asked, smiling. "Devious?"

"How can I answer that?" asked Barzel, returning her smile. "If I say yes, I incriminate myself. If I say no, I corroborate your suspicions."

"What a marvelously devious answer."

"You're not on trial here, Prime Minister," said Livingstone quickly. To a former prosecutor, the word *incriminate* set off warning bells.

"Don't worry, Senator, Mrs. Goldberg and I are merely teasing one another," Barzel said blandly. "What is it you think I'm being devious about, I wonder?"

Goldberg shot his wife a warning look which Barzel caught, as he was meant to; they had rehearsed this moment all morning. "I find your support for Governor Childes devious. And mysterious."

"Supporting Governor Childes? I've never even met the man. Besides, I wouldn't consider involving myself in American politics—"

"Larry, this might be a good time for the prime minister and me to talk alone," said Goldberg smoothly. "Why don't you and Didi give Mr. Vilk a tour of the White House."

"I've been here before," said Motke. "Besides, this is more interesting."

"Go ahead, Motke," said Barzel. "Try not to break anything."

In silence they watched Livingstone, Didi and Motke

leave. Then Goldberg turned to Barzel and smiled. "Alone at last."

"Alone, yes," said Barzel, in a harder voice than before. "I understood that you didn't want to see me alone."

"Mr. Prime Minister, let's talk turkey," said Goldberg.

"*Tachlis*, as Motke would say," said Barzel, using another of Fat Fred's favorite Yiddish expressions. "Yes, by all means."

"Didi got carried away, but I can't say she was wrong."

"Can't you? Well, I can, and I do. I have absolutely no intention of supporting Governor Childes. As I told your friend Mr. Walker in Jerusalem a few weeks ago."

"Well, of course I accept your word, Mr. Prime Minister—"

"But you don't believe me," said Barzel, his blue eyes twinkling. "No, no, it's all right. We're both men of the world. I admit I've mentioned to one or two of our friends that it might be a good idea to hold off political contributions until you and I had a chance to talk." He paused for a moment. "I want to ask you a favor. Please call me Elihu, or Eli if you prefer."

"By all means, Eli. And you call me Dewey."

"Thank you, Dewey," said Barzel, leaning forward and lowering his voice slightly for dramatic effect. "This is a unique moment—an Israeli prime minister meeting for the first time with a Jewish president. Right now we're making history. In fact, two histories—yours and ours, American and Jewish. It is too important an occasion to squander on trivialities. Not that your election is a trivial matter. But there are issues of life and death that need to be clarified. That's why I'm going to ask your permission to speak to you as one Jew to another. I promise that I will never do this again, but it must be done now."

"Go ahead," said Goldberg, warily.

"Dewey, the prime minister of Israel has a unique role. He is the head of his government, but he also bears the responsibility for the survival and welfare of the Jewish people throughout the world. If a Jew is tortured in Iran, I must go to his aid. If a Jew is imprisoned in South Africa, I search for ways to free him. I tell you honestly, it's a responsibility I didn't seek, but it comes with the job. It is impossible to escape. Do you understand that?"

"I understand it. I'm not certain what you're getting at, though."

"There are millions of Jews in the United States. They consider themselves to be Americans. I understand this—I lived in this country for twenty years. But that doesn't alter my own responsibility toward them. They are Jews, just like the Jews of Iran or the Jews of South Africa."

"Hardly," Goldberg snapped. "We don't consider ourselves Americans, we *are* Americans. My family has been in this country for a hundred and forty years. I'm the president of the United States, for Christ's sake."

"And you feel totally comfortable as an American? As much as any other of your predecessors?"

"Of course."

"Then why was it so hard for me to get an appointment to see you?"

Goldberg flushed. "I'm not sure I like your implication—"

"Why did you want witnesses to our conversation? Why did you ban television cameras from our dinner? Tell me honestly: Would you have behaved the same way if I were, for example, the prime minister of Italy?"

Goldberg paused, staring into the hard face of the old man across from him. "No," he said finally. "I wouldn't. Of course there are certain special sensitivities here. I can't deny that."

"Look, Mr. President—Dewey—I haven't come here to lecture you about your responsibilities as a Jew, or to the Jews. That would be presumptuous, and besides, as I said before, that responsibility is on my shoulders, not yours. But I do need to make absolutely certain that you won't bend over backwards."

"I don't bend so easily, Mr. Prime Minister," said Goldberg. "In politics there are certain compromises you make. I noticed, for example, that you brought Rabbi Bloch with you to Washington—"

"Touché," murmured Barzel.

"—but there's a difference between political compromise and principle. America's relationship with Israel goes back fifty years. It's based on mutual values and mutual interests. I would never do anything to harm that."

"I'm sure you wouldn't," said Barzel quickly. "But there are sometimes disagreements even among friends. When they crop up, I need to know that I am dealing with an American president, period. That there are no, as you say here, curveballs."

"I played football, not baseball," said Dewey. "If we have any problems, I'll come straight at you, don't worry."

"I'm not certain if I should be reassured or frightened," said Barzel. "You are a very powerful man."

"Eli, can I tell you something? I really think you're making too much out of this Jewish thing. The polls show that most Americans don't care. Sure there are a few people who'll vote against me because my name's Goldberg, just like there are some who will vote for me because of it. That is," he added with a smile, "if you don't scare them off."

"I have no intention of doing that," said Barzel. "This has been a very satisfactory conversation, from my point of view. I have every confidence in our relationship. And I will, eventually, find a way to convey that confidence to our American friends here."

"Eventually?" said Goldberg. "Don't take too long. The election's in November."

"I have the date circled on my calendar." Barzel smiled. "By coincidence it is almost exactly two months before our own election."

"I see," said Goldberg, although, more precisely, he heard;

it was in Barzel's voice, the unmistakable sound of a politician looking to trade favors. "How are your chances?"

"Oh, I think we'll win," said Barzel easily. "Of course, as I told Mr. Walker, good relations with America are always a powerful selling point at home. It reassures our voters to see I have a warm rapport with the president of the United States. Our American friends, too."

"Yes," said Goldberg. "Listen, I have an idea. Why don't we change the ground rules for tonight and allow press coverage of the speeches?"

"Splendid," said Barzel, as if it had never occurred to him. "It might solve several problems at once."

"I, ah, I'd like to show you a copy of my remarks in advance," said Goldberg. "If you have no objection. I have them right here."

"I'd be honored," said Barzel. He waited just long enough to disconcert Goldberg before adding, "And of course, I'd like you to read mine. As you will see, I left the Jewish business for our private discussion."

Goldberg and Barzel beamed at one another from across a gap of four feet, twenty-five years and two lives as different as the lives of two men could be. And yet, despite all these differences of age and culture, experience and temperament, they shared, at that moment, a single timeless politician's thought: "Gotcha."

CHAPTER TWENTY-TWO

BROUN AND LEVRAN SAT IN THE MOSSAD CHIEF'S SPARTAN
office and watched the final stages of the White House dinner
live on CNN. As senior White House correspondent Doug
Parker went on about the historic nature of the occasion, the
two Mossad chiefs viewed the scene through expert eyes, picking out things that Parker would never notice.

"Looks like our information about Pouissant was good,"
said Broun. The Secretary of State, looking miserable, was
seated between Rabbi Bloch and one of his sons—despite protocol, which dictated alternate male-female seating, the rabbi
refused to sit next to a woman. "Goldberg must really hate
him."

"It's a cruel thing," agreed Levran cheerfully. "That's what
he gets for being a black Republican."

"Vilk's got his tie off," said Broun disapprovingly.

"Look at him talking to Boyd French," said Levran. "You

think Boyd likes Yiddish folk tales? He doesn't seem to be laughing."

"There's Reshef," said Broun. "With Snowden."

There was no need for elaboration. In the weeks since Charlie Walker's visit, Broun and Levran had become increasingly suspicious of the Project and Reshef's role in it.

"Barzel seems to be enjoying himself," said Levran. "Mrs. Goldberg is really something. Not like the Mrs. Goldbergs I knew when I was a kid."

"What's that on Barzel's head?" asked Broun.

"What? I don't see anything."

"Wait till the camera pans back on him. There. See?"

"A yarmulke?" said Levran. "What's that all about?"

"He's wearing it for Bloch, I suppose," said Broun sourly. He didn't care for religious politicians.

"The meal is concluding, and we're getting the signal that President Goldberg is about to begin his remarks," said the CNN reporter.

Levran and Broun saw the president rise and take his place at a small podium at the head table. "Prime Minister Barzel, distinguished guests, ladies and gentlemen . . ."

"He's lost a few pounds," said Levran. Ever since Clinton, the Mossad had tracked the weight of American presidents as an indicator of their moods. Levran didn't actually believe the psychological data this method produced, but it was fun to follow, like team standings in the newspaper.

"He weighs one hundred and three kilos," said Broun with automatic precision. "I understand he and Barzel spent an hour alone this afternoon. And there was no protocol of the conversation."

"Reshef wasn't there?"

"Reshef went to a synagogue with Rabbi Bloch."

"You're kidding," said Levran.

Broun gave his friend a flat, brown-eyed stare. "Apparently

they've been spending quite a lot of time together lately. Not just in America, either."

"Really?" said Levran. Broun was telling him that Reshef was now being followed.

Broun and Levran shared the spy's gift of talking and listening at the same time; together they heard President Goldberg wind up his predictable remarks to polite applause. "Barzel's turn," said Levran. "I see he's got a prepared text. That's not like him."

Barzel rose, took the president's hand in both of his and beamed warmly into the cameras. Then he moved to the lectern and gazed out at the assembly. "President and Mrs. Goldberg, distinguished guests, friends. I have some remarks here that I want to read, but first, with your permission, I'd like to ask Rabbi Bloch, our venerable Minister of Interior, to lead us in the traditional Jewish prayer after meals. Mr. President?"

Goldberg nodded, struggling hard to retain his composure, as the rabbi, accompanied by his two sons, marched to the lectern. All three were dressed in long black coats and wide fur-brimmed black hats. All three had curled sidelocks and wild, untrimmed beards, the sons' salt and pepper, Rabbi Bloch's a shade of tobacco-stained yellow that matched his teeth.

"What the hell?" said Levran.

"Shhh—I want to see this," Broun said.

The rabbi cleared his throat and began to chant in a thin, high-pitched voice. The camera showed Goldberg looking on in flushed silence and Barzel, head bent devoutly, lips moving. From the angle, it was impossible to see the expression on his face.

Suddenly one of the rabbi's sons walked over to Goldberg and unceremoniously plopped a black fedora on his head. Goldberg grabbed the hat, started to snatch it off and then thought better of it. For a long moment millions of Americans saw their president, hand poised on the brim of the fedora, face mottled with indecision and anger, as the Hebrew wailing continued in the background.

"Very moving," cooed Boyd French to Motke Vilk. "Extremely, ah, evocative."

"His Honor the rabbi looks so distinguished," exclaimed Mrs. Bloch—who always referred to her husband in the third person—to her daughter-in-law.

"Get a close-up of Goldberg's face and keep it there," screamed the CNN producer to his cameraman.

"Barzel just cut off Dewey's cock on national TV," hissed Willis to Cassidy. "I warned him not to trust that motherfucker."

"Just stay calm, Dewey," Didi Travers Goldberg whispered under her breath. "We'll deal with this later."

Broun and Levran heard none of these observations. They sat, staring at the screen, as Rabbi Bloch droned on. Both men knew they were witnessing something extraordinary—a televised sneak attack by the prime minister of Israel on the president of the United States.

"Walker was right," Broun muttered. "Barzel wants Goldberg out of the way."

"Yeah, but out of the way of what?" asked Levran. The question was rhetorical; both men knew that it could only be the Project. After a pause he said, "I don't think we can afford to wait any longer."

"What do you propose doing?" asked Broun.

"Barzel records all his conversations," said Levran. "I suggest we listen to them."

"Out of the question," said Broun. "I will not authorize you to spy on the prime minister under any circumstances."

"Okay, then let's get into Reshef's safe."

Broun shook his massive bald head. "It amounts to the same thing," he said. "I can't authorize any such thing."

"Who can?"

"The prime minister."

"Then let's get his permission."

"Fine. When he gets back from Washington in five days, you can ask him personally."

"I don't need to wait five days," said Levran. "I can go see him right now. In Jerusalem."

Broun looked at his friend blankly. "Yarkoni," said Levran. "He's acting prime minister. In a national security emergency he can authorize it."

"Who says this is an emergency?"

"You do. The head of Mossad."

"He won't agree."

"Leave Yarkoni to me," said Levran. "We go back a long way together. I even went out with his sister for a while. He trusts me."

Broun sat staring into space. "All right," he said finally. "Go ahead, see him. But I don't want you doing anything until I hear from him personally."

"Don't worry," said Levran. "We'll get over to his office right now."

"We?"

"Me," said Levran. "And Chanele."

CHAPTER TWENTY-THREE

"YOU LOOK LIKE SHIT," SAID CHARLIE SYMPATHETICALLY when the president got back from the damage control session with his advisers. "What'd they say?"

"Good news, bad news," said Goldberg. "According to Graff, we've lost eleven points nationally in the past seventy-two hours. In some of the southern and western states I'm running behind the Flat Earth Party. Among the adjectives most commonly associated with my name, we now have 'foreign' and 'weird.'"

"We can win without the South. Or the West," said Didi.

"At the moment we're way ahead in Michigan, leading in New York and New Jersey, and that's just about it."

"A debacle," said Charlie.

"You said there's good news," said Didi hopefully.

"Right, the good news. Well, the good news is that this will be the best-financed debacle in American political history.

Money's pouring in. Barzel said he'd open the tap and he did. Of course, he didn't mention that it would splash sewer water all over me, but then again, I didn't ask. Christ, how could I have been so damn stupid?"

"If anybody's to blame, it's me," said Charlie miserably. "I was the one who came up with the he-just-wants-some-attention theory. I wonder if Howard Grant set me up."

"It was me who wanted to throw him a big dinner party," said Didi. "That was my bright idea."

"Whatever happened to 'defeat is an orphan'?" asked Goldberg with a pained smile. "Everybody wants the blame around here. Except Willis and Cassidy, who keep saying 'I told you so.'"

"Maybe you should have listened to them," said Charlie.

"Fuck it," said Goldberg, pouring himself a shot of Wild Turkey. "You know the worst part? Two days ago I was sitting downstairs telling Barzel how he's all wrong, Americans aren't anti-Semites. And now it turns out the old bastard was right. One lousy prayer and half the country thinks I'm some sort of illegal alien."

"This will blow over in a few days," said Didi.

"I don't think so," said Goldberg. "Hell, I know it won't. Cassidy can't even get Reverend Silas on the phone. I guess the folks in the Bible Belt like their Chosen People sunny side up."

"Speaking of Chosen People, your mom called," said Didi glumly.

"Great, what'd she have to say?"

"She said, quote, That's what you get for inviting undesirables to the White House, unquote."

"Good old mom." Goldberg took a swig of the bourbon. "Jesus, I was so close. So goddamn close. Ah, well, maybe it's for the best."

"What do you mean by that?" asked Charlie.

"You remember after the inauguration, that pep talk you gave me about what a good president I'd make? Well, you were wrong, Slim. I knew I wasn't presidential material, I told you at the time. A real president would never have let himself get sandbagged like this, especially not with all the warning signs I had."

"I should have come back with better information," said Charlie.

"Bullshit, Charlie. I sent you because I don't even know how to use the CIA. Maybe I'm lucky—after all, at least nobody's dead. What if this had been a real crisis? America can't afford a president like me."

"That's the most ridiculous thing I've ever heard," snapped Didi. "What happened to you could have happened to anybody. You think Kennedy wasn't screwed by the CIA in Cuba? Reagan didn't get suckered into Lebanon? The difference is, they didn't give up. And you are. It makes me sick, if you want to know the truth."

"Besides, you're a hell of a lot better qualified than Childes," said Charlie. "At least you aren't a lunatic."

"Thanks," said Goldberg sourly, but his mood was lifting. "Look, I never said anything about giving up. I'm going to campaign like hell. I even agree that I might be better than Childes. But I'm not fooling myself—I don't have a real shot, not anymore."

"Campaigns have lots of twists and turns," said Didi. "You've already made your mistake—Childes's are still ahead of him. And I think you're overestimating this Goldberg factor. Give people a chance to see you and let them make up their minds. That's all I'm saying."

"Didi's right," said Charlie. "In the immortal words of Aretha, it's TCB time. For both of us. You've got to put this behind you, go out and kick Childes's ass."

"Okay," said Goldberg. "Just out of curiosity, while I'm doing all this ass-kicking, what business are you going to be taking care of?"

"Barzel business," said Charlie grimly. "He's mine."

*   *   *

On the way home, Elihu Barzel reflected on the economics of air travel. When he had returned to Israel from his years of exile in Europe and the United States, he had flown in his own private jet. Nowadays, he traveled on El Al, upstairs in first class. Still, he was rich enough to buy a jet if he wanted one, and it occurred to him that maybe he should. After the Project got under way, he'd need his own plane.

"Motke, when we get home, find out how much a 767 costs, will you?"

"New or used?" asked Motke.

"New. It's for me, so be sure you get a good price. Ask the American ambassador if he can get us the internal specs on Air Force One."

"You think the Americans are still talking to us?"

"Starks is. He's a Republican," said Barzel. "Do you think I was too hard on Goldberg?"

Motke shrugged. "According to the *Times*, he's taking a bad beating in the polls."

"And that's my fault?"

"Well . . ."

"I suppose it is," said Barzel in a tone of playful rumination. "After all, I forced President Goldberg to commit the unpardonable crime of looking like a Jew in public."

"There's Jews and there's Jews," said Motke. "Rabbi Bloch is enough to scare the whole Talmud."

"Yes, he is a bit ripe." Barzel chuckled. "Still, all he did was recite a prayer on television."

"Don't forget the fedora," said Motke. "Whose idea was that, anyway?"

"Now that you mention it, I believe it was mine," said Barzel blandly.

"That's what I thought," said Motke. "Bloch's too cheap to spring for a new hat. Those things cost money."

"A man should never save on his hat, his shoes or his

bed," said Barzel. "You wind up spending a lot of time in all three."

"I don't think Goldberg's the hat type," said Motke.

"No," agreed Barzel. "I suppose not."

"So, you going to tell me why you did it?" There was no censure in Motke's voice, just curiosity.

"Because I could," said Barzel. "And I can't afford an American president who's that vulnerable. If appearing Jewish for thirty seconds on television can get him in this much trouble, imagine what would happen if he had to actually stand up for Israel on something critical."

"I see what you mean," said Motke. "Still, he's been fine so far."

"So far it's been easy," said Barzel. "Now it's going to get harder."

Chapter Twenty-four

Amos Levran began listening to Reshef's tapes at Mossad headquarters, along with Broun and Yarkoni. Within a few minutes, the foreign minister rose and began pacing the small office.

"Barzel's gone completely insane," he said. "This is a recipe for catastrophe."

"Let's take our time, think this through," said Levran.

"There is no time," said Yarkoni. "I'm going to call a press conference, blow the lid off, expose this madness before it goes any further. Barzel will be forced to resign, but I'm confident I can put together a new coalition—"

"Yarkoni, listen to me," said Levran in a soft, persuasive voice. "If you call a press conference, you'll have to play the tapes. Otherwise no one will believe you."

"That's the whole point," Yarkoni said. "I want people

to hear what's going on. This is a democracy. The people have the right to know!"

"Of course, you're right, but there are some implications you have to consider. How do you suppose the extremists will react? It could start a *jihad*. Maybe even a nuclear *jihad*."

Yarkoni shook his head. "When the extremists see what I'm doing, they'll realize that not every Israeli leader is a war-monger. This might even have a favorable long-term impact on our relations. It could build confidence."

Levran felt Broun's stare, but he kept his eyes focused on the foreign minister. "What you're saying is perfectly logical," he said, "but I don't think we can count on the mullahs being so, ah, rational. It's too risky, believe me."

Yarkoni turned to Broun. "What do you say?"

"I say absolutely not, no press conference," said Broun. He was almost as concerned about the Iranian response as he was about the scandal that would follow the disclosure that the Mossad had stolen tapes from the safe of the prime minister's security adviser.

"In that case, the only honorable thing for me to do is resign," said Yarkoni. "If my party leaves the coalition, the government falls and Barzel will have to drop the plan."

Not for the first time, Levran wondered how Professor Yarkoni had gone so far in politics. "It's possible that Barzel might have already thought of that," he said. "With a scheme like this, he'll be able to replace you with the hawks. They'd go along."

Yarkoni sighed. "When will people in this country real-ize that military force only makes matters worse? That the only solution is diplomacy? That the Iranians, for all their ex-tremism, have some valid concerns, too—"

"Right," said Levran. "But my point is, if you resign now, the reason's bound to come out. That's the worst of both worlds. The extremists will know about the Project and you won't be in the government to keep Barzel under control."

Yarkoni paused, considering. "I see what you mean," he said finally. "Well, what do you suggest?"

"You're the acting prime minister," said Levran. "Give us your authorization to deal with this." Broun looked at Levran but said nothing; both men were aware that such an authorization was meaningless.

"All right," said Yarkoni decisively. "You are so authorized."

"Good," said Levran. "Now, I want you to promise me that you won't discuss this with a soul. Not your wife, not your children, not Ronnie Adler, no one. Will you promise me that?"

Yarkoni gave Levran a sharp look, flushed briefly and then nodded.

"Good. The Project's at least half a year off, so there's no immediate danger. At the end of the month I'll call you and we can review the situation. At that point, if we haven't come up with something, we might have to consider the press conference option after all."

"I'll expect to hear from you," said Yarkoni.

The door closed and Broun turned to Levran. "Who's Ronnie Adler?"

"Ronnie Adler was in the scouts with Yarkoni. He was twelve, Yarkoni was seventeen, the troop leader. Yarkoni molested him."

"How do you know that?"

"I told you, I used to go out with Yarkoni's sister. Yarkoni's father paid off the Adlers, and that was that. One of those little Tel Aviv scandals nobody remembers."

"Except you," said Broun.

"And Yarkoni. And Adler."

"You know where to find Adler?" Levran nodded. "And Yarkoni knows you know?" Levran nodded again. "All right, then," said Broun. "Let's get down to cases. The Project. What do you think?"

"The same thing you do," said Levran. "Barzel's a genius. If he could pull this off, it would be the biggest thing since the fall of the Soviet Union."

"You don't think it can be done?"

Levran shrugged. "Maybe it can, who knows? If Childes wins, if Barzel can keep him on board, if the initial phase goes like clockwork. But one misstep and it turns into a total disaster. It would put the country in jeopardy. We can't justify a risk like that."

"In your opinion," said Broun evenly.

"What do you mean by that?"

Broun cleared his throat and gazed dolefully at his only friend. "Amos, the one thing you sabras have never understood is that Israel is a country. Not a boy's club, not a big kibbutz, not an extended family—a sovereign country, with laws and institutions. A democratic country."

"You sound like Yarkoni," said Levran impatiently.

"You think of us as warriors, heroes, secret agents," said Broun, unperturbed by the interruption. "But that's not what we are. We are civil servants. Servants of the state. And in a democratic country, the authority of the state is exercised by the elected government. We are bound to serve that authority. You may think whatever you like about Barzel's decisions, but no one voted you in."

"I see," said Levran. "So we just sit here and do nothing."

Broun hauled his bulky frame out of the chair and went to the window. For a moment he stood staring out at the lights of Tel Aviv. When he turned back, Levran could see the lines of tension on his smooth face.

"No," the Mossad chief said quietly, his German accent more pronounced than usual. "We're going to stop it. There's no one else to do it. But what we're doing is wrong. I don't want it to become a precedent, which means no one must ever know. I don't want some young agent to hear about it and think it's heroic. So. After we shut down the Project, you will submit your resignation to me, and I will submit mine to Barzel. Is that clear?"

Levran looked at Broun intently and the charming smile slowly spread over his face. "It's clear," he said.

"Then what are you smiling at?"

"At you," said Levran. "I'm going to break a rule of ours and say something personal. All right?"

Broun nodded. "Go ahead."

"All these years, you've wondered why I chose you to be my friend, haven't you?"

"Yes," said Broun thickly. "I wondered."

"This is why," said Levran.

Chapter Twenty-Five

THE FIRST THING KENNY WYKOWSKY SAID TO CHARLIE Walker was, "Have you had your lunch yet?"

"It's a little early for lunch," said Charlie, looking at his watch. The time was nine-thirty A.M.

"Depends on when you wake up," said Wykowsky. "Hamtramck people get up early. I've been on my feet since five. Come on, I'll take you for the best kielbasa you've ever tasted."

They drove from Wykowsky's office in the small, neat city hall on Lech Walesa Plaza down to the main drag, a wide street of auto dealerships, old-fashioned storefronts and mom-and-pop diners. Charlie noticed that many of the names on the shops and eateries were Polish. There was Polish polka music on the car stereo, too. "I always play the old-timey stuff for visitors," Wykowsky said with a booming laugh. "It gets them in the Hamtramck mood." The laugh caused his massive stomach to bounce up and down against the steering wheel.

"Makes me feel right at home," said Charlie. "I'm from North Dakota. Lawrence Welk territory."

"You're not a Polack, though. You don't look like one. Too skinny," said Wykowsky cheerfully.

"No, afraid not. Just a standard-issue American."

"That's what I figured," said Wykowsky. "Well, look around you. We're driving through beautiful downtown Hamtramck, a little city famous worldwide for the three B's—bowling, babushkas and kielbasa."

"Kielbasa starts with a *k*," said Charlie.

"You mean it only counts if the letter is at the beginning of the word?" Wykowsky waited until he caught Charlie looking at him with consternation before bursting into laughter. "Okay, you got your polka music, you got your dumb Polack joke, now it's lunchtime," he said, easing his car into the vacant space in front of a small restaurant. "Dewey said to give you the full treatment."

"He's got a very high opinion of you," said Charlie, although he didn't necessarily share it. The pudgy, clownish mayor seemed like the last person who could help Charlie get what he needed—the real deal on Elihu Barzel.

There was something off about Barzel; Charlie had gone back to his notes and seen it. Sara Epstein calling him a lone wolf and a stranger. Howard Grant's vagueness about Barzel's business in New York. The big hole where the decade of his twenties should have been.

"It all fits together," he had told Goldberg. "Or, I should say, it doesn't. The guy's been in public life for years. He's the prime minister of Israel, for Christ's sake. And his bio's Swiss cheese."

"Like what?" asked Goldberg. He was back in Washington after a campaign swing through the Midwest, still trailing in the polls in the aftermath of the Barzel dinner. Childes's reaction hadn't helped him any. "Hell's bells," the Arizona governor had told reporters, "maybe he's got some funny-lookin' fellas in his synagogue, but that doesn't necessarily mean anything. It's like ole Martin Luther King said, you got to judge people by their character, not their color—and he got himself a national holiday named after him."

"For one thing, Barzel's not his real name," said Charlie. "He changed it from Leibowitz."

"A lot of Israelis took Hebrew names," said Goldberg.

"And for another, nobody knows where he's from exactly. The story is that he's from some Polish village near Kracòw that was destroyed by the Nazis, but I called Sara Epstein, had her do a little investigating and found out something interesting. Nobody knows the name of the village."

"That doesn't necessarily mean anything," said Goldberg. "I once asked my father's mother where she was from and she said, 'The old country, it's all gone now.' So if you want to get technical, I don't know where my family's from, either."

"Yeah, but you weren't born there, he was. Sara checked with the Yad V'Shem Holocaust archives—they have no record of his family. On the forms he filled out when he arrived in Israel he listed no relatives, living or dead. None of the immigrant groups from around Kracòw know anything about him. His file at the Jewish Agency is missing. And there are no pictures of him before he joined the Israeli army."

"Charlie, this was fifty years ago—"

"Do you know what his nickname in Europe was? Avi Har-el told me—the Angel of Death. He had a reputation for brutality."

"What are you getting at?"

"Dewey, I've been in this business a long time and my gut tells me there's something Barzel's covering up. Something he did in the war."

"Like what?"

"Do you know what a Jewish capo was? In the concentration camps?"

"Come on, Slim. You can't be serious."

"Damn right I'm serious."

"How come nobody ever recognized him, then? One of the survivors?"

Charlie shrugged. "The man's a chameleon, everybody says so. Maybe he changed his appearance." He paused, and said, "Or maybe everybody who could have recognized him is dead. It's the only explanation that makes sense. And I'm going to prove it."

"How?"

"For openers, I'm going over to Kracòw, look around, talk to old-timers, see if anybody remembers anything about him. Meanwhile, I've got researchers combing archives—the Wiesenthal Center in L.A., Yad V'Shem, even the files the Russians have released. Something will turn up. But I'm going to need your help."

"What kind of help?"

"Poland's one of the few places I've never worked. I have to find someone who knows the territory, a good investigator. Can you get the embassy to give me a hand?"

Goldberg frowned. "Forget it. The ambassador's one of Boyd French's golfing buddies." He thought for a moment, running his hand through his thinning hair. "I think you should talk to Kenny Wykowsky."

"Who?"

"He's the mayor of Hamtramck, a little town next to Detroit. It's like Warsaw with streetlights. If you need somebody to fix you up in Poland, Kenny's your man."

"You're sure?"

"Yeah," said Goldberg. "Just don't tell him what you're up to. All I need right now is a story in the press about how I'm carrying on some vendetta against Barzel."

"You don't trust him?"

"I do, but these things have a way of getting around. I still don't believe this theory of yours, but if anybody can help, it'll be Kenny."

Now Charlie watched as the mayor of Hamtramck grunted his way out of the car and stood rubbing his hands before a plate-glass window that read: ALICE'S SOUL FOOD KITCHEN. "We're here," he said happily. "Let's chow down and you can tell me what you need."

The restaurant was crowded, and Wykowsky waddled among the customers, greeting each one by name. "You, I don't know," he said to a young man at the counter, dressed in Sears maintenance overalls. "I'm Kenny Wykowsky, lord mayor of Hamtramck."

"Phil Gromak," said the kid shyly, uncomfortable at having been singled out.

"You live around here, Phil?"

"In Warren," he said. "My grandparents still live here, though."

"That would be Stan and Mary Gromak, of two thirteen Myrtle?"

"Hey, how did you know?"

"I went to school with your old man," said Wykowsky, grabbing the kid in a bear hug. "He ever tell you about the time him and a couple buddies got lost coming back from a Wings game and wound up in Flint?"

"I don't believe so, no sir," said the kid.

"Never drink and drive, son," said Wykowsky with mock solemnity. "Seriously, tell your old man I said stop by sometime."

Wykowsky slid himself into a booth with difficulty. A black woman, almost as fat as the mayor, appeared out of nowhere with a plate of kielbasa. "Alice, say hi to Charlie Walker. He's a personal friend of the president of the United States."

"That right?" said the woman. "The—you tell Dewey I know he's gonna be in town Labor Day and I expect him to come by, stir me up some free publicity."

"Dewey was a regular," Wykowsky explained.

"Good customer, too," said Alice. "Between him and Kenny, they could empty out some refrigerators. What can I get for you, Charlie?"

"Coffee," said Charlie. "I just had breakfast."

"Late riser," Wykowsky explained.

Charlie let his gaze wander around the room, which was decorated with old Motown posters. Over the cash register hung a large color photo of Pope Paul II. "A Polish soul food restaurant," he said. "Is this another Hamtramck joke?"

"You wouldn't ask that if you tried some of these," said Wykowsky, his mouth half full of kielbasa. "Alice is Africa's gift to Polish cuisine. She learned cooking at a joint near the Chrysler factory. But serving it here, in her own place, that was my idea."

"Yours? Why?"

"Because a lot of Polacks happen to be prejudiced against black people," said Kenny. "And I don't like prejudice. It's bad for business, it's bad for the schools and it's bad for the city's tax base. Plus it's just plain bad. My ma always said 'The way to a man's heart is through his stomach.' That's why I helped Alice set this place up."

"Has it done any good?"

"It's given me a hell of a place to eat lunch," Wykowsky said with a laugh. He took another bite of kielbasa, washed it down with a swallow of Schlitz and burped daintily. "So. What can I do for you?"

"It's sort of an odd request. . . ."

"You don't know what odd requests are until you run a town like this. Go ahead, ask me anything."

"Well, I'm going to Poland in a few days and I need someone there who's reliable, smart, speaks English and can help me look for something. Know anybody over there who fits that description?"

"Plenty," said Wykowsky. "Hell, I'd recommend myself if

it wasn't for the reliable and smart part. I'm about due for a trip
to the motherland. But sure, I know lots of people. Warsaw?"

"Near Kracôw," said Charlie.

"Down south," Wykowsky said. "What are you looking
for?"

"I'm working on a book about Elihu Barzel."

"Dewey's pal," said Wykowsky, with a sardonic grin.

"Yeah, right. According to everything I've read, he was
born and raised in a village near Kracôw. I doubt very much if
there are any records left, but I thought I could poke around,
maybe find someone who remembers him or his family. Even if
I don't, it'll be helpful just to see the place, sort of set the
scene."

"There were two Polands, the Jewish one and the Polish
one," said Wykowsky. "Even in the cities they didn't mix much.
Stupid, but that's the way things were in the old country. You
might be better off with a Jewish guide."

"There aren't many Jews left around Kracôw," said Charlie. "Besides, I need a journalist or a cop, somebody with some
investigative experience."

"Stick with a cop, then," said Wykowsky. He thought for
a moment and then snapped his stubby fingers. "There's a
widow here in town name of Pauline Barr, used to be
Barkowsky. She comes from around there and she's got a
nephew who's a police detective in Kracôw. He was here a couple of years ago on a visit. Nice guy, speaks good English—a
lot better than his aunt, as a matter of fact. I think he's your
man."

"Would he be willing to take off a few days and help me,
do you think?"

"For hard currency? He'd leave the Church."

"You know how to get in touch with him?"

"No, but Pauline does. She's probably home now; these
babushkas do their shopping nice and early. You want, we can

stop by her place, drink a little coffee and get the phone number."

"That'd be great," said Charlie.

"And then after, I'll take you by the Polish Yacht Club for lunch. They got terrific meat loaf."

"Fine," said Charlie, examining Wykowsky's clean plate. "I'll be hungry by then."

"I'm hungry now," said the mayor of Hamtramck. "But I'll restrain myself for an hour. Business before pleasure, that's my motto. Besides, Pauline's probably got cookies."

Pauline Barr was a stout, alert old woman with rough, wrinkled skin and a shy smile. She greeted Wykowsky and Charlie with the diffident hospitality of the chronically lonely and led them into a small front room crammed with overstuffed furniture and bric-a-brac. Dozens of family photos in cheap silver frames stood on a shelf. Over them, like a household god, hung a picture of the pope.

Mrs. Barr said something to the mayor in Polish, disappeared into the rear of the house and returned with a walnut coffee cake. Wykowsky took a bite and breathed a sound of sincere appreciation that made the woman blush.

"Charlie, I'm going to speak to Pauline in Polish, if you don't mind," he said. "Her English is perfect, but I like to practice my Polish."

Charlie nodded. It was obvious that Mrs. Barr's command of English was far from perfect; she hadn't uttered a single word in the language since they arrived. He sat back in the overstuffed chair and munched the coffee cake as they conversed. After a while he heard the name "Elihu Barzel" and sensed a sudden intensity in the tone of the conversation. Charlie looked closely at the mayor, whose expressive face was rapidly, almost comically, undergoing a transformation from polite disbelief to amazement.

"What is it?" asked Charlie.

"I think I just saved you a trip to Poland," said Wykowsky.

"What do you mean?"

"There's a woman Pauline knows, Ida Lenkowsky. They go to church together. Actually I know her, too; her husband belonged to the same lodge as my father."

Charlie nodded impatiently. "What about her?"

"She's from a village near Kraców, called Pinczow. That's Barzel's hometown."

"She knew him there? In Pinczów?"

"Pauline here says she did," said Wykowsky. The old woman nodded emphatically.

"How well?"

"Pretty well," said Kenny Wykowsky. "She's his sister."

Charlie caught up with Goldberg and Didi on a campaign stop in Milwaukee. "How'd it go in Hamtramck?" Goldberg asked.

"Good," said Charlie.

"Kenny find you somebody in Poland?"

"I'm not going to Poland," said Charlie.

"Oh?"

"Yeah, you were right," he said. "That theory of mine, that he was a Jewish capo, doesn't stand up."

"It sounded far-fetched to me," said Goldberg. "But what the hell, you tried. Don't worry about—"

"He was never in a concentration camp," said Charlie, allowing the excitement to creep into his voice for the first time. "Know why?"

"Why?"

"Because Mr. SuperJew, the prime minister of Israel, Elihu Barzel, is a fucking Roman Catholic."

"What are you, crazy?" demanded Goldberg.

"His real name isn't Barzel and it isn't Leibowitz. It's Elia Lenkowsky from Pinczów, Poland. His sister lives in Hamtramck. She told me the whole story. Jesus, I knew there was something crooked about his bio—I told you that, remember? Didn't I say there was something off—"

"Charlie, you gotta calm down," said Goldberg. "Have a drink, sit. You're not making sense."

"Okay," said Charlie. "Yeah, let's all sit down." He lowered himself onto the couch and then jumped up again, leaping into the air with a clenched fist. "Goddamn, I've got him!" he cried.

"What are you talking about?" asked Didi.

"Just listen to this. Barzel was born in 1926. His father was a Polish Catholic and his mother was German."

"A Jewish German," said Goldberg. "Which would make Barzel a Jew according to Jewish law—"

"No, a Catholic German. Nobody was Jewish. Not his mother, not his father, not even a grandparent. Nothing, nobody. It was a regular Polish family. When the Nazis invaded, Elia's folks took to the woods with the partisans. He was thirteen at the time, and he went with them. The sister, Ida, the one in Detroit, was fifteen. She was in a convent school and they left her there.

"Anyway, the Nazis killed both Barzel's parents. He survived. Somehow he must have gotten hooked up with Jews after the war and wound up in Palestine. Ida managed to get out in 1956 and came to the States."

"She's in touch with him?"

"No," said Charlie. "She hasn't seen him since 1939."

"Nineteen thirty-nine? That's sixty-one years."

"Yeah, I know, I was skeptical, too. But she's got pictures of him as a kid. I compared them to a photo from when he was in the Israeli army in the forties. It's the same guy, no question about it.

"Now listen to this," Charlie continued. "In 1982, Barzel was in Detroit on a book tour. Ida saw him on TV, recognized him and wrote to him in care of his publisher."

"And he wrote back?"

Charlie shook his head. "No, never. But that Christmas she got a cashier's check for twenty-five thousand dollars in the mail, drawn on a New York bank. And she's been getting one every Christmas since then. Indexed for inflation, no less. But no note, no card, nothing."

"Wait a minute," said Didi. "This woman finds out her brother is the prime minister of Israel, not to mention a multimillionaire, and she doesn't tell anyone? How come it hasn't been in the papers? How come nobody knows?"

"Because she's ashamed," said Charlie. "To her, becoming a Jew is a mortal sin. It took me a while to get that out of her—she's what Wykowsky calls a babushka, real old-fashioned, not too bright—but that's what she thinks."

"So she kept it a secret," said Didi.

"Not exactly. She told her priest and a few old crones she goes to church with. That's how Pauline Barr found out."

"You say the last time she saw her brother was 1939?" asked Goldberg.

"In person, yes. But she sees him on television. She told me she watched him at the White House dinner the other night."

"She must have loved that," said Didi.

"She lit a candle for him the next day."

"Jesus H. Christ," said Goldberg. "Elihu Barzel is a goy. He's got to be the greatest con man of the twentieth century. Too bad we didn't know this ten days ago."

"It still might not be too late," said Charlie. "Maybe we can use this to turn things around."

"How?" asked Goldberg. "For one thing, there's no real proof—"

"We've got his sister," protested Charlie. "And the pictures. I'm telling you, there's no doubt."

"Not in your mind," said Goldberg. "And none in mine, either, if you say so. But if he denies it, it's his word against hers. Face it, Slim, not too many people are going to believe an old lady in Hamtramck, Michigan, who claims the Israeli prime minister is a Catholic."

"We could let him know privately," said Didi. "If it's true, it would sure as hell concentrate his mind."

"So that he'd do what? Endorse me? That's all I need. Like I said the other day, it's spilled milk. If I get elected, a piece of information like this would come in handy, but under the circumstances, it's not very useful."

"It's useful to me," said Charlie angrily. "I'm going to wait until about two weeks before the Israeli elections and publish the whole story. Let's see how the voters over there feel about being duped."

"Well, I have no objection to that," said Goldberg. "Sure, cut his balls off. But wait until after November. I've still got a chance—not much of one, but who knows? A story like this is bound to make people think that Jews are even weirder than they already seem. I don't want a bunch of articles about how maybe I'm not Jewish, either, you know?"

"With a face like yours, I don't think there's much doubt," said Didi. "But you're right. It's better to wait."

"I'll wait," said Charlie. "What is it the Mafia guys say? Revenge is a dish best eaten cold."

"That's what my mother says about shrimp," said Goldberg. "I should have listened to her."

"About shrimp?" asked Charlie.

"No, about the Jews," said Goldberg. "She always said stay away from Jews, they're trouble."

"I've never understood that about her," said Charlie. "I mean, she's a Jew herself."

"And Elihu Barzel's a Polish Catholic," said Goldberg. "You go figure it out."

Chapter Twenty-six

Since boyhood, whenever Amos Levran had faced a hard decision, he had come to the Thinking Tree. The tree was a giant eucalyptus that stood alone on a small rise overlooking Lake Kinneret, not far from the kibbutz where he was born and raised. Sitting under its branches as an eighteen-year-old recruit, he had decided to pass up flight school and join an infantry commando unit instead. It was there, too, that he had made other fateful choices: to marry Rina Leshem; to leave the army for the Mossad; to quit the kibbutz and move to Tel Aviv; and finally, to divorce Rina.

Levran wasn't superstitious; he didn't ascribe any particular powers to the tree. It was simply a quiet place where he felt rooted, a piece of land he trusted. And so he had come back now to the tree, a man in late middle age dressed in sandals and jeans and a white T-shirt, sitting on the ground wondering how to prevent the prime minister of Israel from plunging his country and the world into a disastrous adventure.

In a spy movie he would simply have eliminated Barzel by some clever means—poison in his soup, perhaps, or a mysterious accident. Levran loved spy movies for just that reason: Their solutions were always so neat and easy. But there was no such option here. Levran could no more kill the prime minister of Israel than he could kill himself.

Nor could he force Barzel's hand by confronting him. A different prime minister might be intimidated, but then, a different prime minister wouldn't have conceived the Project in the first place. Barzel wouldn't scare, Levran was certain of that. And, although he tried to repress the thought, it crossed his mind that if he tried to stand in Barzel's way, it might actually be dangerous. Levran knew the unspoken rules and constraints of the Israeli intelligence community; he couldn't imagine an agent of the Shin Bet agreeing to assassinate the deputy head of the Mossad. But he also knew that Barzel himself was perfectly capable of doing the job. He was at once amused and embarrassed—and even a bit awed—by the fact that he was physically afraid of a seventy-five-year-old man.

Still, Barzel alone couldn't implement the Project; he needed the cooperation of an American president. The tape made it clear that Earl Childes would be a willing, even enthusiastic partner. He was ahead in the polls and, although Goldberg was running hard and making up lost ground, five weeks before election day it looked almost certain that Childes would win. Stop Childes, Levran thought, and the Project would die. But how?

Reshef's tape gave him the ammunition; it cast the Republican candidate as a dangerously naive adventurer. The problem was how to use it. Making it public could inflame a worldwide Moslem crusade against Israel. But if he approached Childes privately, the Republican candidate might blow the whistle, making it seem that the Mossad was trying to intervene in an American election to help a Jewish candidate. If he did that, the damage to Israel would be incalculable.

For weeks Levran had puzzled over the problem, listening to the tape again and again, trying to find a safe, effective course. The plan he had finally arrived at was complicated and risky—anytime foreigners were brought into an operation there was risk—but possible. If it worked, the Project would be stopped without serious damage. If not, he'd have to try a more confrontational approach and risk the consequences. One thing was clear: Under no circumstances could he allow the Project to go forward.

Levran sat under the tree, staring out at the Kinneret and beyond it the Golan Heights, barely visible through the haze. He had come here to make a final decision and he had reached it. Tomorrow he would fly to the States. Normally he would have used a go-between, but he didn't want to involve a single person more than necessary. And he couldn't afford any misunderstandings. When he made his pitch to Charlie Walker, he wanted to be looking directly into his eyes.

It was a little past six and Charlie was dressing, with his usual combination of trepidation and excitement, for a dinner date with a young Justice Department litigator named Sandra Kleindiest. He was running late and when the phone rang he almost let the machine answer it. Only the possibility that it might be Goldberg, calling from the road, made him take the call. A light, mildly accented baritone voice said, "Charlie? It's your dancing partner."

"My dancing partner? Oh. My dancing partner. Right. Where are you calling from?"

"Not far," said Amos Levran. "Can you see me in half an hour?"

"I've got a date," said Charlie, aware of how juvenile the phrase sounded.

"I don't want to interrupt your social life—"

"No, I'll get out of it," he said, feeling a certain relief. "Where shall we meet?"

"Your place will be fine," said Levran casually. "If it's convenient."

"Okay, sure. Let me give you the address."

"Never mind," said Levran. "I know where you live."

While he waited for Levran, Charlie watched the nightly news. The election had begun to turn ugly. Childes was hammering away at his "American Values" theme, accusing Goldberg of cultural elitism. At one point the governor had even referred to Dewey as "exotic," although he later claimed to have been misquoted. But Childes didn't need epithets to get his message across: Dewey Goldberg wasn't quite a real American.

There had been a row among Goldberg's advisers over how to respond. Willis wanted to address the Jewish issue directly, the way Kennedy had his Catholicism before the Baptist ministers in Houston in 1960, but Cassidy argued for an elliptical approach. "We've got to drive the message home—college football star, Vietnam vet, congressman from a Catholic district, blond wife—let the voters see you as a regular guy," he said. The remark had infuriated Goldberg, who wondered aloud why the president of the United States had to prove his credentials as an American. Still, he realized that Cassidy was right, and he reluctantly went along, sidestepping the Goldberg factor.

Ironically, the high-road strategy alienated Jewish voters. A group of militant New York rabbis, the "Coalition for Jewish Pride," held a press conference and derided Goldberg as a sellout. "After what they did to our people in Auschwitz, the president lets the goyim spit in his face and pretends it's rain," said one of the rabbis in an oft-played sound bite. It was the worst thing that had happened to Goldberg's campaign since the Barzel dinner.

Charlie had followed the campaign with frustrated fury, unable to do more than offer long-distance encouragement.

Goldberg still clung to the hope that Reverend Silas, who had yet to make an endorsement, would swing his votes behind him, but it was a thin reed—the rumor Charlie heard was that Silas was planning to come out for Childes a few days before the balloting.

With Goldberg's chances slipping away, Charlie found himself contemplating what might have been. He was honest enough to admit that America wasn't losing a great president. Goldberg was too cautious, too plodding, too lacking in vision. He would never lead the nation in a great crusade or inspire sacrifice from his countrymen. His style was compromise and consensus at home, care and coalition-building abroad. Still, compared to Earl Childes, Goldberg was Abraham Lincoln.

The doorbell rang and Charlie let in Amos Levran. The Israeli smiled his charming smile and wordlessly handed Charlie a small package.

"State secrets?" asked Charlie.

"Riesling," said Amos. "It's from a winery in the Golan. I thought you'd like to try it."

"I'll open it right now," said Charlie.

"Please wait," said Levran. "Let's talk first. What I want to discuss, it's better if we're both completely sober."

"Sounds serious," Charlie said.

"Do you know the name Adam Reshef?"

Charlie shook his head. "I don't think so. Should I?"

"He's the prime minister's adviser for what we call special operations."

"You mean he's a spook."

"No, not exactly. He's a former pilot who's been with Barzel for a long time. An amateur."

"What about him?"

"He's about to start World War Three," said Levran in an unemotional voice that succeeded in dramatizing the words.

"What?"

"Before I say anything more, we need ground rules," said

Levran. "What I have to tell you is completely off the record. You can't report it or discuss it with anyone, not even President Goldberg, unless we mutually agree on how and when. We must be partners on this story."

"No way," said Charlie. "I'm a journalist, not a Mossad agent."

"Okay," said Levran. "You can open the Riesling now."

"No, wait. I want to hear this. But what you're asking is a violation of journalistic ethics. Maybe that sounds silly to you, but it's something I take very seriously."

"The only reason I'm here right now is because I know that about you," said Levran. "And I respect it. If it makes you feel better, telling this to you violates my professional ethics, too. Not to mention Israeli law. But this is an exceptional case—a matter of stopping a war, maybe a nuclear war. In such a case, my personal ethics come second."

"Amos, I like you," said Charlie. "But you're the deputy head of the Mossad, for God's sake. I have to assume that you're manipulating me."

"Of course you do," said Amos. "I understand that. But you aren't under any obligation to use what I tell you. My condition is that, if you do use it, we must both agree on when and how. I wouldn't ask such a thing if it wasn't a question of life and death."

"All right," said Charlie slowly. "I'll listen. But I have a condition of my own. I want you to promise me that what you're about to tell me is the truth."

"You think the promise of the deputy head of the Mossad is worth something?" asked Levran with a slight smile.

"I want your word as a man," said Charlie. "That's worth something."

"All right. I promise I won't lie to you."

"That's not quite the same thing," said Charlie.

Levran nodded. "We understand each other," he said.

"Yes," said Charlie. "All right, tell me about World War Three."

Levran took a deep breath. "For the past few months, maybe longer, Adam Reshef has been meeting secretly with Reverend Bobby Silas and Governor Childes on something Reshef calls the Project. Silas calls it Operation Armageddon."

"Operation Armageddon?"

"That's right," said Levran. "Reshef originally met Silas in Jerusalem, and Silas took him to Childes. That's how it started."

"Go on."

"According to the Project, sometime next year, after Childes becomes president, Israel will launch a preemptive, simultaneous strike against the Islamic nuclear facilities in Iran and Egypt, similar to the attack on Osirak in 1981."

"Those facilities are supposed to be invulnerable to air strikes," said Charlie.

"To conventional air strikes," said Levran. "But we have the technique to pierce them."

"Holy Christ," said Charlie.

"That's only step one," said Levran. "Next, Israeli ground forces will move west, into Egypt, as far as Cairo. Naturally, the other Islamic countries will come to Egypt's aid. At which time the U.S. will strike against Iran, Iraq and Syria."

"What do you mean, 'strike'? How?"

"Air attacks, missiles, naval bombardment and a rapid mobilization of ground troops. Within a few weeks the entire Middle East will be under American and Israeli occupation, from Sudan to the Persian Gulf."

"That's insane," said Charlie. "For one thing, Congress would never allow it. You can't just launch a war like that."

"In the first days of the operation, when Israel is moving toward Cairo, an American battleship in the Persian Gulf will be attacked and badly damaged by MIG-21s that presumably belong to Iran. You know how public opinion works here, you saw it in Desert Storm. Americans will demand war, especially since they already believe that Islam is the number one threat in the world. Which is true, by the way, but that's not the point."

"No, it's not," agreed Charlie. He was trying hard to absorb what Levran was saying, but a dozen questions buzzed in his brain. "What would all this accomplish?"

"Accomplish? It will destroy the extremists' nuclear capability. It will give the United States total control over Middle East oil reserves. And it will put a stop to Islamic expansion. Those are the goals."

"Yes, but what about afterwards? The Moslem world will find some way to counterattack."

"There is no 'afterwards,'" said Levran. "The United States will stay. Permanently."

"You're talking about the re-colonization of the Middle East."

"That's right," said Levran. "That's exactly what I'm talking about."

"Impossible," said Charlie. "The world will never let that happen."

"What world? The Europeans? You think they give a damn about the Moslems? The Japanese? The Russians? There's nobody to oppose the United States anymore, and frankly, when it comes to dealing with the extremists, nobody wants to. As long as they have oil and nuclear weapons, they're dangerous. But if they're disarmed, who cares about them?"

"Well then, I don't see what you're worried about," said Charlie. "From Israel's point of view it sounds great."

"I'm worried about two things," said Levran. "First, when it comes to a war, you know how things start but you're never sure how they end up. The preemptive strike could fail. Or Childes could lose his nerve and leave us hanging like the French and British did in '56. And even if it works, the invasion of Egypt alone would cost us thousands of casualties. That's number one."

"What's number two?"

"The long run. There are only two constants in the Middle East—memory and geography. If we wait long enough the extremist mood will pass, just like Nasserism did. Fashions change, even ideological ones. But in our part of the world, nobody ever forgets a grievance. Maybe the U.S. can colonize the Arabs for twenty, thirty, even fifty years. But eventually you'll get tired or the oil will run out, and you'll leave. And we'll still be there, only this time the Moslems will be crazy for revenge."

"This is the goddamnedest story I've ever heard," said Charlie. "You're saying that Earl Childes has agreed to this thing?"

Levran reached into the inside pocket of his jacket and took out a small audiocassette. "Have you got a tape recorder?" he asked.

For the next hour Charlie and Levran sat in total silence, listening as Reshef, Childes, General Hunter and the Reverend Bobby Silas calmly discussed their conspiracy to conquer the Moslem world. Charlie snorted when Childes proclaimed that there was no connection between politics and the Project, and he rolled his eyes when Silas talked about God's plan for the End of Days, but these were conditioned responses to political cant and religious lunacy; his attention was focused on the smooth, rational-sounding way that Reshef and Hunter talked about the details of the scheme. He was so absorbed that when the tape clicked off, he jumped slightly in his seat.

"That cassette hasn't been doctored?" Charlie asked. "Remember, you promised not to lie, and anyway I can have it checked."

"Thank you for your confidence," said Levran. "The tape is absolutely authentic. No doctoring."

"Can you tell me where you got it?"

"No," said Levran. "But it doesn't matter."

"Okay, then let's talk about what's not on the tape."

"What's that?"

"The name Elihu Barzel."

"That's right, it isn't," said Levran.

"You're saying Barzel doesn't know about this? That Reshef's acting on his own?"

Levran looked at the journalist steadily, his soft brown eyes wholly devoid of expression. This was what he had prepared for. "It's conceivable," he said finally.

"Anything's conceivable," said Charlie. "But Israel isn't about to launch a war on the Moslem world on the say-so of some adviser. Nobody has the authority to do that except the prime minister."

"That's true," Levran said carefully. "But let me give you a hypothetical case. Supposing Reshef was a rogue agent who thought up the Project alone and tricked Childes and Silas into believing that he was speaking for Barzel. And suppose further that he planned to get their agreement and then use it to convince Barzel to go along."

"That's what you're telling me actually happened? That's bullshit, Amos. If Barzel didn't know, you'd have gone to him with this tape and Reshef would be in jail right now."

"I told you we were speaking hypothetically," said Levran mildly.

"That works both ways," said Charlie. "Suppose, hypothetically, I take what you just told me and publish it. What then?"

"You wouldn't," said Levran confidently. "You promised me, for one thing. And for another, without the tape, nobody would believe you. Everybody knows you're Goldberg's best friend. You come out with a wild story like this a couple weeks before the election, what would people think?" The look on Charlie's face told Levran that he had scored a point, and he pressed his advantage. "Let me offer you a scenario, Charlie, just as a possibility. Supposing someone went to Barzel and told him you had this tape and what's on it."

"He already knows what's on it," said Charlie.

"You're not positive of that, are you?" asked Levran. "You may assume it, but you have no proof. Right?"

Charlie nodded. "No proof, no."

"Okay. And suppose Barzel said, 'By God, Reshef's been acting on his own. He's out, as of this minute. This so-called Project of his is dead.' Then the story would be that Barzel had caught a renegade Israeli official plotting a Christian holy war with Silas and Childes, wouldn't it? And you'd have the proof. That's a hell of a story."

"That's exactly what it is—a story."

"I want to point out one more thing," said Levran imperturbably. "I don't imagine Childes could get elected if his role in this came out. He might even be forced to withdraw his candidacy."

"American presidential candidates don't withdraw," said Charlie. "That's science fiction."

"All right, but a tape like this, with him talking to Silas about Armageddon, would mean President Goldberg's election. Or am I being naive?"

"I wouldn't choose the word 'naive' to describe you," said Charlie.

"You know it makes me uncomfortable to get involved in an American election like this," said Levran, ignoring the sarcasm. "But frankly, I'd be even less comfortable seeing a man like Earl Childes in the White House. Wouldn't you?"

"How am I supposed to feel about a man like Barzel as head of the Israeli government?"

Levran shrugged. "It's not the same. An Israeli prime minister doesn't have the same power. Besides, Barzel's old. He won't be around much longer."

"Let me think about this," said Charlie. He sat staring at the cassette on the coffee table, considering his options. Levran's deal was clear: If he went along, Barzel would get credit for acting responsibly. The world would be spared a terrible war. America would be saved from an irresponsible president.

Dewey Goldberg would be elected in November. Charlie would have the scoop of the decade. Everyone came out a winner. All Charlie had to do was to publish a story he knew to be false.

Given these circumstances, Charlie knew, most reporters wouldn't think twice. But he had spent a lifetime nurturing a certain view of himself and his profession. He considered lying, even in a good cause, to be a professional sin. And so he paused, almost ten full seconds, before nodding his head and saying, "All right, we've got a deal."

CHAPTER TWENTY-SEVEN

OCTOBER 27 WAS BROUN'S BIRTHDAY. NO ONE WAS AWARE OF it except his wife, and she knew better than to mention it. She had long since learned that her husband had no interest in birthdays or anniversaries. His only concession to the occasion was to allow her to kiss him on his bald skull at breakfast. It was merely a peck, but in their undemonstrative relationship that peck was a dramatic departure from the established order. Every February 11, on his wife's birthday, she got a similar kiss on the forehead.

This morning, Broun seemed even more preoccupied than usual. He never discussed business with his wife, so she had no way of knowing that he was still trying to digest yesterday's conversation with Elihu Barzel.

To avoid taping, Broun had asked to see Barzel at a Mossad facility in Jerusalem. It was an unusual request, and he had been prepared with an explanation about the need for top secrecy, but none had been necessary. The prime minister had simply agreed without asking any questions. It wasn't like him, and it had made Broun wonder if what he had to say would come as a complete surprise to the old man.

Barzel had arrived, looking fresh and composed, at exactly ten-fifteen. Broun put a very high premium on promptness and normally he would have been gratified, but this was a conversation he wasn't looking forward to. Levran had volunteered to break the news, but Broun felt that it was his duty.

"Prime Minister," he said in his formal way, "it's come to my attention that an American journalist named Charlie Walker has a copy of a damaging tape."

"What sort of tape?"

"A conversation between Adam Reshef and some Americans, including Governor Childes. They talked about something called the Project."

A look passed fleetingly over Barzel's face. Broun assumed it must be alarm, although the prime minister didn't seem alarmed, merely curious. "Really?" he asked smoothly. "Have you listened to it?"

"Yes sir, I have. Reshef and the others discussed the possibility of an Israeli-American military operation against the Islamic extremists sometime after the American election."

"An operation," said Barzel, his face expressionless now. "How did Walker get the tape? Do you know?"

"It could have come from a Goldberg spy in the Childes campaign. Or from the CIA," said Broun.

"Could have," mused Barzel. "Yes, I see. Tell me, how do you happen to be involved in this? The press isn't your concern."

"Charlie Walker isn't a regular journalist. He's President Goldberg's close friend."

"So we have to assume that President Goldberg knows about this tape. Is that what you're telling me?"

"Yes, Prime Minister. I think we have to assume that."

"Well, then. You still haven't told me how this particular matter happened to fall in your lap."

"Walker knows Amos Levran. Considering the, ah, inflammatory nature of the conversation, Walker decided to verify it with him before going any further."

"Very conscientious of him," said Barzel with a droll smile. "You don't meet many journalists with such a highly developed sense of responsibility."

Again, Broun was puzzled by Barzel's light tone. Actually, the prime minister often confused him with his moods and whimsies. Broun was exceptionally good at collecting and shifting through intelligence data, but analyzing human nuance was not his strong suit and he knew it.

"Why isn't Amos here himself?" asked Barzel.

"I decided it would be best if this discussion was limited to the two of us," said Broun. "I thought perhaps you'd prefer it that way."

"Most considerate. Well, what did Amos tell Mr. Walker?"

"That Reshef was acting entirely on his own, without your knowledge or approval."

"And Walker believed him?"

"He was skeptical."

"Skepticism is admirable in a journalist. How about you, Broun? Are you skeptical, too? Do you think I've been cooking up a military operation behind your broad back?"

"Prime Minister, I—"

"There's no need for you to answer that," said Barzel, his voice turning hard. "What's Walker going to do with this story?"

Broun was grateful for the reprieve. He had come into the conversation determined to resign rather than tell the prime minister a direct lie. Equivocations and evasions he could rationalize. "He's going to publish it," Broun said.

"What's he waiting for?"

"Our reaction. Amos assured him that you'd fire Reshef and give Walker an exclusive statement, making it clear that this so-called Project was a rogue operation."

"Amos assured him of that? Well, we can't make a liar out of the deputy head of the Mossad, can we? Do you by any chance know where Reshef is now?"

"In his office, I believe," said Broun. "Shall I send for him?"

"There's no need for that," said Barzel, carefully arranging his long, beautifully manicured fingers on the knees of his trousers. "I'll attend to him later. I assume this tape will be highly embarrassing to Governor Childes?"

"I'd say so, yes."

"Pity," said Barzel. "I don't trust Goldberg. Ah, well, those are the vicissitudes of politics. It's a terrible profession, Broun. You were wise to stay in intelligence."

"Yes sir," said Broun, blinking at the suggestion that he might have contemplated a political career.

"All right, then," said Barzel briskly. "Congratulate Amos for me on a job well done. I want him to come to me today at four, for a full account. Together we can draft a statement for Mr. Walker. And I want to be kept fully informed about any reactions by the extremists. I think it might be prudent to order the army on partial alert. What do you think?"

"I think it might," said Broun. "Although, if your statement makes it completely clear that you had nothing to do with this, I don't foresee serious repercussions."

"I suppose you're right," said Barzel. He gazed into space and a faint smile spread over his face. "We go back together, don't we Broun? You were prepared to kill me in Buenos Aires."

"If I had to," said Broun heavily. "I was under orders."

"Orders," said Barzel. "Do you know, that's the reason I decided to keep you on as head of the Mossad. I can't say I enjoyed being thwarted in Argentina, but I was very impressed by your sense of duty."

"Yes sir," said Broun uncomfortably.

"Well, if that's everything," said Barzel, rising spryly to his feet, "I have a speech to give to a group of UJA stalwarts at the King David Hotel. They're here on something called the Prime Minister's Mission. Very impressive title, wouldn't you say?"

"I don't know anything about the UJA," said Broun, relieved to have gotten through the meeting but still perplexed by the prime minister's blithe reaction.

"No, I don't suppose you do," said Barzel. He walked to the door and paused. "You and Reshef and I have been busy with our own sort of missions. We have that in common," he said quietly. "Perhaps mistakes have been made, but they were made to safeguard this country. Never forget that."

"Yes, Prime Minister," said Broun, although he didn't know whose mistakes Barzel was referring to—Reshef's, Broun's or his own.

CHAPTER TWENTY-EIGHT

CHARLIE CAUGHT UP WITH GOLDBERG IN TYLER, TEXAS, ONE OF A dozen states that Goldberg had to capture in the last ten days of the campaign in order to win. What had looked like a Republican rout in September was now tightening into a close election. Childes was still ahead, but he had lost momentum, especially after the press had uncovered the extent of his heavy gambling. Willis and Cassidy were working the angle hard, running ads that showed a spinning roulette wheel and a voice asking: "Can we really afford a president who will gamble with our future?"

Goldberg greeted Charlie with a hug and a smile. "Welcome to the campaign trail, Slim," he said. "Today's itinerary includes Jackson, Mississippi; Huntsville, Alabama; Knoxville, Tennessee; Louisville; and a rally tonight in South Carolina. Or maybe North Carolina. Some Carolina, anyway. As James Brown once said, 'All aboard for the night train.'"

"Campaigning seems to agree with you," said Charlie. Goldberg had shed ten pounds and he seemed more relaxed and cheerful than at any time since the Tragedy.

"You know what? It's been a hell of an experience," said Goldberg. "A month ago I wasn't enjoying it much, but we're in a horse race now. Everybody should try it at least once. Maybe if I lose I'll set up a fantasy camp; simulated runs for the presidency. How does that sound?"

"I hate to spoil a good business opportunity, but you're not going to lose," said Charlie. He took a small tape recorder from his briefcase and loaded a cassette. "I brought you something to listen to."

"A little Joe Tex to lift the presidential spirits?"

Charlie pressed the play button and Goldberg heard the voice of Earl Childes: ". . . you're saying, then, that these facilities could be destroyed in one stroke?"

"With low-yield, laser-guided nuclear bombs, absolutely," said a second voice.

Goldberg looked sharply at Charlie. "That's Adam Reshef. Barzel's adviser."

"Charlie, what the hell—"

"No, just listen," said Charlie.

". . . like the plagues of old visited by God Almighty on the Egyptians. His servants will deliver the eleventh plague so as to make His will manifest."

"That's Reverend Silas," said Charlie.

"Shut that thing off for a minute and tell me what this means," Goldberg commanded.

"It means that Earl Childes is going to lose in November," said Charlie. "And Elihu Barzel is fucked, too."

"Come on," said Goldberg impatiently. "Skip the riddles. Talk."

As the campaign jet flew eastward toward Mississippi, Charlie told Goldberg about the tape and the deal he had made with Amos Levran. Goldberg listened in fascinated silence. "This is incredible," he said finally.

"You got that right," said Charlie. "I'll break it in my Sunday column and go on one of the talk shows. By Monday morning, Governor Childes will be a cross between a national laughingstock and Dr. Strangelove. Even you ought to be able to beat him."

"Thanks," said Goldberg. "But I can't let you do that."

"What?"

"Charlie, publishing this could start a war. You know what the extremists are like."

"I don't see it," said Charlie. "Not if it's a rogue operation—"

"Do you actually believe Barzel didn't know anything about this?"

"No, but—"

"Then what makes you think the Iranians will? Christ, they see conspiracies where there aren't any. And this time there happens to be one."

"Which includes Governor Childes," said Charlie.

"I know you think this tape will blow him out of the water, but there aren't any sure things in politics. In fact, making it public could hurt me more than him," Goldberg said.

"How do you figure that?"

"Let me ask you something. What are you going to say when people ask where the tape came from?"

"That I don't reveal my sources. Naturally."

"Right. Which means they'll be left to speculate. They'll assume that you didn't find it at Tower Records. Somebody gave it to you. To you, specifically, my best friend. Now, who would do that? It would have to be someone who recorded the conversation, or had access to the tape. Childes? Why would he sabotage his own campaign? Hunter? He's about to be appointed Secretary of Defense. No, people will figure I got the FBI to bug Childes's house, which makes me the new Richard

Nixon. Or they might even suspect that the tape came from the Israelis."

"Why on earth would the Israelis want you to have the tape?"

"That's a funny question under the circumstances."

"Levran gave me the tape unofficially—"

"Are you positive?"

"I'd bet my life on it," said Charlie. As he said the words he remembered the shirt in Tel Aviv with the seven buttons. "Well, I'm damn sure, anyway. Besides, why would anyone think the Israelis leaked the story?"

"To get me elected president," said Goldberg quietly. "The Jewish conspiracy. People will say the Israelis set up Childes, gave you the tape ten days before the election and bingo—four more years for President Goldberg."

"Jesus," said Charlie. "I never thought of that."

"That's because you don't think like a politician. I do."

"Aren't you exaggerating the conspiracy angle?" asked Charlie. "Sure there may be some nuts who buy the Elders of Zion crap, but most Americans are way past that."

"You'd like to think so, wouldn't you," mused Goldberg. "You know, in the last few months I've learned a lot about how people in this country feel about Jews."

"You're saying you're surprised by the anti-Semitism you never knew was out there?"

"Not anti-Semitism," said Goldberg. "Confusion. It doesn't matter how many Holocaust documentaries people see, how many Jewish sitcom characters they watch, even if they have Jewish friends or relatives. They're still never quite sure what Jews are."

"You're not sure yourselves," said Charlie. "Who's a Jew? That Rabbi Bloch character? Amos Levran? Hell, the most famous Jew in the world is a Polish Catholic. How do you expect the people to know what Jews are when the Jews don't even know?"

"I guess you're right," said Goldberg. "But I've sensed in this campaign that they're trying to figure it out. Like it or not, I've become a symbol. If they elect me, this country gets past a barrier. That's important to me as an American. And frankly, as a Jew. That's why I can't take a chance on releasing the tape. If I lose without it, well, too bad, one of the candidates loses every time out. But if I lose because of it, it could set things back a long way."

"So the tape is worthless," said Charlie.

"Not at all," Goldberg replied. "For one thing, it puts a stop to the Project; if Childes wins, you can be sure I'll play it for him before he takes office. And for another, I think it might help turn Reverend Silas around. His endorsement would pretty much wrap up this election for me. I'll get it, too, if he decides he'd be better off with me in the White House."

"How are you going to do that?"

"I'm not," said Goldberg. "Barzel is."

"Barzel?"

"Yeah. But I'm going to need that Polish story you uncovered. I know I asked you to hold off publication until after November, but this changes things."

"You want me to publish it now?"

"If what I intend to do works, you won't be able to publish it at all."

"Christ," said Charlie. "This damn election is going to cost me another Pulitzer."

"It's your call, Slim. Whatever you decide will be okay with me."

"Naw, take the story," said Charlie. "And ram it up Barzel's ass."

CHAPTER TWENTY-NINE

WHEN BARZEL RETURNED FROM HIS MEETING WITH BROUN, he summoned Motke Vilk. "Reshef is not to be allowed in the building, starting tomorrow," he said. "And let everyone know he has no security clearance, effective immediately. When you're finished, tell him to come see me. Make sure the security people seal off his office and collect his briefcase. Then come back yourself; I want you to sit in on the meeting."

It took Motke fifteen minutes to erase the authority and access that Adam Reshef had acquired over a decade. When he was through, he buzzed the young adviser, told him Barzel wanted him right away and returned to the prime minister's office.

"That was quick," said Barzel.

"Nobody asked any questions," said Motke. "Adam isn't a very popular person."

"No," agreed Barzel. "You never liked him, did you?"

"An understatement," said Motke. "You never liked him, either."

"What makes you say that?"

"I've known you a long time. It's obvious."

"Obvious?" said Barzel with his shadowy smile. "How disconcerting. I sometimes forget how well you know me, Motke. It could be a dangerous quality in someone less loyal."

"Loyal. You make me sound like a cocker spaniel," said Motke.

"Sorry," said Barzel. "By the way, there's something I want you to do for me. I'm expecting a visitor. Reverend Silas."

"*Oy vey.*"

"Precisely," said Barzel. "He'll be arriving in Israel later today and he'll call for an appointment. Tell him to come at midnight."

"Midnight?"

"Yes. I want you to round up a few things. I've made a list."

Motke took the paper from Barzel; it was written in the Old Man's neat, unembellished Hebrew and it contained half a dozen items. "What do you want with this stuff?"

"You'll see tonight."

"Tonight? Don't tell me you want me here. I've got theater tickets. The revival of *My Fair Lady* at Habima."

"Give them away," said Barzel. "Don't worry—I think I can promise you a show at least as entertaining as *My Fair Lady.*"

There was a sharp knock on the door and Adam Reshef entered. He scowled at Motke, took a seat across from Barzel and gave the prime minister an inquiring look.

"Adam, I'm afraid we have some bad news," said Barzel. "It seems that President Goldberg knows about your meetings with Governor Childes. His friend Charlie Walker is going to publish the story in a day or two."

"That's impossible. How could he know?"

"I intend to find out, but that isn't the point now. We've got to contain the damage."

"Give me a few hours to think about this and I'll come up with something," said Reshef.

"I've already done the thinking," said Barzel. "What you planned was totally without my knowledge or approval. It was a rogue operation. Do you understand what I'm saying?"

Reshef stared speechlessly at the old man.

"Just nod if you understand," said Motke, unable to suppress a grin. Barzel shot him a sharp look and Motke ducked his head.

"You're selling me out," said Reshef in a shaky voice.

"I'm afraid so," said Barzel. "There isn't any other alternative."

"No alternative? I was the one who convinced you to go into politics. I worked for you for ten years, did whatever you asked. I'm your heir, you said so yourself, right here in this room—"

"I told you something else that day, too," said Barzel. "To be prime minister of this country a man has to be hard. You said you understood, but you didn't. Now, perhaps, you do."

"You used me," said Reshef in a muffled voice.

"Of course I did," said Barzel. "You wanted to be used. And I used you for a noble purpose. The Project was a good idea, Adam; it might have worked. But it was a gamble and we lost. That's the risk you take if you operate on this level."

"I won't let you destroy me," said Reshef, suddenly furious. "I'll go to the press—"

"No you won't," said Barzel evenly. "You're a patriot. Going public would put the country in jeopardy."

"Fuck the country and fuck you," snapped Reshef, leaping from his seat.

"You don't really mean that," said Barzel. "The part about me, perhaps; that's understandable. But you love this country too much to endanger it."

"We'll see about that," said Reshef, heading for the door.

"Wait," commanded Barzel in a soft, metallic voice that froze the young man. "Listen to me, Adam. You're angry right now and you're not thinking clearly. Don't force me to do something I don't want to do."

"Are you threatening me?"

"Yes," said Barzel, fixing Reshef with an icy stare.

The two men faced one another, locked in a silent tug of wills that ended abruptly when Reshef lowered his gaze. "What do you want me to do?" he asked in a choked voice.

"Leave the country, now," said Barzel. "Go to Zurich. Someone will contact you there with a new passport and enough money to allow you to live comfortably. You can send for your family, but stay out of sight, especially while the Project is in the news."

"When will I be able to come back?"

Barzel sighed. "I'm an old man. When I'm gone, my successor will get a letter from me exonerating you. What he decides to do about it will be his business."

Reshef opened the door and turned to Barzel. "God damn you," he said.

"There is no God," said Barzel. "If there were, I wouldn't have to do these things."

The building in Jerusalem's government complex that housed the prime minister's office was dark and forbidding at midnight. Two uniformed policemen peered through the late October fog at Bobby Silas, said something in Hebrew to the young security man at the wheel and waved their car through.

The security man led Silas down a long, unlit corridor to the bulletproof glass partition that separated the inner sanctum from the rest of the building. A buzzer sounded, the door opened and Silas found himself standing alone in the gloom. Suddenly he felt a hand on his elbow and a familiar voice: "He's ready for you. Come with me."

"Brother Vilk!" said Silas, relieved to see the cheerful little aide. "God bless you."

"Reverend Silas," said Vilk in a solemn, formal tone that Silas had never heard him use before. *"Kish mir en tochis."*

When they came to Barzel's door, Motke waited a beat to build suspense and then ushered the preacher inside. The room was dark, illuminated only by three tall white candles that threw long shadows and made Elihu Barzel's face glow an eerie shade of reddish yellow.

"Thank you for coming to see me," said Barzel. "Are you rested from your flight?"

"I'm fine," said Silas. "What's the matter, you having a power failure?"

"We have things to discuss that are best said in the dark," Barzel intoned. "Ancient secrets passed down from generation to generation. I have brought you here to reveal these secrets to you, but only if you give me your sacred oath that you will never reveal what you hear tonight to a living soul. Do you swear it?"

"Yes," said Silas, "I swear it."

"Two thousand years ago," said Barzel in a soft, hypnotic voice, "when the Temple lay in ruins, three men escaped from Jerusalem and fled into the desert of Judea. They took with them the Ark of the Covenant and hid it in a cave in a remote place in the wilderness. Two of these men were Jews. The third was a follower of Jesus Christ named Silas." He paused, letting the name hang in the air, and then continued.

"As they grew old, these men feared their deaths would mean the Ark would be lost. And so they decided to choose three younger men who would continue to protect it until the Temple was restored. Two of these guardians would be Jews, the third a Christian. And so it has been, generation after generation, from then until today."

"You're saying that the Ark of the Covenant still exists?" asked Reverend Silas in an awed voice.

"Regrettably, it does not," said Barzel. "In the year 1001, a group of roving bedouins stole the Ark and slaughtered two of the Guardians. The third survived. Legend tells us his name was Malachi.

"Malachi traveled by foot to Jerusalem. There he found two men—one a Jew, one a Christian—who were worthy to become Guardians. He took them to a dark spot in the forest outside the city and told them the secret of the Covenant, just as I am telling it to you now. He asked them to pledge that they would not rest until the Ark was found and restored to its rightful place. And he commanded them to appoint successors—always two Jews and one Christian—to follow in their footsteps.

"And so it has been, from then until now. I am a Guardian. Motke is a Guardian. The third was a French priest. Word has reached me that he is dead. Motke and I are old men. The time has come to anoint a new generation."

"This is overwhelming," said Silas.

"Surprising, yes, but somehow I do not think you are overwhelmed," said Barzel. "You are a man who has experienced divine mysteries. That is why it is you who is the Christian chosen to be a Guardian of the Covenant."

"I am unworthy," said Silas.

"No, you have been tested. The Project was your test. Like Abraham of old, you were asked to sacrifice all you hold dearest—loyalty to your country, the lives of fellow human beings, even, ah, common sense—and you did not hesitate. You were prepared to risk everything for your faith."

"You mean Operation Armageddon was just a test? It isn't real?"

"Correct," said Barzel. "Of course, what God Himself chooses to do is a mystery."

"I—I don't know what to say," Silas stammered. "This is so unexpected. What will I tell Governor Childes?"

"There is no need to tell him anything," said Barzel, "if

he does not become president. We must see to it that Dewey Goldberg wins the election. I believe you have that power."

"I've always had the feeling that you didn't trust Goldberg," said Silas.

"He, too, was being tested," said Barzel. "He, too, has been found worthy."

"You mean—"

"Yes. President Goldberg will replace Motke. After the election, I will be the first Guardian—a senior partner, in a manner of speaking. Goldberg will be the second. And you, Reverend, will be the third."

"What happens then?"

"What God directs," said Barzel solemnly. "His will be done."

Silas stared into the candlelit face of Elihu Barzel and suddenly felt the room tip and sway. He fell to his knees, chanting strange words that welled up in his throat and poured from his mouth like sacred water. He felt the Spirit within him, tearing with powerful, triumphant fingers at the fear that gripped his heart. He howled and writhed, oblivious to everything and everyone, crying and praying in the unknown tongue God had made his gift. And then, all at once, he felt a great peace and he was bathed in light, like the light that had enveloped him on the road to Broussard. He opened his eyes and saw Motke Vilk standing over him with a flashlight, a concerned look on his face.

"Are you all right?" Motke asked. "Do you need a doctor?"

Silas smiled at the little man. "Praise the Lord," he said weakly.

"I'll bring you a glass of water," said Motke.

"Thank you," said Silas. He rose to his feet, lightheaded but clear in his mind. Barzel, still seated at his desk, seemed entirely unconcerned by his spasm. The old man's face expressed an inner serenity that Silas recognized as pure holiness.

"The Lord has spoken to me," he said simply. "He has told me to say yes. I will become a Guardian."

Barzel removed a gold signet ring from his finger and held it out to Silas. "Take this ring. When the time comes, you will pass it along to your successor. In the meantime, wear it as a symbol of your pledge."

Silas slipped the ring on his finger. It fit perfectly, a sign that things were as they were meant to be. "Does President Goldberg have the same ring?" he asked.

"Not yet," said Barzel. "He does not yet know that he has been selected. I will approach him after the election. When you see he is wearing the ring, you may speak to him of this. Until then, say nothing."

"I understand," said Silas.

"Good. Now, when are you scheduled to make your endorsement?"

"On Saturday," said Silas.

"What network?"

"ABC," said Silas.

"Prime time?"

"Eight P.M.," said Silas.

"Excellent. Rouse your Christian soldiers, Reverend. Send them to the polls. There is much we will do together, President Goldberg, you and I. And now, the hour is late. I have kept you too long. You'll need your strength for the days ahead." He rose, seized the minister by the shoulders in a powerful grip and squeezed. "Go with God," he said, pushing him gently toward the door. "The security men will take you to your hotel."

Motke waited until he heard Silas's steps echo down the empty corridor before switching on the light and blowing out the candles. "Poor Irv Stein," he said. "He should have held out for a ring."

"I don't think Mr. Stein has the requisite, ah, spiritual

qualities to be a fully fledged Guardian," said Barzel dryly. "Besides, the Jewish slots are already filled, as you heard."

"I don't know where you come up with this stuff," said Motke. "How does a moron like that get so powerful?"

"Silas isn't a moron, he's a mystic," said Barzel. "A naive mystic, I grant you, but sincere. History is full of such people. Some of them inspired millions."

"He doesn't strike me as a Gandhi type," said Motke.

A small, sardonic smile passed over Barzel's thin lips. "I was thinking more along the lines of the Children's Crusade," he said.

"When he started wiggling around on the floor and barking, I thought he was having an epileptic fit."

"He was speaking in tongues," said Barzel. "It's a common practice."

"I can't wait till he tries it out in the Oval Office. What will you do when he talks to Goldberg, one Guardian to another?"

"Do? Why should I do anything? On Saturday Reverend Silas will endorse Goldberg. On Tuesday he'll be elected president. What he does about Silas after that is his business. Although I suppose that if the good reverend goes around insisting he's a Guardian of the Covenant, Goldberg might be disposed to think he's a bit touched. In any event, I don't involve myself in internal American affairs."

"You didn't want Goldberg," said Motke. "What made you change your mind?"

Barzel looked at Motke and sighed. "I'm afraid I underestimated him," he said. "He knows something about me. It's an old story, and I imagine you're going to have a hard time believing it, but you deserve to know. I'm not who you think I am."

"Yes, you are," said Motke. "After sixty years I know who you are and what you are. Nothing Goldberg knows about you can change that. I don't want to hear it."

"You know who I am and what I am," said Barzel softly. "All right, then, little brother, tell me. Who am I?"

Motke Vilk looked into his old friend's blue eyes and smiled. "You're a Guardian," he said gently. "The rest is just commentary."

CHAPTER THIRTY

PRESIDENT GOLDBERG AND DIDI WERE IN THE MIDDLE OF A light election-day lunch when Willis burst in with the news. "We got it, Dewey," he said excitedly. "According to the exit polls, we're way ahead in New York, Pennsylvania, New Jersey and Illinois. And we're running slightly ahead in most of the South. Graff figures the margin's going to be a hundred and twenty electoral votes, maybe more. You owe Bobby Silas big-time."

"I owe nobody but the American people," said Goldberg sharply. "I don't want you to talk to Silas or anyone else, including the press, without consulting me first. Tell Cassidy and the others, too."

"Yes, Mr. President," said Willis in a chastened tone. "Anything else?"

"You've got Boyd French's job, if you want it."

"Yes sir," said Willis. "I want it."

"Good. Get ahold of Kenny Wykowsky, tell him to come

see me as soon as possible. I want him to work with you on staff appointments. He can have congressional liaison or special counselor, whichever he prefers. We're getting rid of these Creole Republicans and getting some honest-to-God Democratic Wolverines in here."

"It's about time," said Willis. "What about Cabinet posts?"

"Livingstone will be in charge of putting together a short list," said Goldberg. "If you think of anybody for the CIA, let me know. And Willis, get somebody you trust into the Oval Office, and have him go over the place for bugs. From now on, when I talk I want to know who's listening."

"Yes, Mr. President," said Willis. "I'll get right onto it."

"Well," said Didi when he was gone, "you did it."

"Piece of cake." Goldberg grinned. "Never any doubt in my mind."

Didi put her arms around her husband and hugged him. "I love the way you talked to Willis just now. I'm a sucker for decisive men."

"Think I overdid it?"

"No. A man's entitled to a testosterone high on election day. Just don't go blowing up the world or anything."

Charlie arrived around three. "I hear you've got it, Textile," he said, embracing his old friend.

"Thanks to you, Slim," said Goldberg.

"I just found the ammunition. You're the one who knew what to do with it," said Charlie. "You ran a hell of a campaign."

"I did, didn't I?" said Goldberg happily. "Well, now it's time to get down to business. How would you feel about coming to work for me?"

"As what?" Charlie laughed. "Court scribe?"

"Secretary of State," said Goldberg. "I want somebody I trust, and that's you."

"That's a hell of an offer, but I'm not qualified to be Secretary of State."

"So what? Was I qualified to be president? It's something you pick up as you go along, like roller-skating. How about it?"

"Nope," Charlie said. "It's flattering, but I'm not the government type. I've been on the other side too long. Of course, if you happen to have any interesting information lying around, I wouldn't mind hearing about it first."

"Yeah, I owe you a couple," said Goldberg. "All right, try this. It has been learned from highly placed sources that President Dewey Goldberg's first foreign visitor will be Prime Minister Elihu Barzel of Israel."

"Barzel? Is that a good idea? I mean, considering everything."

"You think I can't handle him?"

"I didn't say that. But there are easier ways of starting a new administration."

Goldberg paced the office in silence for a moment. "What kind of a president do you think I'm going to make?" he asked.

"A damn good one."

"I wonder. I know you were disappointed in me last year—"

"You inherited an impossible situation," said Charlie. "Nobody could have done any better."

"No, I was shaky. I felt like an intruder. Sometimes I'd look at the portraits of the presidents, Washington, Adams, all those imposing old bastards, and think to myself, *Goldberg? How the hell did you get here?*"

"President Sandwich," said Charlie.

"Huh?"

"That's what Howard Grant called you. He said President Goldberg sounds like a sandwich at the Carnegie Deli."

"President Sandwich," Dewey repeated. "How come you didn't tell me that before?"

"It skipped my mind," said Charlie. "Besides, it's not exactly a confidence builder."

"No. Well, I don't feel that way anymore. This election was a referendum on the Goldberg factor, and I won. I've earned the right to be president. And I'm going to use it, you can be damn sure of that."

"Dewey Goldberg, closet radical? Now, there's a real scoop," said Charlie.

"You know me better than that," said Goldberg. "But I've got a few things that I'd like to accomplish. I may not be Mount Rushmore material, but I can make a difference. If I'm not distracted."

"By what?"

"By Barzel, for example. I twisted his arm hard on the Silas thing. He's a formidable man like you once said, and I don't need him as an enemy. That's why I want to see him, to get things straight between us."

"What's done is done," said Charlie. "I don't think an apology will help much."

"I have no intention of apologizing for anything," said Goldberg in a surprisingly sharp tone. "He's the one who tried to fuck me, remember? Not to mention plotting a world war."

"You did blackmail him into getting you the Silas endorsement," said Charlie.

"Maybe so, but he asked for it. The point is, he's mad right now, he's scared of what I know and he's got a guilty conscience. That's a nasty combination, especially in an operator like Barzel. I want him to know that he's got nothing to fear from me. Then I won't have to worry about him."

"How are you going to do that?"

"I don't know exactly," said Goldberg. "But I've got between now and the inauguration to figure it out."

On January 11, Elihu Barzel was reelected. His Tzedek Party won forty-nine seats in the Knesset. Along with the Rabbinical Party of Rabbi Yehuda Bloch it was enough to form a ruling coalition, even without Yarkoni's doves, who refused to join the government. It was a pleasant victory for Barzel, if unexciting; the polls had predicted the outcome almost exactly.

Shortly after the results became public, Barzel received a call from Dewey Goldberg. "Congratulations, Mr. Prime Minister," he said. "The people of Israel have chosen wisely."

"Thank you, Mr. President," said Barzel formally. It was the first time they had spoken since Goldberg's call in late October.

"I'd like to take this occasion to invite you to Washington," said Goldberg. "At your convenience, of course. There are some things we need to discuss."

"Are there?" asked Barzel mildly.

"I think so, yes. I'd be interested in hearing your views on extremism."

"I'm at your service, Mr. President," said Barzel. It didn't escape him that Goldberg hadn't qualified "extremism" with the usual "Islamic"; he wondered if the president was being snide. "Of course, this is a busy time for me, setting up the new government. But when the moment is right, I'd be honored to pay you a visit."

"Good. Would early in April suit your schedule?"

"Passover is in early April."

"I'm aware of that," said Goldberg. "I'm having a seder at the White House."

"Are you?" said Barzel, sounding genuinely surprised.

"Yes. Perhaps you'd like to attend."

"Well," said Barzel, speechless for a moment. "It's an intriguing invitation—"

"You can even bring Rabbi Bloch if you like," said Goldberg easily.

"No, I believe the rabbi will be spending the holiday in Israel," said Barzel. "And, for that matter, so will I."

"Pity," said Goldberg, hardening his tone. "Well, then, immediately after Passover."

It was no longer a request, Barzel realized; it was a summons. "I'll have Motke Vilk get in touch with your people about the date," he said.

"Fine," said Goldberg briskly. "I'm looking forward to your visit."

Barzel put down the phone and buzzed Motke. "We're going to Washington in April," he said.

"Good time," said Motke. "The cherry blossoms are out in April."

"Goldberg invited me to a seder at the White House."

"He did? In the White House? I don't think that chef of his would be much on gefilte fish."

"It was a warning," said Barzel. "He was letting me know he's not vulnerable on the Jewish issue anymore."

"You think it's going to be trouble, this meeting?"

"It could be," said Barzel. "I underestimated Goldberg once. I won't do it again."

"I thought things were settled between you," said Motke. "He got elected, you got elected, it all came out even."

"Even, perhaps, but not settled," said Barzel. "Goldberg wants something from me."

"What?"

"I don't know," said Barzel. "But there's something that he doesn't know."

"What's that?"

Barzel gazed impassively at his aide, and a tiny, almost imperceptible smile crossed his face. "I want something from him, too."

CHAPTER THIRTY-ONE

THE AMERICANS LAID ON THE FULL TREATMENT FOR PRIME
Minister Barzel. He was effusively greeted by Vice President
Livingstone at Andrews Air Force Base, serenaded with the
"Hativka" and the "Star Spangled Banner," marched down a
red carpet past a crack unit of army rangers, and then whisked
by armored limousine from the airfield to the White House.
"A little different than last time," said Barzel, referring to his
grudging reception of the previous summer.

"A lot of things are different, Mr. Prime Minister," said
Livingstone.

"So I understand. From what I hear, President Goldberg
has been making quite a splash lately."

"It's the difference between being a caretaker and having a
mandate," explained Livingstone eagerly.

"Is that right?" said Barzel. "Yes, I can see how that could
make all the difference." Motke, who was sitting next to Barzel,

shot Livingstone a look, but the young vice president seemed unaware of the prime minister's pale sarcasm.

Goldberg was waiting for Barzel in the Rose Garden. They shook hands enthusiastically for the cameras, waved to the small crowd of staffers and guests assembled on the grass and then walked into the Oval Office. It had been agreed, at Goldberg's suggestion, that the first part of their meeting be one-on-one; later, they would be joined by their aides. The arrangement expressed Goldberg's new self-confidence, and it suited Barzel as well. Flanked by secretaries and generals, Dewey Goldberg was the president of the United States with all the power that implied. Face-to-face, he was just a man. Not a weak man, Barzel realized now, and far from a naive one. Meeting Goldberg one-on-one didn't erase the disparity in power between them, but it diminished it just a little, and perhaps that would be enough.

"At our last meeting, you suggested we call one another by our first names," Goldberg said.

"Yes, by all means."

"Shall I call you Elihu? Or Elia?"

Barzel had expected Goldberg to feel him out before going on the attack. The sudden jab made him blink with surprise. Goldberg saw it and smiled.

"No one has called me Elia since before you were born," said Barzel. "It's a name that no longer belongs to me."

"You know, it's funny," said Goldberg in a relaxed, conversational tone. "My mother always hated the name Goldberg. For years she tried to get my father to change it to something more American. But he would never do it. 'A Jew can change his name, but he's still a Jew,' he used to tell her."

"In Poland, before the war, I remember people saying the same thing," said Barzel. "They were anti-Semites who believed that the Jews were an inferior race. Of course, I'm certain that doesn't apply to your father."

"He thinks you're a Jewish hero," said Goldberg.

"And you think I am an imposter."

"What if I do? I promised you in October that I won't reveal your secret. What do you care what I think?"

"It happens that I care very much," said Barzel. "You are the only person, with the exception of my sister, who knows the truth. Since you and I are going to be doing business together for the next few years, I don't want you to feel that you're dealing with a liar. I'd like for you to understand why I did what I did."

"I'm interested in hearing what happened," said Goldberg.

"Well," said Barzel, taking a deep breath, "it was after the war. I was nineteen years old. I had spent six years in the woods with the partisans. My mother and father were dead. I thought my sister was, too. My house was destroyed. There was nothing to go back to. Poland was a giant cemetery. I wasn't thinking clearly, but I knew I had to escape, and escape meant moving west. And so I moved. I had become very good at moving by that time, like an animal in the forest. I scavenged for food, I slept where I found a roof. When someone showed me kindness, I tried to feel kindness in return—I was raised, I believe, as a kind boy—but I had lost kindness. I was aware that it was gone the way an amputee knows he is missing a limb, and like an amputee I was reconciled to living without it. I had lost so much during the war that I didn't mourn the loss of my kindness. I simply moved ahead, to the west.

"One night, in Germany, in the woods, I saw a farmer prepare to shoot a group of Jewish children. I killed the farmer by throwing a metal sliver through his skull. Killing meant nothing to me. In the war I killed dozens of people, perhaps hundreds. And I wasn't trying to save Jews. I knew what the Nazis had done to the Jews, and if I had any sympathy left I would have felt sympathetic, but I had no sympathy, just as I had no kindness."

"Then why did you kill the farmer?" asked Goldberg in a hushed voice.

Barzel shrugged. "I suppose I thought he had food in his cabin. Or perhaps it was a reflex. A German with a rifle. I don't recall why. But I remember the faces of the children. They looked at me like I was their savior. One especially. His eyes were so large and black and full of gratitude for his life. That boy was Motke Vilk."

"Vilk? I thought you said no one knows who you really are," said Goldberg.

"He spoke to me in Yiddish and I answered in Yiddish. My mother was a German—the languages are very close—and I learned to speak Yiddish from the Jewish partisans. He thought I was a Jew, and I let him think so."

"Why?"

"The Jews were heading for Italy, in order to go by boat to Palestine. The roads were full of them. I thought that by attaching myself to them, I might get passage to Palestine and go from there to America or Australia.

"That night in the farmhouse, after we had eaten the German's dog and divided his possessions, we lay down on his floor to sleep. I closed my eyes, but I felt someone looking at me. I had the instincts of an animal and I could actually feel the gaze on my face. When I opened my eyes, I saw Motke. He was fourteen then, but tiny from malnutrition. He seemed ten or eleven, not more than that. And looking into his eyes I felt something. It came and it went like a shock of electricity, but I recognized it. It was kindness. That's when I knew that I wasn't dead. Mutilated, yes; for life. But still alive, still human."

"Jesus," Goldberg breathed.

"We walked all the way to Italy together," said Barzel, talking in a low monotone, seemingly unaware now of Goldberg's presence. "And all the time we walked I thought about what would become of me. Not how I would survive—I had no doubt that I could survive anything—but, literally, what I would become. You see, I didn't want to be a monster.

"When we arrived in Palestine I joined the army. The officers who recruited me were like children. They were brave, but they knew nothing about war. They wanted to kill the Arabs and be loved by them at the same time. I had been in the woods for six years. I had seen human nature. I had never met an Arab, but I knew about war.

"What the Jews wanted was just. After Hitler, they could have claimed half the planet and it would have been just. I felt that if I could use my hatred in a just cause, it might be transformed into something human. And so I fought. I thought, in the back of my mind, that after the war I would go to America. But first I would become human again by killing in a just cause.

"And then David Ben Gurion called for me. He sent me abroad to kill Nazis. For ten years I was neither a Jew nor a Pole. I was a German living among Germans, killing Germans. During this time I was neither Lenkowsky nor Leibowitz nor Barzel. I was a man suspended in air, floating in blood.

"I was closing in on Adolf Eichmann. And then the Mossad stepped between Eichmann and death. They wanted him alive. They ordered me to stop, to go home to Israel. But Israel was no longer my home. Instead, I went to America. I had a friend there, Howard Grant. He was in business and he took me in as a partner. Together we made millions of dollars. I was an American, finally, after all those years. I even had an American passport. But it was then that I discovered something shocking—I had become a Jew. I knew I had been born Elia Lenkowsky. I never lost touch with reality. But somehow I had become a Jew."

"You never converted, though," said Goldberg.

"What for? I'm not a religious man—I'm afraid that after

the war I can't take the idea of a supreme being seriously. The world already considered me a Jew. I had no need for rabbis."

"You stayed in New York," said Goldberg. "You didn't return to Israel."

"That's true," said Barzel. "I was making money, I had Motke with me. My life was fulfilling. But I suppose I always knew that eventually I'd have to go back."

"You make it sound unpleasant."

"Since I'm telling you all my secrets, I'll tell you one more—I have never particularly liked living in Israel. It's a small country and, to my taste, provincial. Perhaps I'm a bit of a snob. I liked being in the wide world, doing business on a grand scale. I enjoyed the openness of America. People here are carefree. It's a quality I appreciate, even if I myself lack it. Perhaps especially for that reason."

"Well then, why did you go back?"

"Out of obligation," said Barzel. "I sat in America and watched the U.N. declare Israel a racist state. I saw powerful governments pandering to the Arabs because of oil. I listened to the lies people told about Israel to justify their greed, and I understood that the world wasn't finished yet with the Jews."

"You really believe that, don't you?"

"Yes, I do. But you don't." Barzel said it flatly, a statement rather than a question.

"I don't deny that Israel has enemies. All countries do. But I don't believe there's an international conspiracy against the Jews."

"When you put it that way, no," said Barzel. "I also don't believe in an organized conspiracy. Let's just say that there is a certain predilection for mistreating Jews. It affects different people at different times. When I was a boy it was the Poles. Later it was the Germans. Then the Arabs and the Russian Communists. Now it is the Moslem extremists. Did they come together and divide the task among themselves? Of course not.

They have nothing in common, no shared denominator. And that, Mr. President, is the point. The hatred of Jews is not a plot, it is a disease. It is no more organized than the bubonic plague. And no less deadly."

"If it were true, I wouldn't be sitting here right now," said Goldberg.

"In a plague, not everyone becomes sick at once. Those with strong constitutions may even be immune. But for the healthy to deny that the plague exists doesn't alter reality."

"You're getting the metaphor confused," said Goldberg. "The victims of your plague are anti-Semites, not the Jews."

"You think Jews aren't infected with anti-Semitism?" Barzel laughed dryly. "You should try governing Israel for a while. The Jews are like battered children—they despise themselves without knowing it. Half the country thinks the extremists are justified—my own foreign minister believed this. He felt that their hatred for us must be our fault. The other half, the hawks, are incapable of trusting the world."

"Only you are healthy," said Goldberg quietly.

"I prefer the term 'clear-sighted,'" said Barzel. "Perhaps my biography gives me a perspective others lack."

"And the Project was an example of your 'clear-sightedness'?"

"Ah. I wondered when we would come to that," said Barzel. "Yes, I believe it was. Frankly."

"Well, as long as we're being frank, allow me to tell you frankly that I think it was a goddamn irrational and dangerous scheme," said Goldberg.

"Mr. President, with all due respect, I was living in New York in 1962, when President Kennedy almost destroyed the entire world because of Russian missiles in Cuba. Was that a rational act? America has never hesitated to defend its interests, not to mention its national survival, by whatever means necessary. Nor would you shrink from it today. Or am I mistaken?"

"That's entirely different," said Goldberg. "America is the leader of the free world."

"You may recall that in our last conversation I spoke of my obligation to the survival of the Jews," said Barzel. "Of course it doesn't compare to yours, but it is, nonetheless, an obligation. What you would do to protect your people I will do to protect mine."

"Up to and including unilaterally starting a world war," said Goldberg, his voice rising.

"Mr. President, I had no intention of acting unilaterally. As you know."

"You went behind my back."

"I would prefer to say we sounded out Governor Childes to ascertain his views on something that would be beneficial to both our countries."

"Well if it was so goddamn beneficial, how is it that you neglected to mention it to me when we met last year?"

"Because I knew you wouldn't agree," said Barzel. "A Jewish president could never cooperate so closely with Israel."

"So you tried to defeat me."

"If anyone has intervened in another country's politics, it is you. Imagine if I had tried to blackmail you as you did me."

"This is getting us no place," said Goldberg. "What happened, happened. The important thing is that we understand each other from now on. I want you to be absolutely clear that I will not countenance any military adventures in the Middle East. I want your promise that you won't try anything like the Project again."

"Is that an ultimatum, Mr. President?"

"No, of course not," said Goldberg, struggling to keep his temper in the face of this implacable old man. "It's an appeal to common sense."

"Common sense. Let me ask you: Am I wrong in thinking that the extremists want to destroy Israel?"

"No," said Goldberg. "Probably not."

"Am I wrong in thinking that they are arming themselves with nuclear weapons?"

"I really can't discuss specifics—"

"Am I right or wrong, Mr. President? We're talking about the life of my country. If America was facing such a prospect, what would you do?"

"I don't say do nothing," said Goldberg. "There are other ways to deal with this. And you're not alone. We're committed to Israel's security."

"Mr. President, with respect, you are not. I realized that when you turned down our request for ASII."

"ASII?" said Goldberg, in a conversational tone that he hoped masked the fact that he had no idea what Barzel was talking about.

"Your Advanced Strategic Intelligence Information package," said Barzel. "On-line satellite imaging and thermal sensors that would enable us to spot missiles as they are fired."

"I turned that down?" asked Goldberg.

"General Snowden assured our military people that you were categorically opposed," Barzel said. "Under the circumstances—"

"General Snowden was mistaken," said Goldberg. He lowered his voice to a confidential whisper. "He never even told me about this."

"I see," said Barzel. "So you'd be prepared to reconsider?"

"Reconsider, yes. Promise, no. I want to know what the navy's objections are and discuss it with the Secretary of Defense. But if this, ah, ASII system can protect Israel from nuclear attack, I'd be inclined to find some way to provide it. Would that satisfy you?"

"Me, yes. But I'm afraid it won't satisfy the Pentagon. You see, they're concerned that if you provide us with ASII, we might actually use it. Unless . . ."

"I'm listening," said Goldberg.

"Unless the United States were to make a formal declaration that an attack on Israel would be tantamount to an attack on Washington, D.C."

"I see," said Goldberg. "Let me ask you a hypothetical question: Suppose we were to make such a commitment?"

"Would such a commitment be in writing? Speaking hypothetically."

"Yes," said Goldberg.

"And would it be ratified by Congress?"

"That wouldn't be necessary," said Goldberg. "An executive order would be sufficient."

"Executives come and go," said Barzel evenly.

"All right, I suppose it could be sent through Congress."

"It might even be a good idea if it originated in Congress," said Barzel. "I know nothing of American politics, but it seems to me that it might make the president's position easier. Particularly a Jewish president."

"No," said Goldberg. "If a Jewish president were to duck responsibility, an Israeli prime minister might think that he was untrustworthy. And if he were a certain kind of prime minister, that might cause him to go behind the president's back. Again."

"But there would be no reason for such skepticism," said Barzel, peering into Goldberg's eyes.

"None," said Goldberg, meeting his gaze and holding it.

"In that case, I could assure you that Israel wouldn't undertake any initiatives without American approval," said Barzel.

Goldberg extended his hand. "We understand one another," he said.

"Yes," said Barzel, returning the grip. "It appears that we do."

At the state dinner, Motke Vilk shared a table with Charlie Walker. They were sitting, separated only by the slightly tipsy wife of a southern senator, when President Dewey Goldberg rose and made his dramatic announcement. "For too long the state of Israel has been forced to live with the threat of military aggression from its neighbors. For too long, the enemies of democracy in the Middle East have nurtured the hope that Israel might someday be exterminated. Tonight, it is my intention to end that hope forever. I want to make it crystal clear that Israel's physical security is a vital interest of this country. With that in mind," he said, pausing to bow slightly in the direction of the prime minister, "I have informed my good friend Elihu Barzel that, from this day forward, an attack on the state of Israel will be tantamount to an attack on the United States of America itself. Moreover, I am directing a review of our strategic assets in the region. . . ."

"Howard Grant," Charlie muttered to himself.

"What about him?" asked Motke over the shoulder of the senator's wife.

"There never was any Project," said Charlie. "Grant told me that Barzel always creates a problem so he can solve it and get what he wants. This is what he was after all the time, isn't it?"

"I don't know what you're talking about," said Motke.

"Goddamn," Charlie said, "your boss *is* the biggest con man in the history of the world. And I mean that as a compliment, I guess."

". . . deeply appreciate this gesture, Mr. President," Barzel was saying, his wineglass held before him. "The children of our country will sleep well at night knowing that they are as safe as the children of this, the greatest democracy in the world. And so, I raise my glass to you, sir, and salute you and your country with a heartfelt toast: God Bless America."

"Thank you, Mr. Prime Minister," said Goldberg, raising his own glass. "And let me say to you, in the language of your people—and my people—*le'chaim*, 'to life,' for both our countries."

As the audience burst into cheers, Motke leaned over toward Charlie. "Maybe there was a Project, maybe there wasn't," he said. "With Barzel I can't be sure, even after all these years. With him, anything's possible. Know why?"

Charlie shook his head. "Why?"

"Because he's got a *Yiddishe kopp*, a 'Jewish brain.'" Motke grinned, pointing to his own noggin. "No offense, Mr. Walker, but it's something you've got to be born with."